A Smack of Jellyfish

FEAR, FISH & FINDING YOURSELF IN ALASKA

a novel

Lynda Sather

CHEECHAKO PRESS

A SMACK OF JELLYFISH: Fear, Fish & Finding Yourself in Alaska
Cheechako Press • Fairbanks, AK
copyright © 2024 Lynda Sather
LyndaSather.com

This is a work of fiction. Names, characters, businesses, places, events, locales, and incidents are either the products of the author's imagination or used in a fictitious manner. Any resemblance to actual persons, living or dead, or actual events is purely coincidental. Except, of course, Petersburg is a very real and wonderful town.

COVER DESIGN
Kellee Ratzlaff • Awedore Studios • awedore.com
Cover art: Stein Egil Liland • pexels.com/@therato/collections/

PRE-TATTOO SKETCH OF WINGED HEART
Lyle Tuttle Tattoo Parlor (c. 1970)
Chapter Icon: Brenna Carlson • Carlson Creative

AUTHOR PHOTO
Timothy J Parks • Timothy Park Photo & Video • timparkstudios.com

INTERIOR DESIGN & PRODUCTION
Eva Long • Long On Books • longonbooks.com

Print ISBN: 979-8-9907789-0-0
eBook ISBN: 979-8-9907789-1-7

Printed in the U.S.A.

For Per

Home is the sailor, home from sea,
And the hunter home from the hill.

Robert Lewis Stevensen

Alaska isn't about who you were when you headed that way.
It's about who you become.

Kristin Hannah

Contents

Au Revoir

Wʜᴇɴ ᴍʏ ғʀɪᴇɴᴅ Rᴀᴄʜᴇʟ Cᴏʜᴇɴ ғɪʀsᴛ mentioned going to Alaska after graduation, I laughed. Snorted in disbelief would be more like it, except my mother taught me young ladies don't snort. Nor do they sweat. Or fart.

Sadly, I do all three.

"Alaska?" I snorted in disbelief. "Isn't that where Jack London froze to death? No thanks."

"It was Sam McGee who froze to death in a Robert Service poem," she replied in that know-it-all voice I hate.

"Still, freezing is freezing," I said, zipping up my sweatshirt for emphasis.

An hour earlier, Rachel had shown up on my doorstep looking like something the cat drug in, as my mother would say: eyes bloodshot, hair greasy, wearing a dirty poncho with an Indian print skirt hanging off her skinny frame.

"I need a beer," she said, brushing by me. "But first, a pee."

I found two beers in the back of the fridge, and we took them down to the Santa Cruz beach two blocks away. I wanted to ask a million questions, but I'd learned over the last four years I was more likely to get answers if I didn't appear too curious. As we skirted the edge of the surf and the level in the beer can lowered, she started talking. She said she had to get out of the City, said she needed to get away from her boyfriend and the life there. Her dad, a professor, and her mother, a professional drunk, were divorcing and her younger sister was running feral. She was needed at home, her father said, and he'd wired her money for bus fare which she'd pocketed in favor of buying smokes and hitchhiking home.

"So, enough about me," she said, turning her back to the wind to light a joint. "What will Maddie Maguire do next?"

I took two steps away from the persistent surf trying to nibble my sneakers while I thought about how to answer. Rachel passed me the joint and didn't seem to notice, or care, that her shoes got wet.

"Go back home to Mommy and Daddy?" she asked when I stayed silent. "Go shopping for career clothes and a husband? Sunday brunch at the country club?" She put on a fake la-te-dah voice. "They do a mah-vellous Eggs Benedict, don't you know, with a side of young lawyer."

"Don't be mean," I said, squirming.

"Well?" she demanded in a gentler tone.

"Well, I don't know!" I wailed, sounding pathetic even to my own ears. "Everyone keeps asking, but I only know what I *don't* want to do. I *don't* want to move back to L.A. I *don't* want to start a career. I *don't* want to get married, even if I had a boyfriend which, as you know, I don't. Not since, well…you know."

We watched another wave rush up the shore only to retreat, exhausted. I kicked at the remains of a collapsed sandcastle. "I wish I could travel, but where would I get the money? Not from my folks, that's for sure. Not for that." I looked at Rachel sideways. "Maybe for career clothes."

She smiled briefly, then turned serious. "Listen, Mad. We could earn enough money this summer in Alaska to travel to Mexico in the winter."

I don't remember the last time I saw her this excited. Maybe when we were sophomores and she'd scored tickets to a Grateful Dead concert at the Cow Palace; before she'd dropped out and gotten into that whole San Franscisco scene and I'd gone off to study in France and all that.

I hated to burst her bubble, but I equated Alaska with Siberia, with Eskimos and dog sleds, and the idea of working in a cannery was ridiculous. "Alaska? No way," I repeated, and turned back.

"Well, I'm going," Rachel said defiantly, flinging the roach into the waves. "Call me if you change your mind."

A month later, I was on a ferry to Alaska. I used the small bequest my grandmother had left me to fund my escape, as I called the bus ticket from L.A. to Seattle and the ferry ticket from there to Petersburg.

I left my horrified mother and bemused father back in Southern California, along with my newly married sister ("one down, one to go," my normally taciturn dad said after one glass of champagne too many). I left behind my newly inked diploma in French Literature and Scruffy the stuffed dog who had consoled me countless times during my angst-ridden adolescence. I'd thrown out the stack of Seventeen Magazines; abandoned the closet full of bell bottoms, miniskirts, one hideous bridesmaid dress, and a crocheted prom dress I rather liked. I left it all behind and took only what fit in my new red backpack.

I also took my banjo in its battered case, although I could only play six tunes. I'd discovered it was a good prop. I would play my six tunes, then put the banjo away in an ostentatious display of false modesty, steadfastly refusing to play an encore. By that time, the banjo had served its purpose, had broken the ice, got the conversation going. Well worth lugging around even if I could barely play it.

So, there I was. Twenty-one years old. A banjo, a backpack and, oh yes, a tattoo. I could hardly leave *that* behind, indelibly inked on my right hip.

All Ashore

"Petersburg, Alaska. All ashore going ashore," the ferry's loud-speaker boomed.

I looked around for Rachel whose flamboyant presence would have been unmistakable among the locals in their drab wool jackets and faded caps. Not surprisingly, she was nowhere to be seen. After three days on the ferry from Seattle, I thought we would take our first steps on Alaskan soil together, but I was wrong. Surprise, surprise. You could use a lot of words to describe my friend, but reliable was not one of them.

The small crowd surged forward as soon as the giant cargo door opened. I started to push my way back to wait for Rachel, but stopped. This trip was supposed to be my debut as a confident woman of the world: the star, for a change, not the sidekick. I was tired of waiting for my life to begin. I zipped up my new blue rain coat and went with the flow, a dreamy girl with a sleeping bag and backpack trying to look like she knew who she was and where she was going.

I was so preoccupied trying futilely to keep my banjo dry, I stepped right into a large mud puddle at the bottom of the ramp. "*Zut alors!*" I swore under my breath, the French coming naturally after my year abroad.

I hurried to the shelter of the ferry office to take stock. My new raincoat, although stylish, was no defense against the rain which fell relentlessly. My new white tennis shoes were white no longer. My banjo case was damp. The town, or what I could see of it, was one of the smallest I had ever seen, perched precariously between tall mountains on one side and the dark, swift channel that people on board called the "Narrows," part of the Inside Passage running between mainland America and Alaska.

This coast didn't look a thing like the shore back home. There, the Pacific rollers came in one after another, throwing themselves on shore in a futile attempt to get on dry land. Here, the water rushed by like it meant business, like it had somewhere urgent to go but would be back, as it would be, every twelve hours when the tide changed.

There was no white sand or colorful sun umbrellas on this beach, only wet, algae-covered boulders and strings of stranded bull kelp begging to be popped. No sailboats or yachts in the marina, just commercial fishing boats of every size jammed two- and three-deep in the harbor.

A handful of vehicles drove gingerly off the ferry before accelerating quickly away, throwing water up behind them like the wake behind a speeding skiff. Passengers on foot hurried into waiting cars and vanished. Lights in the ferry office blinked off, and a man in rubber boots and yellow raingear disappeared out the back. I tried the front door, but it was locked.

The ramp leading to the ship beckoned like the portal back to the known world, back to the warm and familiar ferry that could take me home. I wished I were back on it, going somewhere, but not yet arrived.

I collided with Rachel at the bottom of the ramp.

"Where are you going?" she asked in surprise.

"Where were you?"

"Saying goodbye to John. He's going on to Sitka." She fingered the hickey on her neck like the fresh notch on a gunfighter's belt.

Two deep blasts on the ferry's horn announced its quick departure from the dock, eager to leave the Narrows before low tide.

Your ship has sailed, my mother proclaimed.

Even 2500 miles away, I still heard her voice in my head.

You've made your bed, now sleep in it. Your goose is cooked.

"Stop it!" I commanded.

"Stop what?" Rachel asked.

"Never mind." I'm pretty sure Rachel never heard her mother, even when she was right in front of her.

We splashed back to the deserted ferry office. I tucked *Gravity's Rainbow* deeper into my pack among the extra pair of Wrangler jeans and the cotton underwear from Sears so it would stay dry. I wished I had a garbage bag to wrap around my banjo case, but I didn't. Besides, it would have spoiled the effect.

Rachel took a cigarette from her pocket and lit up, looking cool even while doing nothing.

I'd known Rachel since we'd been assigned to share a room our freshman year at U.C. Santa Cruz. She arrived at the dorm long after orientation was over, a tall girl with long, wavy dark hair and an aquiline nose. Although not pretty in a classical sense, there was something compelling about her, maybe her confidence or her careless attitude. She might as well have said, "Hi, I'm Rachel, and I don't give a damn." She came from a large, noisy dysfunctional Jewish clan, the opposite of my small, uptight upper-class Protestant family. My dad was an aeronautical engineer, my mother a stay-at-home housewife. Her father was a professor, her mother a drunk.

I was a French lit major; Rachel majored in rebellion. I took notes in class, studied hard and had panic attacks before each test. Rachel skimmed books and skipped class but still got the answers right.

Rachel was the free spirit I wanted to be, and at her side I tried exotic things like yoga, curry, and foreign films. I even dropped LSD once but only took half a tab, just enough to make things sparkly, but not alarming. Rachel swallowed her tab and the remainder of mine. She preached a healthy lifestyle but candy wrappers fell out of her macrame bag, pizza boxes littered the dorm room, and empty beer cans rolled around the floor. I know she had even been smoking heroin last year while I was in France and she was slumming in San Francisco. We didn't talk about it, but I think that was the main reason she'd left California. Her boyfriend, Reb, had started shooting up. She had just enough will power to leave, but not enough to stay without getting sucked in.

Her tobacco habit now seemed benign by comparison, so I contained my impatience while she practiced blowing smoke rings. When I grew tired of nibbling my cuticles, I finally spoke. "Well, we can't just stand here. Isn't there a phone number on that letter you got? There's a pay phone at the end of the parking lot."

"You should know, you've read it enough," she grumbled, thrusting the crumpled letter toward me.

I clenched my hands in my pockets. "Your letter. Your call."

Rachel shrugged and sloshed over to the pay phone, pretending not to notice—or maybe really not noticing—she was getting soaked. She inserted the coin, held the receiver to her ear for a few minutes, then sloshed back.

"No answer."

"Shit. It's getting dark." I took a deep breath as though going underwater and hurried across the parking lot to the only other person around, a man loading boxes into his pickup.

"Hello, excuse me," I tried a disarming smile. "We just got here on the ferry, well, obviously…" The man glanced at me, nodded, then threw another soggy carton into the pickup. "So anyway, do you know where Petersburg Processors is? The cannery?"

He jerked his thumb toward town. "That green building over there, but they haven't started up yet."

Seeing my disarming smile slip into a grimace, he added, "Allen Taylor, the manager, lives in the white house across from the cannery. On Hill Street. Can't miss it." He slammed the tailgate decisively, climbed into the cab, and drove off quickly in the other direction. I sloshed back to Rachel.

"We can try hitchhiking," she said.

"We can try walking. I don't think it's very far."

We shrugged into our backpacks and started walking. "Voila!" I announced when we came to the green warehouse perched over the water, a worn sign announcing it was indeed Petersburg Processors. We slogged down the plank boardwalk to find the office dark, the door locked.

"*Merde*," I said.

"Shit," Rachel agreed.

"Okay, that man said the manager lives across the street in a white house," I said.

"All the houses are white."

"Yeah, but we want the white one on Hill Street."

We trudged up the hill, then hesitated in front of a white house.

I thought about walking up to the front door, but before I could talk myself into it, Rachel marched up the steps and knocked.

A middle-aged man wearing a sweatshirt and blue jeans cracked opened the door. He held a sheaf of papers in one hand and reading glasses in the other, and used his legs to block a curious toddler from escaping. "Yes?"

"Hey, hello," Rachel spoke quickly. "Are you Allen? I'm Rachel. Sorry to bother you but my friend Sage suggested I write and you wrote back saying I could work at the cannery this summer."

He stroked his toddler's head absently. "Sage?"

I stepped forward. "Hello, Mr. Taylor. I'm Maddie. Her name is *Nancy*, not Sage. Nancy worked at the cannery last year and suggested we write."

"Oh yeah, Nancy." He peered past me like someone else might be lurking in the shadows. "There's two of you?"

The letter mentioned a job for one person, probably because Rachel had only asked about one person. Coming all the way up here without knowing for sure I had a job was probably the boldest thing I'd ever done. I nodded. "Yep, two of us."

"Well, I guess that's okay. We need the workers."

I started breathing again.

"I'll get my keys and drive you down to the house. You can stay there with a couple of the other gals, when they get here." He shut the door and reappeared a few minutes later shrugging into a gray wool jacket.

"Everyone around here wears wool jackets," Rachel whispered as we followed him to his pickup truck. "Must be some kind of uniform."

"Like you know fashion," I hissed back. All her clothes came from the thrift store.

Allen slapped the bed of the pickup truck. "Throw your bags in back and climb inside. That guitar of yours going to be okay?"

Without waiting for an answer or a correction, he slapped the back of the pickup truck.

"Call me Allen," he said.

My heart sank when the truck stopped at a small dilapidated blue house only slightly larger than a playhouse perched on the sidewalk beside the cannery. Luckily, Allen led us past it down a plank walkway to a larger white house perched over the water.

He unlocked the front door and motioned us to follow. "House has been closed up all winter. You can stay here and get the place cleaned up. Two other girls will be arriving soon. Cleaning supplies are around somewhere. If you need something else, pick it up at the Trading Union and charge it to the cannery." He showed us around the two-bedroom house, turning lights on and off, and plugging in the refrigerator as he went.

"When do we start work?" I asked.

"There'll be an opening in a few days." Seeing my blank look, Allen shook his head. "An opening means the seiners go out and when they come back with the fish, we start canning. I don't charge rent, but you work at Processors whenever you're needed. Could be ten or twelve hours a day if the seining is good. Could be nothing. You worked a slime line before?"

I shook my head. Rachel stood next to the coffee table flipping through a pile of old magazines, but I could tell she was listening.

"Well, it's not rocket science. Make sure to wear rain gear and rubber boots, it'll be wet work," he said looking at my saturated shoes.

"Yeah, Sage mentioned we'd need them," Rachel said casually. What else had Sage/Nancy mentioned that Rachel hadn't bothered to share with me?

"Don't wear anything you ever want to wear again," Allen said. "Unless you like *Odor Fish,* as my mother used to say." He chuckled.

"Eau du fish!" I exclaimed. "Fish water!"

"What? No. Fish odor."

I started to correct his French, but Rachel dropped the pile of magazines onto the coffee table with a loud thud.

"Bob and Jim stay in the little blue house, work at the cannery," Allen continued. "Talk to them tomorrow, they'll know what's going on. Work hard and you'll make good money." He looked at us for a moment. "Don't blow it all in the bar."

A Penny for Your Thoughts

THE HOUSE HAD BEEN SHUTTERED ALL winter. Now, the stale air smelled like burnt dust as the furnace slowly rumbled to life. Rachel and I toured the house again slowly. A fine layer of dust had sifted onto the surfaces, but the threadbare carpet was fairly clean. Two easy chairs, a sofa and two rickety side tables filled the living room, along with the coffee table whose beer can rings and cigarette burns suggested survival rather than decor. In the kitchen, a large Formica table surrounded by six mismatched chairs presided at the window with a view over the Narrows. The pink bathroom was hideous, but functional.

"I've lived in worse," Rachel said.

"You sure have," I agreed, imagining the drafty loft in San Francisco where I'd visited her when I got back from France: the cavernous warehouse divided into dark stalls, thin mattresses on floors, the communal bathroom no one ever cleaned, the empty light sockets.

"And you haven't," she stated, like there was something wrong with that.

I thought of the sprawling house in Encino, the beach house at Newport Beach, the dorm room in Santa Cruz, the student apartment in Paris.

"Nope, this is really slumming it."

Rachel rolled her eyes.

"Rach," I asked, "what else did Sage tell you we'd need besides rain boots?"

"Oh, I don't remember. She just said everything is expensive in Alaska but you can make good money." She grinned at me. "Oh, I do remember something! She said to bring birth control, the guys are hot."

I had tucked several packets of birth control pills in my pack, hoping to need them.

"In fact, that's why she's not up here again this season. She's prego."

We chose the large back bedroom jutting over the water and deposited our bags on the twin beds on opposite sides of the room. I didn't feel like unpacking yet and wasn't sure Rachel ever would. I did open the banjo case to let the damp instrument inside dry out. I wasn't sure it would ever be the same. I wasn't sure I cared.

I wandered back into the living room to investigate the bookshelf. Mostly old paperbacks and magazines like *Popular Mechanics*, *Mad Magazine*, and *Rolling Stone*. A small pocket-sized yellow booklet on the middle shelf caught my eye: 1972-73 Tide Table. Inside, in tiny print, page after page detailed the exact time and height of high and low tides for every day of the year in locations all around Petersburg. The corner of every page was torn so you could easily find the most recent day. I peered at the entry for a year ago.

"Hey Rach, did you know the tide rises and falls twenty-feet every twelve hours!"

Rachel's muffled voice came from the kitchen as she opened and closed cupboards. "I hope there's something to eat in here."

I wandered into the kitchen and peered out the back door. "I bet at high tide the house will be surrounded by water…we live in a house boat. Get it? House. Boat."

Rachel ignored me, intent on the hunt for food.

"No food, but someone left a couple of beers!" Rachel said, emerging victorious from her quest.

I didn't like beer, especially not warm, cheap beer—but Mom always said *beggars can't be choosers*. I took one of the cans and we made ourselves comfortable on the back deck, me on a rusty folding chair and Rachel perched on an upended plastic carton.

The clouds had dumped their load of rain and fled, leaving remnants of tattered fog caught in the treetops like sodden pennants hastily abandoned. Dusk was falling, but a few retreating sunbeams stabbed the mountaintops as they withdrew. I closed my eyes, breathed deeply, and relaxed for the first time since leaving the ferry, or maybe since leaving California. Maybe since forever.

I still wasn't sure what I was doing here, but I had breathing room for once to figure it out.

"A penny for your thoughts?"

My eyes flew open, half expecting to see my mother there probing my psyche with her favorite hackneyed expression. Luckily, it was only Rachel staring at me curiously. I started to tell her my thoughts were worth at least a quarter, but Rachel didn't usually care what anyone thought and now she had actually asked.

"I feel like I've spent the last few years of my life trying to be someone I'm not," I replied cautiously, "making sure people approve of me, even people I don't especially care about."

She took a swallow of warm beer and nodded.

"Now, I can be who I really want to be, do what I want instead of what's expected," I said.

"Leave behind the people you don't care about," she said.

I thought about that for a minute.

"Like Reb," she said.

"Like Brad," I added, trying to convince myself.

Brad was my friend Leslie's older brother. My ex-boyfriend. I'd had a crush on him since high school. He was smart and musical and good-looking in a blond, blue-eyed Beach Boys kind of way that had me doodling his name on my notepaper when I should have been paying attention to Madam Dubois conjugating verbs at the blackboard.

Brad didn't notice me until I came home from college after my sophomore year with clear skin, long straight hair pulled back with a leather hairclip, and a tight crop-top shirt. No bra. I knocked on the door of Leslie's house, after first making sure her car wasn't in the driveway and Brad's was. When he came to the door, I put my hands in the back pockets of my short shorts, knowing that would thrust my boobs forward, and asked if Leslie was home. She wasn't—surprise, surprise—but he motioned me inside to wait.

Before I left—without having seen Leslie—he asked me out to dinner at a small Italian restaurant with wax dripping down real Chianti bottles. The next night we went to the movies. When I choked up because Butch and Sundance ran out of luck in Bolivia, Brad put his arm around me and whispered, "You remind me of Katherine Ross." We were inseparable the rest of the summer.

When I returned to U.C. Santa Cruz that fall, Brad moved to Berkeley so we could see each other on weekends. I usually hitchhiked there with Rachel, as Berkeley was a lot more fun than a dorm room on a quiet campus. He got a waterbed, a part-time job in a record store, and protested weekly against the Vietnam War.

While politically opposed to the war, there was also an element of personal desperation to his protests. Having graduated from college the year before and with no student deferment to protect him, Brad tried everything his wealthy parents could afford to be declared unfit for military service. Pricey doctors searched in vain for evidence of high blood pressure or fallen arches, and expensive lawyers advised Quakerism or Canada. With his draft number growing ever closer, Brad applied frantically to law schools. He got accepted that spring.

"But Boston University?" I protested. "In Boston? Why not somewhere in California?"

"Because that's where I got accepted." He traced the tears down my cheek. "It's Massachusetts or the Mekong, baby," he said in a pseudo-gangster voice.

I held it together for the rest of the semester, using the time to make sure he would miss me when he was gone. After I returned home for the summer and he left, I fell apart. No longer able to see the reflection of a beautiful, vibrant woman in his eyes, I became dull and listless. Without his gaze on me, I felt invisible. Without his touch, I had no body. Without him to hear my words, I grew quiet.

"So, study in France for a year," my older sister Charlene said, exasperated by my lengthy depression. "Just think. The Sorbonne! The Louvre! Cheap red wine in Paris cafes!"

She ignored my sullen expression. "You can miss that boyfriend of yours just as well from France as California."

I had to admit she had a point. That fall I studied existentialists at the Sorbonne while Brad enjoyed being one in Boston. I sent him long letters and romantic love poems. In return, he sent occasional missives describing his latest political epiphany or philosophical dilemma. While I appreciated being given a window into his head, I would have preferred a glimpse into his heart.

I came out of my reverie when the back door slammed and Rachel came back outside with two more beers.

"Brad wasn't a schmuck," I repeated. "At least, not at first."

Rachel lit a cigarette. "They never are, at first," she said.

We watched three smoke rings wobble away into the night sky.

What did they signal? I Love You? Be Back Soon? SOS?

Valkommen to Little Norway

THE NEXT MORNING, I LOCATED A broom, a dingy mop, a box half full of crusty detergent, and a vacuum cleaner that belonged in a museum. I wasted no time plugging it in and vacuuming the threadbare carpet in our bedroom. Rachel, who was still asleep—or pretending to be—moaned and burrowed deeper into her sleeping bag like a caterpillar refusing to leave its cocoon.

I rammed the vacuum into Rachel's bed frame and said cheerfully, "Rise and shine, sleepy head! I made you a cup of coffee, but you have to go in the kitchen to get it." I did not mention the coffee came from a jar of stale instant powder. "Bus for town leaves in fifteen minutes. Be on it or be left behind!"

"A bus? Really?" Rachel emerged cautiously from the sleeping bag with tangled hair and wrinkled tee shirt.

"No, silly. Does this look like the kind of place that has a bus running down the street? But there *is* a cup of coffee in the kitchen."

"Ugh, Nescafe," Rachel said when she tasted it. "I want real coffee. With cream and sugar. And I'm hungry. I want waffles and bacon and eggs!"

"You don't eat meat," I reminded her. "Come on, drink your coffee-like substance and let's go. I've made a grocery list. I think we can charge the cannery for Windex, cleanser and sponges. What do you think about toilet paper?"

"You should use it."

"Ha ha. We'll buy some, but we probably shouldn't charge the cannery." I tapped the pen against my teeth, watching Rachel. I could almost see the moment the caffeine reached her brain and the wheels engaged.

"Don't forget what Allen said about getting rain gear and boots," she said.

I added those to the top of the list.

We walked for half a mile along the road's edge toward town. Rain clouds had snuck back overnight and now surrounded the town like they had no intention of leaving until they reclaimed lost territory.

"More wet than dry," I observed.

"More puddle than pavement," Rachel responded.

It was a game we played in California to pass the time while hitchhiking to Oakland from Santa Cruz so that Rachel could disappear into The City and I into Brad's bedroom in Berkeley. My romance hadn't survived, but our game had.

Rachel would say, "More cars than pickups." And I'd say, "More Fords than Chevys." Or I'd say, "More couples than singles last night." And, after thinking a minute, she'd say, "More making out than marking time."

Last night, the buildings I'd seen raised on stilts along the beach had looked faintly ludicrous, like long-legged shorebirds out-of-place on dry land. Now at high tide, the same buildings looked faintly smug, high and dry above water that lapped ineffectually at their pilings.

The buildings were of two types. A few consisted of warped planks, rusty parts and faded blue tarps. They looked like ancient shipwrecks washed ashore and stranded at high tide, now resigned to a slow decline. To my amazement, however, most were tidy and well-kept two-story houses looking out of place in the Alaska wilderness. The houses were painted white and the green lawns freshly mown, and flowers bloomed in window boxes. Stylized flowers were painted on the wooden shutters and across the eaves. The Scandinavian rosemaling reminded me of costumed folk-dancers transplanted to foreign soil but determined not to assimilate.

We reached the intersection of Main Street and First Avenue.

"Wow, what original names," Rachel observed. "Who would have guessed this main street was named Main Street?"

"And look, First Avenue. I wonder what the next street up is called?"

"Tenth?"

"Main Street isn't even paved."

"There are sidewalks, though."

"Boardwalks," Rachel corrected. "They're made of wood."

The downtown looked like a movie set with false fronts to make the stores look bigger. Instead of horses tied up in front, old pickup trucks sagged at the curb.

"Norway meets the Wild West," I observed.

"More wilderness than civil-ness," Rachel added.

The buildings sported perky tole paintings along the storefronts. Even the names were Norwegian: the Scandia House, Sigrid's Flowers, the Kaffe Cafe. I saw lots of Viking this and Norse that as we walked all three blocks of the downtown: Viking Travel, Viking Insurance, Norse House. Red, white and blue banners and patriotic buntings hung everywhere. I'd never seen so many flags in one place.

"I'd forgotten the Fourth of July is coming up," I said.

"Yeah, it'd be nice if they decorated," Rachel said sarcastically.

I poked her in the ribs. "Notice how the bars have nautical names?" I mimicked a deep male voice. "Yes, dear, I'll be right home. Just have to stop by "The Harbor" first!"

"Okay sweetheart," she chirped in response. "I'm at "The Cannery" but will see you soon."

At the end of town, two large general stores faced each other like bookends propping up the buildings on their side of the street. The far end of town was dominated by a bright blue cannery with the picture of a Viking ship prominently displayed. A collection of bright blue buildings with Viking signs clustered around the central cannery.

I couldn't help but wish we were working there, instead of the shabby-looking cannery where we'd landed.

What had I gotten myself into? Usually when I asked myself a question, I heard my mother answer. But all I heard now was the squawk of seagulls, the passing of an occasional pickup truck, a distant foghorn. Sounds which only served to reinforce how far I was from home, too far, perhaps, to hear my mother's voice.

We entered a large grocery store advertising merchandise upstairs. The "clothing department" turned out to contain canvas pants, wool jackets, and flannel shirts—what I would call work clothes but up here seemed to be everyday wear. Packages of long underwear teetered on shelves next to work gloves and wool hats.

"More wool than cotton," Rachel observed.

"More functional than fashionable."

"But look at all these different colors of wool jackets. Green or gray or red plaid. If that's not high fashion, I don't know what is!"

I chose a pair of heavy rubber bib rain pants and a rain jacket. Then I thought about having to remove my jacket and pull those bibs down every time had to go to the bathroom. I exchanged the bib overalls for pants with elastic at the waist.

The shoe section featured rows of ugly rubber boots called "Extra Tuffs."

"Looks like it's Extra Tuffs or Extra Tuffs," Rachel observed.

"We need something other than tennis shoes, but look at the price!" My small savings wouldn't last long at this rate.

The clerk was a matronly-looking woman with frizzy brown hair that had never known conditioner or a blow dryer. She wore a paisley blouse, mustard-colored polyester pants, and a beautiful but worn knit cardigan with pewter clasps. She looked at me and then at my small stack of purchases. "You new to town?"

"Yes, we're starting at Petersburg Processors soon."

"Allen's a good man."

"You know Mr. Taylor?"

"Honey, everyone knows everyone around here."

"I'm from L.A." I admitted. "We don't know anyone."

"I'm sorry," she said. "Well, you'll need those red rubbers around here."

I checked to make sure Rachel hadn't slipped a packet of condoms into my pile.

"I'm not getting red rubbers," I stammered.

"What we call those Extra-Tuff boots," the woman said. "Red rubbers. Waterproof, but not very warm. You should get some felt insoles and wool socks, too."

I looked longingly at the display, my feet in their wet tennis shoes growing colder by the minute. Then I noticed the price. "Guess I'd better wait."

"I'd take one or the other if I was you," the woman insisted. My cold feet seconded the motion. "And get the boots a size larger so you can wiggle your toes and keep the blood flowing."

I exchanged the boots I'd selected for a larger pair and added a package of insoles to my purchases. They were cheaper than wool socks.

Rachel watched with interest as I counted the necessary bills and replaced the much-depleted stack in my wallet. "How much do you have left?" she asked.

"Not much," I replied, thinking I didn't want her to start mooching off me.

"So much for being able to afford breakfast," she grumbled as we took our purchases downstairs and went into the grocery section. Rachel steered the cart up and down the aisles while I checked off the items on my list. I scrupulously separated the cleaning supplies from our meager pile of groceries: Pop-Tarts, bananas, toilet paper, paper towels. We couldn't agree on anything for dinner, at least nothing we could afford. So, I grabbed a can of chicken soup and Rachel, Top Ramen, which is what we'd eaten during our student days. After much debate, we decided we couldn't afford real coffee and settled on instant. At least this jar would be fresh, or fresher.

I started chewing my nails in the checkout line. "What if they don't let us charge this stuff to the cannery?" I whispered to Rachel. "That would be so embarrassing."

Rachel shrugged. "They can keep the cleaning supplies, as long as we get the food."

When it was our turn, Rachel smiled at the teenage boy working the register and tossed her ponytail.

"So, Peter," Rachel said, peering at his nametag. "Okay if I call you Pete?"

He nodded and blushed, not an attractive combination given his acne.

"Allen at Processors said to charge this stuff to the cannery," she said breezily.

"Okay, sure," he stammered. "No problem."

"Not the groceries," I hastened to add. "We're paying for those."

I ignored the dirty look she shot me before she turned back to the teenager. "How much for a donut? This chocolate one sure looks good but we don't have much money."

The clerk glanced around. "Help yourself. It's on the house!" he announced grandly as though treating her to a glass of champagne.

He watched, mesmerized, as Rachel slowly licked the icing off the donut, a bit more licentiously than necessary. While he was engrossed in her performance, I took a jelly donut from the display case, wrapped it in a napkin, and stuffed it in my pocket to eat later.

"Hey, Pete, I haven't got all day," groused the woman behind us and he snapped to attention. Turns out all we had to do was sign the receipt for the cannery's share which he put into the register like a check.

Outside, rain was falling with a vengeance. I took off my wet sneakers and put on my new boots.

"I never had rain boots before, did you?" I asked, wiggling my grateful toes.

"In California? Are you kidding?" Rachel hesitated while pondering whether to have wet feet or follow my lead. She opted for dry feet.

I'll clean the kitchen, you take the bathroom," Rachel said after we got back to the house.

"*Mais non.* I'll take the kitchen. You do the bathroom." When we were roommates, I'd end up cleaning the whole house when I got tired of waiting for her to help. But we weren't in college anymore and that was one pattern I was determined to break.

"You do the toilet; I'll do the basin and shower," she countered.

"Only if we both clean the kitchen."

"Deal."

When the house was reasonably clean, we walked next door to check out the cannery. I halted at the sign reading: NO VISITORS BEYOND THIS POINT. Rachel strode inside and promptly ran into a young man turning the corner. He held a broom in one hand and steadied her with his other.

"Whoa! Do I know you? Girls are always throwing themselves at me. Sorry, I can't keep track of them all."

With his large nose, prominent Adam's apple, carrot red hair and skinny frame, I doubted many women did that. But he had an infectious grin and a great laugh. "You must be the new girls staying in the white house?"

When I nodded, he doffed his baseball cap and bowed with a flourish. "Greetings!" He straightened, put the cap back on his messy hair, shouldered the broom like a rifle and clicked his heels. "Jimmie Campbell at your service. Bob—he's around here somewhere—and I stay in the little blue house next to yours."

"I'm Maddie," I curtsied. "That's Rachel. You've already run into each other."

"A casualty, not a conquest," Rachel said, rubbing her arm, which I knew wasn't really injured.

"Allen said we could start work as soon as the cannery starts," I said.

"Right, we're getting it ready," Jimmie said. "Just a couple more days. Look, the boss doesn't like people wandering around in here. Liability and all. But I can give you a quick tour."

His words were drowned out by a forklift lumbering our way. I was sure we would be in trouble for trespassing but when it stopped, Jimmie gave a mock salute.

"Bob, meet our new neighbors, Rachel and Maddie. They're going to work here. Ladies, meet Bob..." then, after a pause, "...the foreman."

Bob didn't look like a foreman. He was not that much older than us, with friendly brown eyes and laugh lines etched into a youthful face. His powerful build made him look like he spent more time working outside than tooling around indoors.

Bob tipped his black cowboy hat in greeting like it was the most natural thing in the world, although I'd only ever seen cowboys do it in Western shows. "Howdy, nice to meet you. Cannery's not open yet. And won't be unless Jimmie and I get back to work," he said looking pointedly at Jimmie.

"Allen said for me to give them a tour," Jimmie said quickly. "They moved into the white house yesterday."

Bob nodded once, then accelerated quickly away, causing the flattened cardboard boxes stacked precariously on the forklift to slide off.

"So much for a grand exit," Jimmie said under his breath. It was hard to tell in the gloom, but it looked like Bob was blushing. After the pile was restacked and Bob drove off, more sedately this time, Jimmie swept off his cap, made an exaggerated bow, and flourished his cap toward the warehouse.

"Come, my ladies. I will show you the dock out back where freedom beckons but which you will never see again." He ushered us further inside and warmed to his act. "This is the dungeon where you will be enslaved for the rest of your lives—or until the season ends. It will come to feel the same."

He checked to make sure we were enjoying the act. We were.

"Today, when we are done with our tour, you may scurry back across the moat to freedom. But be warned," his voice took on a sonorous tone, "Once you clock in, the cannery owns you and will not let you leave again until the salmon have all been vanquished."

Jimmie shouldered the broom, a court jester mimicking a soldier, and marched us through the dim cannery to the dock. "This avenue to freedom and big bucks is where the boats off-load their catch. Mostly humpies."

"Humpies?" I asked. Rachel was staring after Bob.

"You know there are five kinds of salmon, right?" Jimmie continued.

I shook my head.

'Chum, sockeye, king, silvers and pinks," he ticked them off on his fingers. "Of course, kings are also called Chinooks and sockeye are called reds. Chum are dog salmon because they're used for feeding dog teams. Pinks are called humpies, basically worthless except for catching in large quantities by seiners and canning. Which is what we do."

"I thought salmon were salmon," I admitted.

"No more than a fishing boat is just a fishing boat," he said. "There are seiners, gillnetters, tenders, trollers…don't worry, lovely ladies…you will find I am a veritable fount of knowledge, and I am at your service."

He snapped his fingers. "Brilliant idea! Let's all have dinner tonight. I'll make my famous spaghetti. Famous because it's all I know how to make! Only we need to eat at your house because ours is too small, only fit for a dwarf or two. If that's okay."

"Okay, thanks! That would be great!" I enthused.

"Meatless, I hope?" Rachel asked.

"What?"

"She's vegetarian, well, most of time," I said. "Save some sauce before you add the meat and it'll work. I'll make a salad."

Jimmie nodded. "I'll tell Bob to bring beer. Or wine. Which do you like?"

"Either," I said.

"Both," said Rachel.

"I'll tell him to bring both. It'll be fun bossing *him* around, for a change. He thinks he can boss me around because he's the manager and I'm just a lowly slave." He scowled, then brightened as he continued the tour.

Lurking in the shadows were long steel troughs winding their way between segments of gigantic equipment shrouded in tarps.

"The dragon slumbers today, my lovelies, but not for long," Jimmie warned in a stage whisper. "Take care you do not wake the beast before his time." Then in a normal tone, "We'll get the beast up and running tomorrow. You'll have plenty of time to see it after that. Like, all summer."

I shivered.

"Yeah, it's cold in here," Jimmie said. "Get out while you can."

I was happy to follow him outside to a small black box mounted outside the office door.

"Time clock," Jimmie announced with a flourish. "Very important. Without it, you don't get paid." He patted it affectionately like a small dog. If clocks could wag, this one would have.

"I've heard of clocking in," I said, stroking the machine carefully like it might bite. "How's it work?"

Rachel stared off in the distance but paid close attention.

"Marla, the wicked gate keeper, will have a card here with your name on it. The time gets stamped automatically when you put your card in the slot. No card, no pay. You do *not* want to ask Marla to fix it for you." He shuddered dramatically, then bowed with an exaggerated flourish. "It's back to work for me. See you tonight!"

"Have you ever clocked in?" I asked Rachel after Jimmie left.

"What, is clocking in too blue collar for the Maguires?" Rachel asked.

"Yep!" I replied cheerfully. "We're all doctors, lawyers, engineers, a few teachers. Sometimes my folks go slumming with TV and movie people."

Rachel rolled her eyes, although I knew for a fact her father was a professor. "I need a nap," she yawned.

I was still thinking about the time clock. "Everyone I know tells other people what to do and how to do it. Other people actually do the work. I don't think my mom or dad actually know how to *do* anything."

"My mom can do drinking really well," Rachel said.

The Dinner Party

I WAS MAKING SALAD WITH ONLY SLIGHTLY wilted lettuce when Jimmie banged his way through the door with a pot of spaghetti. Rachel materialized wearing a clean shirt with her hair brushed.

"Where's Bob?" she asked.

"Taking a shower," Jimmie explained.

"Eau de fish!" I exclaimed.

"No fish odor today." Jimmie said seriously. "He's just getting the equipment ready."

There was a knock on the door and Rachel hurried to open it. Bob brought a six-pack and a bottle of inexpensive red wine. I found jelly jars for glasses, but no corkscrew.

"Not to worry!" Bob pulled a Swiss Army knife from the sheath on his belt. "There's a corkscrew on this."

Rachel turned it over admiringly. "Guess you'd better show me how it works," she purred, like this was the first bottle of wine she'd ever seen and not the five hundredth.

"My knife's better!" Jimmie said loudly. "My Leatherman has *two* blades, a file, pliers, *and* a corkscrew."

"Don't worry," Rachel said blithely. "We can admire your tool later."

Jimmie laughed. Bob blushed.

"More hunky than junky," Rachel whispered to me as she grabbed a glass.

"More employer than play toy," I responded tartly.

Jimmie was all arms and legs with a perpetual grin that reminded me of a friendly scarecrow. Bob was different. He had the stocky build and hard muscles of a guy who had grown up doing manual labor. He looked like he could sling a bale of hay as easily as the boys back home swung a golf club.

"So, how long have you guys been working in Petersburg?" I asked.

"My third summer," Bob said. "I grew up on a ranch in Montana, somewhere you've never heard of. Going to take it over from my dad someday. But in the meantime, I'm going to Ag school."

Rachel looked like she found this the most fascinating life story of all time, even though I knew for a fact she hated getting her hands dirty and would have nothing to do with animals of any kind—not to wear, not to eat, not even to pet.

"Yeah, and he's engaged," Jimmie added.

I glanced at Rachel. Her eyes glittered. Might as well wave a red flag at a bull.

"Suzanne and I are getting married after I graduate from college," Bob said matter-of-factly. "Her folks have the neighboring ranch. She came up here once and didn't like it."

"Didn't like it?" I exclaimed. "What's not to like?"

"Just about everything except the money I can make."

I pointed my fork at Jimmie. "Your turn."

"I came up last summer from Iowa. I traded an ocean of soybeans for an ocean of water. I know, crazy." He laughed ruefully. "I wanted to join the Navy, but mom said I'd better make sure I don't get seasick first. So, I came up to Alaska and got a job fishing. And guess what? I got seasick! So now I work in the cannery. Not sure what I'll do next. I might take classes at community college this winter. Might go to Costa Rica. I'm kind of a lazy fare kind of guy."

I knew Jimmie meant *laissez-faire* but he'd gotten the meaning right, if not the pronunciation, so Rachel needn't have kicked my chair leg.

"What brings you fair ladies to our humble land?" Jimmie asked, filling our glasses.

I looked at Rachel, wondering how she would spin the story. "I knew this girl, Sage—" she said.

"Nancy—" I interrupted.

"Who worked at Processors last summer." Rachel said.

"Do you guys remember her?" I asked.

Bob shook his head.

Jimmie nodded. "The girl Steve knocked up."

"Anyway," Rachel continued. "Sage gave me the idea to work up here this summer, make some money to go to Mexico in the winter. I asked Maddie if she wanted to come and she said no way."

"That's true. I didn't want to come at first," I admitted. "But then I did."

"Are you glad you came?" Bob asked, looking at me like I imagined a rancher would assess a cow to separate from the herd.

I wondered what it would feel like to be tackled by him, to feel his strong arms wrapped around me, his hard body falling to the ground on top of me. Would I succumb without a fight—or resist, just to feel the pleasure of eventual submission? I glanced down, sure I was blushing.

"So far, so good," I mumbled.

While Rachel and I polished off the bottle of wine and Jimmie drank three beers, Bob nursed a single beer, friendly but remaining somewhat aloof and in control. When the can was empty, Bob crushed it with one hand, arm muscles flexing. Rachel watched, licking spaghetti sauce off her lips.

Jimmie set a carton of ice cream and four spoons on the table with a flourish. "Ta-da! The piece duh resistance!"

I wanted to correct his pronunciation but stopped myself in time. "Neapolitan, how smart," I said instead. "Something for everyone!"

"Not everyone likes strawberry," he said modestly.

"I'm a vanilla man myself," Bob said, scooping some on his spoon.

"I want some of everything," said Rachel, leaning over and licking some ice cream right off Bob's spoon.

"Why bother with anything other than chocolate?" I closed my eyes as I savored my spoonful. Suddenly, I was with my father at Baskin-Robbins. He always urged me to choose any flavor I wanted—there were thirty-one—but I always chose plain chocolate, like him. He'd hand me my cone like a trophy and I could feel how proud he was of me—not because of the ice cream, of course, but just in general. Did he still think I was special, or was he aghast I'd taken my fancy college degree and gone to work in a cannery in Alaska?

When I opened my eyes, everyone was looking at me.

"Well, I'll leave Madeline to her ice cream orgasm," Rachel announced, pushing back her chair.

Just Another Trip to Town

I WOKE THE NEXT MORNING SCRUNCHED DOWN in my sleeping bag on a strange bed in a strange room, farther north than I'd ever been before, so far from home that it didn't seem like I should still be in America.

In the kitchen, I let the tea kettle whistle shrilly until Rachel appeared looking even more rumpled and grumpy than usual. I thrust a cup of coffee at her preemptively. When she was sufficiently caffeinated, I told her we'd need to go back into town.

"The hell. We went yesterday. Twice."

"*We* went once. *I* went twice."

She stared into her coffee, like the math, or maybe the point, escaped her.

"There's nothing to eat," I tried again. "Or drink."

That got her attention.

We trudged back to town. At the store, I paid for eggs, a can of frozen orange juice, and a stick of butter. Rachel paid for granola and yogurt. We split the cost of bread, brown rice, garlic salt, cheddar cheese, two zucchini and a can of tomato sauce for some kind of stir fry. I wanted to add ground beef to my portion, but meat was expensive. Everything was expensive. Isolation was enchanting until it came time to pay the bill.

Peter perked up when he saw us at the register. At least, when he saw Rachel. He stammered a hello and between ringing up the peanut butter and the strawberry jam, he asked, "You going to the parade?"

"What parade?" I asked.

"The Fourth of July parade. You can read all about it in the *Pilot*."

I took the little four-page newspaper and read the masthead: "PUB-LISHED EVERY THURSDAY. 1450 Happy Readers and Several Critics." I tucked it in my bag to read later.

Peter looked hopefully at Rachel. "I'll see you there?"

She had already turned away, but I smiled. "I'm sure Rachel would love that."

We walked past the Harbor Bar which looked dark and unwelcoming with dingy Norwegian tole painting around the facade. Through the window, I saw a disheveled man with his head on the table, asleep. I shuddered and hurried by. The next bar we passed looked marginally more inviting. This bar's neon sign was supposed to read "The Cannery Bar" but only the part reading "The Can" was lit.

Rachel's steps slowed, then stopped, the siren call of dim lights, cigarette smoke, and a drink beckoning. "Wanna go inside? Have a beer? Maybe play some pool?"

"We don't have any money."

"Who said we were paying? Would you take these groceries back for me while I pop inside?"

I was done making Rachel's life easy at the expense of my own. "It's all I can do to carry my own bag," I said. "See you back at the house."

Jimmie had warned me there were only three public pay phones in town and lots of transients wanting to use them. I figured now was as good a time as any to call my folks, so I detoured up to the one outside the post office. I rehearsed what I was going to say while waiting my turn: the uneventful ferry ride, the gorgeous wilderness, the Norwegian downtown that looked like a movie set, the tour of the cannery. I'd say that Rachel said hello, a little white lie. My mom didn't really like her; she said Rachel was a bad influence. I could never decide whether to correct the record, or continue letting her think it was Rachel's fault I'd turned out the way I was. Whatever way that was.

"Hi, Mom," I said when she picked up.

"Elizabeth, how nice to *finally* hear from you."

"It's Maddie," I said, exasperated right off the bat. Never mind I'd been named Elizabeth at birth and called Liz or Lizzie all my life. I had started using my middle name, Madeline, or Maddie for short, last year when I got back from Europe. After what happened there, I was determined to become a different person than the mousey one who'd left. No more prim and proper "Elizabeth," or dorky "Liz." No goody-goody "Beth" or, worse, "Bessie." Bessie was a cow. No, I wanted to be the kind of free spirit I knew a Maddie would be.

My mother took it as a personal affront.

"Well, excuse me. I thought Elizabeth was calling. How are you, *Madeline?*"

I launched into the cheery travelog I had mentally prepared, but before I was halfway through, Mom interrupted.

"That's nice, dear. Hold on, Charlene wants to talk to you."

That was unusual. My sister and I weren't particularly close, especially once she'd gotten engaged to a young CPA while I was abroad I was sure would be too square for my taste. We met on my first night home from my year abroad.

"Call me Douglas," he said when Charlene introduced us.

"Never Doug or Douggie," Charlene cautioned.

"Call me Maddie," I responded.

"Never Elizabeth or Lizzie" my sister warned.

"*Enchanté, mademoiselle,*" he said, bowing over my hand in mock French courtesy. He handed me a bottle of good Bordeau in honor of my homecoming, *et voilà,* just like that we were *les bon amis.*

At their wedding, I shelved my cynical veneer and did everything I could to make sure Charlene's was perfect. Play silly games at the bridal shower? Sure. Wear a frilly pink dress with puff sleeves? Fantastic. I chatted politely with Douglas's dorky brother and even slow danced with Uncle Arnie despite his bad breath and wandering hands. I smiled until my cheeks hurt and was only too happy to let the other young women jostle for Charlene's tossed bouquet.

My sister's voice came down the line. "Lizard Breath! How are you?" She sounded bright and chipper, which was unusual. She had a tendency toward prissiness bordering on stuffiness.

"I'm fine, Charlemagne," I replied cautiously. "What's up?"

There was a dramatic pause.

"I'm pregnant!" she announced.

I shouldn't have been surprised, but I was. How could she be so grown up already when I was just a young hippie girl, footloose and fancy free? I racked my brain to ask the usual questions: *When's the baby due…How do you feel…Boy or girl?* Charlene wasn't too worried about the specifics yet. She just kept saying how beautiful and wonderful everything was. If I didn't know better, I would have thought she was high.

I had run out of chipper things to say when she passed the phone to Douglas. He called me Aunt Maddie so I called him Daddy Douglas.

"Well, your mom's waving me off," Douglas said after a few minutes. "Time to sign off."

"Wait! Is my dad there?"

Dad came on the line. "Mizzie, how are you?"

"Fine. Rachel and I start work tomorrow. Mom can tell you all about it. Well, if she remembers with all the excitement down there. You're going to be a grandfather!"

"Yes, and I could use some reinforcements down here for the next seven months or so. You'd think no one ever had a baby before, the way they're carrying on."

"And you? How are you?"

"I'm fine. Don't worry about me. Worry about how I'm going to pay for all of this baby stuff."

We laughed together; a companionable laugh like in the old days.

"Dad, can I ask you something?" I said seriously.

I took the silence on the line as assent.

"I've been wondering, what did *you* do after you graduated?"

"Me?" There was a pause. "Well, there was a war on, you know."

"I know."

"So, as soon as I graduated, I joined the navy and quote, *saw the world*. Guam, Guadalcanal, the Philippines. When I got home, I was going to buy a second-hand car and drive across the county. But then I met your mom. Suddenly, all I wanted to do was get married. Start a family. So that's what I did. What's this about?"

"Did you ever want to do something else?"

"It was a different time, Mizzie. After the war, everyone just wanted to get back to normal. I'm glad you're getting a chance to do something different."

I wanted to talk on, tell him all about the doubts I was feeling and how Brad kept getting stuck in my head, but someone knocked on the phone booth.

"I gotta go," I said. "Someone's waiting."

"Well, then, goodbye, Mizabeth. Take care of yourself. Call again soon."

"Dad, wait!"

"What?"

I turned my back to the phone booth door so I wouldn't see the man waiting his turn.

"I had ice cream last night and was remembering all the times you took me to Baskin Robbins when I was growing up. Do you still go without me?"

My father lowered his voice.

"Well, your mom has me on a pretty strict diet since I had that heart trouble. Doesn't keep ice cream in the house. But, once in a while, I sneak away for a scoop. Don't tell!"

"I won't. I love you."

"Love you, too."

I let him hang up first, then listened to the dead air space, nodding as if someone was still talking, ignoring the person outside shifting impatiently from foot to foot. I was overcome with the wish to be back in California—enjoying the warmth, laughing with my family, sneaking a bowl of chocolate ice cream with my dad.

Why did I suddenly feel left behind, even though I was the one who had left?

And Then There Were Four

I saw Allen's battered pickup truck at the curb as I neared the house. Two young women climbed out. One of them took a pink suitcase tied with rope out of the pickup bed, while the taller girl retrieved a dull green duffle bag and slung it over her shoulder.

Allen rolled down the driver's side window and hollered, "Hey, Rachel! Your housemates have arrived!"

I turned around to see if Rachel was behind me, but he'd just mixed up our names. Or maybe all the seasonal workers looked alike to him.

"Tell them what I told you when you arrived," he said, pointing at me. "Any questions, I'll be at the cannery. Work starts tomorrow. 6:00 a.m. Don't be late." He ground the gears and the old truck lurched away.

The girl with the pink suitcase unfurled an umbrella. A pink suitcase *and* an umbrella? I wasn't sure if that made her supremely self-confident or totally clueless.

"My sister loaned it to me," she said defensively.

"That's the first umbrella I've seen since I got here," I said, flushing.

"Well, I don't know why. All it ever does here is rain."

"Because umbrellas on a boat are bad luck," Duffle Bag Girl explained. "Because umbrellas are sissy."

"I suppose it's more macho to get wet," umbrella girl sniffed.

I reached under the mat for the key. "Allen says we should keep the door locked when no one is home," I said, changing the subject.

"Like a burglar wouldn't check under the mat," said Duffle Bag Girl. "Anyway, I'm Maddie, not Rachel," I said ushering them inside.

"And I'm Deb, not Debbie." said Duffle Bag Girl. She was a tall brunette with a pageboy hairstyle that looked cute even when damp from the rain. "Don't call me Debbie."

"I'm Marie," said Pink Suitcase Girl. "Call me Marie. Do NOT call me Marie Catherine Agnes Grace. Only the priest called me that when I was baptized. Or my mother when she was mad. And could remember which kid she was yelling at." Marie took a breath. "Second of seven."

"I'm really Elizabeth Madeline," I admitted. "But everyone calls me Maddie."

Duffle Bag Girl and Pink Suitcase Girl, now officially Deb and Marie, dumped their bags in the living room and looked around.

"Did you two know each other before?" I asked curiously.

"Not really," Marie replied, checking out the view from each window. "Allen put us in touch and we met up at the Army Navy Surplus store to get some gear before coming here. We were going to take the ferry but then Allen called and said to get up here ASAP."

Deb continued. "So, then, *I* said, in that case, he'd better send us airfare. And he did!"

"Gosh, my first airplane ride!" exclaimed Marie. "It was so cool."

I started to say I'd flown up and down the West Coast and even to Europe, but then I remembered Marie's battered suitcase and how I was getting bruised from Rachel jabbing me or stomping on my foot whenever she thought I was acting snotty.

"Rachel and I took the ferry," I said. "I'm so jealous Allen paid your airfare."

"Where do we sleep?" Marie asked.

"I need a smoke." Deb said.

"Not inside!" Marie said, alarmed. "I'm allergic to smoke."

"No, you're not," Deb said good-naturedly. "You just don't like it. Is there a beer around here?"

"Instant coffee or Lipton tea," I answered.

"No diet soda?" asked Marie.

I shook my head.

"Fiddlesticks," muttered Marie.

"Fiddlesticks?" I repeated. I didn't know anyone actually said that.

"She doesn't curse, but she's okay anyway," Deb said in a pitying voice.

Marie ignored her. "I'd love a cup of tea. I don't suppose there's any saccharin?"

"A few hard sugar cubes," I replied.

"Coffee?" asked Deb hopefully."

"Instant."

While Deb went outside for a smoke and Marie went into the bedroom to unpack, I put water on to boil and assembled three mugs, the instant coffee, tea bags and sugar cubes. Ever the hostess. When we were all sitting around the kitchen table with our beverage of choice, Marie pointed with her spoon at the empty chair.

"So, where's she? What's her name?"

"Rachel," I said. "She's…in town." I didn't say she was in the bar.

"Did you two know each other before?" Deb asked.

"For the past four years. We're both from California and were matched up as roommates when we went to college. They gave us a…" I used air quotes, "'personality compatibility test' beforehand with a bunch of stupid questions."

"Like what?" asked Marie curiously.

"Like what hobbies do you have and what do you want to do when you grow up."

"Nothing important, like what is your favorite cookie or your favorite movie?" Deb joked. "Brownies and *Star Wars*, by the way."

"I don't eat cookies," Marie said wistfully. "But if I did, I'd choose Oreos. And *The Sting*. Robert Redford and Paul Newman are so cute!"

They looked at me expectantly.

"Chocolate chip cookies, no contest. But I don't watch a lot of movies," I admitted. Until "The Break Up," I'd considered *Butch Cassidy and the Sundance Kid* my favorite movie but now I hated it. "I like old movies," I said. "You know, like the *Maltese Falcon*."

Deb and Marie looked blank.

"Humphrey Bogart? Detective Sam Spade?" I prompted.

"In Morocco?" Deb asked.

"That's *Casablanca*." I waved my hands dismissively. "The point is, the questionnaire asked whether you like to study at night or in the morning—and then matched me with Rachel, who doesn't like to study at all! Sometimes I think we were just left over when everyone else was matched up."

"You'll fit right in here," Deb said. "Alaska is full of misfits."

"I'm not," Marie protested.

I thought about her pink suitcase, her umbrella, her quaint curses.

"You most of all," Deb said kindly. "And that's a compliment." She dumped her tepid brown liquid in the sink. "I gotta go into town for some smokes and real coffee," she announced.

"And diet soda," Marie said. "I'm broke but Allen said we could get an advance."

I had heard of getting an advance, just like I'd heard of putting clothes you wanted to buy on layaway, but no one I knew ever did it. They used a credit card when they wanted things they couldn't afford. Which, come to think of it, was basically the same.

"I have a little bit of cash my dad gave me for emergencies," I admitted.

"If needing coffee and beer isn't an emergency," Deb said, "I don't know what is."

"Well, here's what I think we should do," Marie said. "We can divide the refrigerator and cupboards into shelves for each of us and the top shelf will be for communal things."

She wrote a list—a woman after my own heart. "Toilet paper, paper towels, dish soap, stuff like that, we should all pay for. Cereal, bread, milk, the stuff you want to eat, you should buy yourself and keep separate so there are no hard feelings later."

"Don't mind her," Deb said good-naturedly. "She's anal."

"Don't mind Rachel" I countered. "She's vegetarian."

If Deb were a dog, she'd be a Great Dane, sleek and self-contained. Marie was a cocker spaniel, her large liquid eyes begging for a pet and her hair going curly in the Peterburg moisture.

What would happen when they met Rachel, the Cat Woman?"

Before I had to find out, I shoved my chair back. "Come on, I'll take you over to the cannery before we go to town."

Walking over to the cannery, I tried to act like an old hand and not like someone who had arrived just two days earlier. *Fake it until you make it* was a motto I decided to take to heart. The new me.

The office was dark and shuttered, but the cannery's double doors stood wide open. As much moisture as daylight blew inside.

"Liquid sunshine," I said knowingly. That's what the locals called the ever-present rain.

The cannery yesterday had been hushed, the equipment a powerful sleeping beast. Today, several workers hurried around under the bright lights, throwing tarps off equipment and prodding the great beast to life.

A forklift chugged by with Bob at the wheel. He stopped beside us but left the engine running.

"Hey, Bob, meet my new housemates, Deb and Marie." I shouted over the engine, repeating the introductions when Jimmie walked by with an armload of cleaning supplies.

"Here to help me clean the bathrooms?" he asked hopefully.

"Yeah, and I'll help whitewash the fence too," I joked.

"We don't need to paint," Jimmie said, puzzled. "We need to clean the toilets."

"*You* need to clean the toilets," Bob said. "The girls don't start until tomorrow."

"Well, then, farewell, lovely ladies. It's back to the dungeon I go." Jimmie made a show of trudging off dragging his bucket and mop dejectedly behind him.

"You'll be spending all your time here soon enough," Bob said as he shifted the fork lift into gear. "Get out while you can."

"I'm going to town," announced Deb. "Look for Brian or at least his boat."

"Who's Brian?" I asked. "A friend?"

"Maybe. Maybe more. We'll see. We only just met before I left Seattle. Friends of friends and all that. I was pretty jazzed to learn he was fishing up here."

Marie's steps slowed. "I'm going to the house. I want to write my fiancé and let him know I got here. Danny and I are getting married as soon as I've earned enough money for the big wedding I've always wanted."

Deb rolled her eyes behind Marie's back. "I'm never getting married," she announced.

"Oh yeah?" Marie retorted. "Just wait until you meet your soul mate. You'll change your tune."

She turned to me. "I've already put my wedding dress on lay-away but I have to lose ten pounds before I buy it. And earn enough money for flowers and a photographer and a place to have the reception." She made a face. "Otherwise, I'll be walking down the aisle in my sister's hand-me-down gown and serving Seven-Up and mints in the church basement."

She shrugged. "Danny said there were more important things to save money for, like an apartment. But I've been reading magazines and planning this wedding ever since I was a little girl. I told Danny you're only married once and I'll earn the money myself. So here I am. But I miss him already."

"You know there's a phone booth in town," I said when I could get a word in. "You could just call."

"Call long distance?" Marie was shocked. "That's too expensive."

"Never mind," Deb said. "Letters are nice."

I wished I had a guy to look for in town, or to send a love letter to back home. Most of the time, I was fine being an independent woman of the world. But sometimes it got lonely.

Since I had no one to visit or to write, I took a long, hot shower. When I emerged from the bathroom, Marie darted inside, making a show of waving aside the steam that billowed out behind me.

"Sorry," I said. "Were you waiting?"

She didn't reply, just wiped the mirror vigorously with a paper towel and then taped a piece of purple paper to it.

DON'T TAKE A LONG SHOWER. OTHERS ARE WAITING.

By the front door, another sign read NO RAINGEAR OR BOOTS INSIDE THE HOUSE. In the kitchen, a note on the fridge warned ONLY FOOD ON THE TOP SHELF IS TO SHARE. Inside the cupboard, each of us had a shelf neatly labeled with our name.

"What's with all the signs?" I asked.

"You've got to make the rules clear right from the start," Marie said unapologetically. "Otherwise, it's anarchy. I know, I come from a large family,"

Just then, the biggest anarchist I knew walked in the front door.

"What's going on?" Rachel asked as she took a package of cigarette out of her pocket and looked around for a lighter.

"I'm Marie," Marie said. "And please don't smoke inside."

Rachel's eyes narrowed.

"She's allergic," Deb said. "Marie's training me to smoke outside. I'm Deb." She pulled a lighter from her pocket. "Follow me!"

I was browning meat for dinner, when Rachel and Deb came back. Marie taped a lavender sign to the front door.

"NO MEN IN THE HOUSE," Deb read aloud.

"You've got to be kidding," Rachel snorted derisively

"Geez, Marie, maybe you've gone a little too far!" I laughed, trying to lighten the mood.

Deb and Rachel were not laughing.

Marie folded her arms primly across her chest. "Well, if I want to lounge around in my PJs, I don't want to worry about who might be here."

As if to emphasize her point, there was a knock on the door and two guys I didn't know barged in.

"Rachel said to stop by," one of them said, waving a six-pack of Bud.

"We come bearing gifts," the other added, lighting a joint to pass around.

"No, no, no," Marie said crossly, making shooing motions. "We are not open. Go away."

The two guys looked at each other and then at us, bewildered.

I thought quickly. "How about this: no visitors when we have to work the next day."

Marie countered. "How about lights out at midnight, work or no work?"

"How about forget it?" Rachel said.

"No men in the bedroom," Marie negotiated.

To my surprise, Rachel didn't object. She merely clapped the two guys on the shoulders and showed them out the door. When she turned back, she had the six-pack dangling from one hand and a joint in the other.

"Good work, sister," said Deb admiringly.

Rachel smirked and waved the joint at Marie. "Don't tell me you're allergic to pot, too?"

A good general picks her battles. Marie sat down silently to write a new sign.

Clocking In

GOOD MORNING!" MARIE CHIRPED THE NEXT morning in the kitchen where Deb and I were gulping tepid coffee.

"God, I hate morning people," Deb said, spreading margarine on a piece of toast. Rachel would have agreed except she was still in bed.

I was neither a morning person nor a night owl. I was a middle-of-the-road, not-too-early, not too-late kind of person—average, as usual.

"Daylight's burning!" Marie made a cup of cocoa and added a teaspoon of instant coffee.

"You know it's five a.m., right?" Deb replied grumpily.

"'Land of the Midnight Sun!" Marie exclaimed. "Maddie, are you going to wake Rachel?"

I started to leave the kitchen, then stopped. "She heard the alarm."

I finished dressing and hurried over to the cannery. The time clock made a satisfying ker-chunk as it stamped 0555 on my card.

Rachel arrived, grabbed her time card, and stamped it. 0605. She looked at it disbelievingly and then at the time clock. If looks could kill, the time clock would be dead.

"Good thing you weren't any later," Deb told Rachel. She jerked her head toward the office where Marla stood with arms crossed outside the door. "Marla's making sure we don't buddy punch."

We milled around inside the large structure that Jimmie had called the "fish house." Through the open door in the back, I glimpsed a large fishing boat tied up at the dock. A crane hoisted a dripping net onto the dock and a worker in green raingear guided it to a white plastic tub the size of a bathtub. Fish tumbled out into the tub and a fork lift carried the tub into the cannery. I couldn't tell who was driving. My stomach roiled from nerves and bad coffee.

Two middle-aged Asian women carrying Styrofoam cups of coffee strolled up.

"Note to self," I muttered to Deb, "There's real coffee somewhere around here."

"Canneries operate on coffee," Deb said knowingly.

Allen materialized beside us looking harried. "Okay, we've been offloading humpies since dawn."

I glanced at Rachel and she gave a tiny shrug.

"Pink salmon. Humpies," said Allen impatiently. "We've already run some through the Iron Chink to make sure everything's a go. Let's get to work." The two Asian women looked bored as they tossed their cups into a trash barrel and disappeared inside. Two sullen teenagers trudged inside after them, yawning. I guessed they were too young to work on a boat or around machinery but old enough to work in the cannery. Their disinterested demeanor made it clear they weren't novices like us. Allen intercepted me as I started into the cannery after them, pointing out a dispenser on the wall labeled "Hairnets." "Wear one of these."

I started to protest. Then I noticed the older women were wearing bandanas to keep their hair out of their faces. Sweet Marie had pulled her ponytail through a pink sequined baseball hat, which apparently passed muster, but Allen made Rachel, Deb and me wear hairnets.

I copied the experienced women as they donned blue vinyl aprons over their work clothes and grabbed rubber gloves from bins marked small, medium and large. Allen looked us over like a drill sergeant reviewing his troops. He didn't look impressed. When everyone was garbed up, he waved toward a large piece of equipment with a conveyor belt at waist level that wound its way around the cannery.

"It does look like a dragon," I whispered to Marie. "That's what Jimmie called it when he first showed us around."

"This, for those of you who don't know, is the Iron Chink," Allen announced grandly.

"Chink?" Rachel repeated.

"It does the work of a dozen Chinks who used to clean the fish by hand."

"I don't think you should use that word," Rachel said.

Allen stared at her. The two Asian women stared at her.

"The word 'chink.' It's disrespectful to Chinese people," she said.

"We're Filipina," said one of the women.

"Whatever," Rachel continued. "The point is…"

"The point is, we have fish to clean and can," Allen said, talking over Rachel. "Unless you're a canning expert as well as a language authority, let me continue."

Rachel crossed her arms over her apron but shut her mouth.

"Here's what you need to know. Fish get offloaded at the dock and brought in to get sorted and placed tail first on the belt. The index machine here cuts off the heads. Harriet will work there today. You others keep away."

The dragon's mouth, all blades and rotors.

Allen continued walking along the conveyor belt.

"The skeins of roe get pulled from the decapitated fish for special processing. You don't need to concern yourselves with this part. We have Japs—," He looked at Rachel. "I mean *workers from Japan* here to take special care of the eggs. I mean caviar." He was enjoying himself, even though no one was laughing.

He stopped by another contraption with clamps, brushes and belts. "Once the eggs are out, the fish get seized by prongs and run around in a circle so the fins and tail can be trimmed off and the belly opened. Most of the guts—that's viscera to you—" he nodded in Rachel's direction, "get cleaned out by the brushes here before the fish are dumped—carefully placed—back on the belt. Don't go putting your hands in here either."

I had no doubt the dragon would gobble our hands along with the fish if given half a chance.

Allen led us past the large machine to where the conveyor belt ran at waist height beside plastic troughs. Narrow water hoses dangled every two feet from a pipe suspended from the ceiling. Water from the hoses drained down into grates running along the trough. About a dozen fish had already been run through the line and were there waiting.

"Now, here's where you come in. We call this the slime line." He looked pointedly at Rachel. "I think it's okay to say 'slime,' right?"

Without waiting for a response, he continued. "If you're working here, you'll use this blunt scraper, grab a fish, make sure it's completely clean, no guts or slime left, then place it back on the belt tail first." He demonstrated on several fish that had already been run through the machinery. "Fish go from here to the cutter machine. Keep your distance from that, too."

He led us past the cutter to another assembly line where the fish pieces emerged. "If you're not working the slime line, you'll be here packing. Other canneries use a machine to pack their cans. We pack ours by hand. Says so on the labels," he said proudly.

"Can't afford a machine, he means," muttered Jimmie who had come up behind me.

"It takes about three pieces to fill a can this size," Allen continued. "Fish pieces circle around in this trough. Empty cans are automatically stacked here. Grab a can, curl two pieces of fish inside and poke a smaller piece in the center, then put the can back on this other belt. Grab a can, fill it, put it back on the belt. Grab, fill, repeat. The cans go from here to get weighed, sealed and sent to be pressure cooked next door in large retorts. Those ovens are large enough and hot enough to boil a person. Stay away from there, too. Okay, off to work!"

"Wait! I don't understand," I blurted out.

"What?" Allen growled. The friendly cannery owner who had driven us to the blue house that first evening was gone, replaced with a man who was all business, who had fresh fish on the dock needing to be processed.

Mom had always told me *there's no harm in asking* so I took a deep breath. "How do you know you've put the proper amount in the can?

"Well, if you fill the can with salmon like I just showed you, it'll be the right amount. And then we weigh it and send it back if it's wrong.

And, if we have to send too many back, you're fired." Allen curled his lips in a fake smile that indicated he was joking. Or maybe not. Hard to tell.

"But it's still got the skin and bones," I protested.

Exasperated, Allen snapped, "Haven't you ever had canned salmon before? It all gets pressure cooked in the can."

No, I thought, but kept my mouth shut. I felt stupid and irritated with my mother. Evidently asking questions made me a good student in the classroom but not here. Maybe in Alaska it was more important to stay quiet and appear competent? Hence Rachel's motto: *fake it until you make it.*

"Mable and Harriett, you work the index and cleaner. You two," Allen pointed to Deb and Rachel. "You're on the slime line this morning with Greg. You two," he said, pointing to Marie and me, "stay here at the canning line with Rusty. They know the drill, follow their lead." The boys straightened up, looking pleased. "Get rid of that gum, Greg. You know better." Greg slouched down again and left the room. "No gum, no candy, no nothing except in the break room, got it? Last thing I need is some housewife finding bubble gum in one of our cans. Trade positions in the afternoon. Jim! Jim, damn it, where are you?"

"Over here, boss!"

"Start this baby up. We'll start off slow until you get the hang of it, and then we'll go faster. Come on, people, we have fish out there getting older every minute we stand here blabbing!"

Allen herded Rachel and Deb out of the canning room and left us alone with Rusty. When he removed his baseball cap to jam it with the bill pointing backwards, I stared at his crewcut. No one I knew had crewcuts.

"If we don't keep our hair short, Allen makes us wear a hairnet," Rusty said defensively.

"It's not that!" I quickly lied. "I was admiring your Petersburg Viking cap. Where'd you get it? I want one, too." That wasn't a lie.

Before he could reply, the conveyor belt came to life and chunks of wet fish came tumbling by. I copied Rusty as he took a can from the queue below, wedged fish pieces inside, and set the filled can on a third belt to be carried into another room.

I didn't know how much fish to put in each can. Sometimes, I took a piece out, chose another, and rearranged them inside for a better fit.

"You don't have time for that," Rusty finally said. "Just stuff the pieces in and they'll weigh the right amount. If they don't pass muster on the scale, they'll come back around and I'll fix them. Just be sure to leave about an eighth of an inch on top for the lid."

Marie worked efficiently beside me, never pausing to adjust her cans. Determined not to be outdone, I forced myself to work faster. Finally, just when I thought my bladder would burst, the conveyor belt clattered to a stop.

Take a Break

"**B**REAK TIME," RUSTY ANNOUNCED AND VANISHED.

Marie and I joined the other workers outside the canning room. Harriet (or was that Mable?) saw us and said, "Put your gloves in the bin there and use a clean pair when you come back." I pulled off my rubber gloves and wiggled my fingers, damp and prune-like—not likely to be featured in a hand lotion commercial any time soon.

I copied the older woman as she took off her apron and hung it on one of many hooks lining the wall between break room and bathroom. Signs warned against wearing outer rain gear in the breakroom.

"Be sure you use the same apron again," said Mable/Harriet. The woman gave the ghost of a smile. "Unless you want to trade up for a cleaner one."

I noticed a piece of pink flagging on the strap of the older woman's apron. After thinking a moment, I tied the ends of my apron in a bow before hanging it up so I could find it again.

The break room held four long plastic tables and a bunch of hard folding chairs. White Styrofoam cups were stacked beside two large coffee urns. A can of powdered creamer, a box of granulated sugar, and several stained spoons were on an orange plastic cafeteria tray beside them.

Newspapers and old magazines were strewn on the tabletop. No *Vogue* or *New Yorker*. Just a Christmas issue of *Good Housekeeping*, back issues of *McCall's*, and several tattered copies of *Popular Mechanics*. Curious,

I picked up a well-thumbed booklet entitled *1972-73 Southeast Alaska/ Yakutat Commercial Salmon Fishing Regulations.* Two hundred pages of small print outlined everything from the size of the mesh on gillnets to how many of each type of species could be harvested in specific bays and coves.

"You need a college degree to understand that thing," said Jimmie, hurriedly pouring himself a cup of coffee.

"Maybe not even then," I said, throwing it back on the table.

I filled up a cup with coffee from one of the two industrial urns and thought about how the only piece of my mother's advice I had ever actually taken was to drink my coffee black to avoid needless calories. Marie came up beside me and dumped both creamer and sugar into her coffee. Either her mother hadn't given her the same advice, or she had ignored it.

Rachel stuck her head inside the break room, still in her rain gear. "Hey, pass me a cup of coffee, will you? Dump a bunch of creamer and sugar in there, too. I'm going outside for a smoke."

Back at work, I wished the time on the canning line would pass as quickly as the break had. Finally, the machinery stopped and Allen announced we had a half hour for lunch. My housemates and I hurried home.

Marie got the peanut butter and grape jelly off our communal shelf. I'm not a fan of peanut butter, and I hate grape jelly. But I was starving.

"Where's the bread?" I asked.

Deb got a funny look on her face. "Oh no! I forgot!" She started opening the cupboards as though a loaf of bread might magically materialize. Instead, she pulled out an unopened box labeled "Sailor Boy Pilot Bread" whose mascot looked like the pudgy Pillsbury Doughboy wearing a jaunty sailor suit.

"What's that?" I asked as she spilled out a dozen large, round crackers onto a paper towel. They rolled around like 4-inch frisbees but didn't crack or crumble.

"You've never had Pilot Bread?" she asked in disbelief. "My dad always kept Pilot Bread and canned Spam around because they never get stale and don't need refrigeration. He said more Pilot Bread is eaten in Alaska than any other state."

"Guam eats the most Spam," said Marie, grabbing two crackers.

"Guam isn't a state, it's a territory," said Rachel. "Hawaii eats the most Spam."

Marie looked hurt and I gave Rachel the evil eye. "How do you even know that?" I asked Marie.

"Jeopardy."

Back at the cannery, I donned my apron and gloves and started toward the canning room.

"No way, Jose!" Rachel said, grabbing my arm. "Allen said to change places this afternoon. I don't want to deprive you of a chance to work the slime line."

"Can't be worse than cramming salmon chunks into cans."

"Oh, no? Then enjoy!" Rachel hurried to the canning line and I followed Marie to the slime line. Greg was there and nodded at us. "Grab a scraper."

"Looks like a cross between a spoon and a knife," remarked Marie.

"A *spnife*!" I joked nervously. Then the machinery rumbled to life and started disgorging decapitated and de-gutted fish. "Eh, Rusty, help me out here?" I said uncertainly.

"Grab a fish. Flush with water. Make sure it's clean inside. Place on conveyor belt so the head—or what used to be the head—is up against the guard so it'll get cut into the right size for canning. Grab another. Clean. Place on belt. Repeat."

"Got it," I replied glumly.

The slime line was wet, messy work. The fish were fairly clean by the time they'd gone through the rollers, but bits of tissue and blood splattered everywhere. "Why do they call this the slime line when there's very little slime on these fish?" I asked Rusty.

He looked like he couldn't believe how ignorant I was. "No slime on fresh fish. No smell, either. Allen's a stickler for fresh."

I realized he was right. I thought a fish cannery would smell fishy, but it didn't.

That was the good news. The bad news was that the room was kept cool and cold water ran constantly from the hoses and troughs that carried the wastewater and fish tissue away. Cold water splashed on the floor, on the fish, and on my apron. I wished I had dressed more warmly.

After only an hour, I was ready to admit the slime line was worse than packing. After two hours, I needed a bathroom break. Three hours later, we finally got one. Then it was back to work.

By then, I was sick of looking at the insides of salmon. How was I going to do this monotonous work hour after hour, day after day, for the rest of the summer? Instead, I could catch the next ferry south, then the bus back to LA. and be home by the end of the week. Surely answering phones in some office or tutoring bored high school students in French would be better than this.

Then I thought of how my mother's face would look, *I told you so* written all over it. And my dad? If he was disappointed in my choice of summer jobs, he would probably be even more disappointed if I quit. I decided I could stick it out another week before going home. That way, no one could say I hadn't tried.

"Hey, pay attention!" Allen barked from behind. "You need to work faster. I told the gals in the canning room to work the slime line for a while. When you're done here, finish up in the canning room. Be back at six o'clock tomorrow morning for more fun."

Rachel came up and grabbed the hose from the station beside me. When Allen turned away, Rachel squirted the outside of my heavy plastic apron.

I yelped but then laughed. "You're right," I admitted. "The slime line is worse."

We finished shortly after 7:00 p.m. I was fuzzy with fatigue and my legs ached. The excitement I had felt at 6:00 a.m. was long gone.

Jimmie stopped me at the exit. "Use this hose to clean your gear first. Once those fish scales dry, you'll never get them off."

Eau de fish, I thought. I gingerly turned the hose on myself to rinse off the fish slime. Amazingly, I didn't get wet. I sprayed myself harder as I realized the water just bounced harmlessly off my thick apron. In

California when it rained, everyone acted like they were made of spun sugar and would dissolve if they got wet. Here, people lived most of their life in water: water from the ocean, from the sky, from cannery hoses—and either ignored it or dressed accordingly.

"Hey, my turn," said Deb. She yanked the hose out of my hands and I started toward the house.

"Not so fast," a voice yelled. Marla was standing outside the office watching. "I'll remind you today, but next time you forget to clock out, you'll only get paid for eight hours, no matter what time you leave. And if someone else clocks in for you, you're both fired. Got it?"

I clocked out exhausted, hungry, aching. After the noise of the cannery, it was a relief to be outside. It was so quiet I heard my mother's voice saying with grim satisfaction, *you've made your bed, now sleep in it.*

I DIDN'T WANT TO WAKE UP the next morning but the thought of my mother saying she told me so and the memory of Marla's grim face pried me out of bed. I swallowed three aspirin and slathered two pieces of Pilot Bread with peanut butter to eat on the way to the cannery. My housemates had already disappeared inside the cannery by the time I clocked in, five minutes late. I fluttered my eyelashes at the time clock, but it didn't succumb to my charms the way Mr. Newberg had when I was tardy for Algebra.

I assumed Rachel was in the canning room while I spent the morning slaving away on the slime line. I was surprised not to see her in the break room when it was time to grab a cup of fresh coffee and a stale donut.

Marla entered and looked around. "Where's Rachel?"

My housemates and I looked at each other.

"Um, cramps?" said Sweet Marie.

Disbelief was etched on Marla's stern face. "Well, you tell her she'd better get to work this afternoon or she can just take her cramps away with her on tomorrow's ferry."

"Yes, ma'am," Marie replied meekly.

Back at the house for lunch, Marie shifted into Big Sister mode, marching into the bedroom, flinging the covers off Rachel's bed, and delivering Marla's message.

"Why didn't you wake me?" Rachel demanded.

"Not our job," I said from behind Marie. The pillow Rachel threw bounced harmlessly off Marie, who threw it back with more strength than I would have anticipated.

"Four brothers," Marie said smugly and left the room.

Rachel groaned, rolled out of bed, and went to work that afternoon.

"This is the real world," I overheard Marla scolding. "Not some fancy schmancey college class you can skip whenever you feel like it. Get real or get out."

After work, Bob drove us to town in the cannery truck. Now that we were making money and had use of a truck, we were able to load up on groceries. While my housemates rolled the cart around the market, I ran upstairs hoping to buy a Viking cap so I didn't have to wear a dreadful hairnet.

"No such luck," said the saleslady. "But we do have these."

The red paisley bandana instantly brought back memories of running around California as a carefree Girl Scout, backpacking in the Sierras or sailing around Newport Beach, always with a red bandana tied jauntily around my dirty, windblown hair. I had seen my bandana as a symbol of cheeky insolence, a banner of non-conformity in a culture that valued coiffed hair, carefully applied makeup, and color-coordinated outfits, a red flag waved in front of my mother, a gauntlet thrown down in our endless mother-daughter wars over bell-bottom blue jeans, loud music, and curfew.

At twenty-one, I thought I had outgrown all that. I thought I had made progress in my life, had transformed myself into the kind of woman I wanted to be: footloose and fancy-free, tragic yet glamorous. As comfortable in Paris as in Petersburg. Wounded in love, perhaps, but open for more.

Now I stared in the mirror. A girl in a red bandana stared back. Had I retreated back to the past instead of moving forward? Or had I lost my way and was now back where I started?

Back at the house, I took my banjo out of its case. One string was broken and the rest completely out of tune. The drumhead had faint but worrisome gray splotches. Mold? I turned it this way and that like I had with Scruffy the stuffed dog before I'd left California. Then I put it away in the case and shoved it under the bed.

Wake, Work, Sleep, Repeat

Wake, coffee, eat, work, coffee, work, eat, more coffee, work, eat, sleep.

I'd never done manual labor before. I discovered time passed more quickly, or rather, less slowly, when I concentrated on each task, whether sliming fish or packing pieces in cans. Unlike abstract schoolwork, the results of my handiwork were immediately apparent. Zen and the Art of Canning.

The cannery routine reminded me of high school, our movements determined by a clock now instead of a bell: harried adults barking orders, girls hurrying from station to station or banging on the bathroom door because there weren't enough stalls, the anticipation and disappointment of lunch.

Rusty sent a salmon eyeball down the conveyor belt. Greg stuck his hand in a fish head like a puppet lamenting the fact it didn't have a body anymore and hadn't gotten to spawn.

I day-dreamed a lot, which my teachers said I did most of the time anyway. When I got bored with my own daydreams, I wondered how my co-workers passed the time.

"What are you thinking about?" I asked Marie while our hands grabbed fish pieces, stuffed them in cans, put the cans back on the conveyor belt.

"Danny," she replied promptly. "Wedding dresses. Cake flavors."

No surprise there. I listened to wedding talk for the rest of the morning and even contributed a few tidbits from my sister's nuptials.

Deb was the next victim in my war against boredom.

"What do I think about?" she asked. "Oh, Brian, I guess. He's funny and hard-working and cute and kind."

"Does he have a brother?" I asked, only half-kidding.

"I know we just met, but I think how nice it would be to jump in his little troller and travel around Southeast, fishing and getting to know each other."

I thought of all the little coves and islands I'd glimpsed from the ferry, the excitement of exploring this vast country, rocking at night on a little boat with someone I loved. "It would be nice," I agreed. "What's he do when the fishing season is over?"

"Over? Trollers work year 'round, not like the seiners. They catch one fish at a time and can make good money, but they have to put in the time."

"Year-round?" No college or career or travel to look forward to? I was—perhaps—willing to do scut work for long hours during the summer in order to have the freedom to do what I wanted in the winter, but if there was no relief in sight? Suddenly, the prospect of hanging out on a troller didn't sound quite so appealing.

I wasn't sure I should ask Rachel. *Don't ask the question if you're not prepared to hear the answer.* But that afternoon on the slime line, I did anyway. She looked at me like I was crazy. "What do I daydream about? Gee, Maddie, I don't know. Whether I like tequila or Jack Daniels better. What I'd do if I won the lottery. Whether we're ever going to get time off to meet guys. And don't tell me your dreams. I'm not that bored."

An hour later, she was.

"What do I daydream about?" I pretended to think. "Oh gee, whether I like chardonnay or cabernet better. What I'd do if I won the lottery which, by the way, is to go around the world. And, oh yeah, I daydream about that cute Dane I met in Paris who's probably in Nepal by now."

I stuffed a couple more fish pieces into cans. "I do *not* think about Brad."

About 4:00 that afternoon, I was elated to hear there would be no work the next day. Or the next. Not until there was another opening and more fish to can.

"Whenever that is," Harriet hung up her apron morosely.

"Well, I'm glad for some time off. I'm bushed."

"Ok for you college girls," Harriet snapped. "What do you care? Maybe you'll have to ask your parents for a bigger allowance or, I don't know, spend a few weeks less in Bali this winter. For me, it means Ivar can't make his boat payment and I owe money for groceries."

Mable came up beside us. "We have to wait until Fish 'N Feathers decides when and where the next opening will be. Educated guesswork, they call it."

"Guesswork, period," Harriet sniffed.

I HAD BECOME THE DESIGNATED CHEF for our household, a role I didn't mind, even if the menu tonight was just tomato soup and grilled cheese sandwiches.

"It's missing a little *je ne sais quoi*." I said, stirring the soup.

"What?" Marie asked, reaching into the cupboard for bowls and plates.

"I don't know," I translated.

"Then why'd you say it?" she asked crossly.

"No, *je ne sais quoi* means…never mind."

Deb leaned against the kitchen counter and began assembling sandwiches.

"No mayo for me, I'm on a diet," Marie said.

Deb rolled her eyes. "I don't know why. You look fine to me."

Deb spread mayonnaise on the other three slices of bread, then pointed the knife she was using in my direction. "So, Maddie, I've been meaning to ask, what's with you and Bob?"

"Me and Bob?' I felt myself blush. "Nothing! Why?"

"I've seen the way he looks at you when he thinks no one is watching."

"Me?" I repeated stupidly.

"Yes, and how you look at him, little Miss Gidget goes to Paris."

"Bob's engaged." I reminded us both. "Off-limits."

"Besides," Rachel said as she snitched a piece of cheese. "Maddie's not interested."

Deb slapped Rachel's hand playfully. "Why not?"

"Because he's not my type," I said, ladling the soup into bowls which Marie took to the table.

"What *is* your type?" Deb asked as we sat down to eat.

"Not a red-neck engaged Montana cowboy, that's for sure."

"More like a blond, guitar-playing, two-timing law student," Rachel inserted.

In my mind, I saw an image of Brad as I'd seen him that day in Greece. Not the blond, long-haired surfer guy I'd fallen in love with in California. Not the passionate lover he'd become in Berkeley. Those images were gone, faded like the polaroid snapshots I'd burned when I got back from France.

The Brad I thought of now was the clean-shaven short-haired guy with wire-rim glasses who'd come all the way from Boston to break my heart at a small café on the island of Amorgos. We'd reunited for what I eagerly anticipated would be a torrid and romantic spring break. The island was the perfect setting, like God had poured gallons of white-wash over the village and then scattered handfuls of vibrant magenta bougainvillea everywhere.

Brad and I sat on the terrace of a small café and ordered ouzo. I sipped the fiery liquid while Brad swallowed his in one gulp. Then he took my hand, told me he loved me, and proceeded to tear my heart to shreds.

He said he also loved a girl back in Boston. He didn't know what to do. He'd come to see me to sort things out. He was so confused, he said, like I was supposed to feel sorry for him.

"So, what you're telling me," I hissed, "is that for the past year, you've been writing me, planning this trip, and now you're here telling me I'm 'on audition' so you can see who you love best? How dare you!"

I wanted to throw my drink at him, smash the glass against the wall, scream bloody murder. Instead, I swallowed my ouzo in one gulp, the way I'd seen the old men do between moves on the backgammon board.

"Well, guess what? I am not auditioning for the part of your lover. I am not playing that game."

And just like that, I threw Brad out of my vacation, out of my life, out of my dreams for happily-ever-after. When he complained there wasn't another ferry for three days, I rose—majestically, I hoped—and said, "Frankly, my dear, I don't give a damn."

In spite of the shock and heartbreak, I was sort of proud of that exit line I'd plagiarized.

"Maddie's heart is broken," Rachel now told Deb and Marie in a solemn voice. "Maddie is determined never to love again."

Deb and Marie eyed me curiously, avid for details but too polite to ask.

"Long story," I shrugged. I wanted to spin it as a tragedy, but Rachel didn't give my heartbreak the gravitas I thought it deserved. Love 'em and leave 'em was her motto. I settled for the abridged version. "A year of bliss, a nasty break-up, a semester of misery...*et voila*, here I am."

Rachel looked like she wanted to add some more detail, but it was hard to argue with the summary.

"Never mind," Marie said. "Someday Maddie will meet the man of her dreams and she'll be as happy as Danny and I are."

"Or," inserted Rachel, "She'll settle for a good roll in the hay with a hunky cowboy, and learn it doesn't have to be forever to be fun."

MARIE WENT TO HER ROOM TO miss Danny, and Deb left to look for Brian. Rachel looked in vain for something to drink or smoke.

"Let's go next door," Rachel suggested.

Jimmie opened the door and ushered us into the cramped kitchen with a flourish. "Welcome, fair ladies. How may I be of assistance on this quiet night?"

"Forsooth," Rachel said coyly, a rare tone for her, "We're bored. We look to our local minstrel for entertainment."

"At your service," he bowed. "Liquid refreshment? Something to smoke? A good story?"

"All of the above," responded Rachel. "Where's Bob?"

"In line to use the pay phone, along with all the other transients in town."

"Not at the cannery?"

"No one's there now."

"Perfect!" said Rachel. "Let's go."

"Go where?" Jimmie said, passing beers and a joint around.

"The cannery."

"Cannery's closed for the night."

"Don't you have a key?"

"Well, yes, there's one by the door in case Bob or I have to run over there after hours."

"I think I heard a noise coming from there!" Rachel said. "Might be a burglar. We'd better check it out!"

Rachel's enthusiasm overcame my normal caution and Jimmie would have followed Rachel anywhere. So, off we went to the silent cannery, dim but for flickering emergency lights left on twenty-four seven.

"What is it you do all day while we're slaving away on the slime line?" asked Rachel as we wandered around the ground floor, checking out the areas we rarely saw.

Jimmie shrugged. "Make cans from strips of aluminum. Make boxes from flattened cardboard. Use the fork lift to move the filled cans into the retort. Then move 'em out of the retort to cool. Stack them, store them. You know, men's work."

Rachel didn't rise to the bait but, instead, led him toward the fork lift. "Show me."

Jimmie and Rachel climbed onto the seat and Jimmie proceeded to give her a lesson in how to operate the fork lift.

"I could do that," she said.

"No way," Jimmie responded.

"Yes, way. I'll bet you a case of beer I can."

"You're on," Jimmie said.

They switched seats and amid much hilarity lurched off deeper into the shadows.

The bright light outside the office switched on and I froze, a deer in the headlights.

"What are you doing?" Marla demanded when she saw me. "Trespassing? Stealing?"

"No! We thought we heard a suspicious noise…".

"We?"

"Jimmie and I. So, we came to investigate."

The forklift chugged into view with Rachel in the driver's seat.

"Joy riding!" Marla exclaimed, horrified.

Jimmie turned off the ignition and, in the sudden silence, Marla's voice rang out. "Jimmie Miller. You ought to be ashamed of yourself. And Rachel…you ought to be fired."

Rachel slid off the forklift. "I was just proving a point."

"And that is…?" Marla crossed her arms: judge, jury and executioner.

"That a woman can operate the equipment. That *I* can drive this fork lift." Rachel glared at Marla like it was all her fault. "I don't know why men get all the good jobs."

Marla's eyes softened. "You're not wrong about that. Men do get the high-paying jobs. They go out on fishing boats…"

"…and drive forklifts," Rachel interjected.

"And drive forklifts," Marla sighed. "That's just the way it is." She yawned and rubbed her eyes. "I'm going to pick up the paperwork I came for and then go home. You three do the same. *After* Jimmie parks the forklift. Lock up on your way out."

"I knew I could operate that forklift!" Rachel enthused on the way home. "You owe me a case of beer, Mr. Miller."

"You almost got us fired, Ms. Women's Libber," Jimmie pointed out. "That negates the bet."

They bickered good-naturedly on the way home. I stayed out of the fray, wondering why *can't* a woman do a 'man's job.' Wondering, why can't I work on a fishing boat?

$$\text{\textasciitilde}$$

The Haircut

I SLEPT IN THE NEXT MORNING AND then went to the laundromat. When I got home that afternoon, Rachel and Deb were sprawled in the living room with an open bottle of rum next to cans of coke.

"Tsk, tsk," I said. "Drinking before 5:00? What would my mother say?"

"If you can't beat 'em, join 'em?" Rachel suggested.

"My mother? Are you kidding?"

"Good thing she's not here," Rachel said, handing me the rum.

Marie wandered in clutching a can of Tab.

"You want some rum in there?" Rachel asked

Marie shuddered. "You know I'm on a diet. Do you have any idea how many calories are in a shot of rum? Sixty-five."

Marie was slightly plump but in a way that only emphasized her heart-shaped face and full figure. Her crooked smile would have been cured with braces in California, but they added a certain raffish charm to Marie's otherwise angelic appearance. No doubt about it, Marie was a dude magnet, even though she pretended not to notice. She'd be good to have at the bar. She would lure the guys in while someone else pounced, most likely Rachel. Rachel was the pouncing type, would even toy with her victim if he tried to escape.

I wasn't a dude magnet. I wasn't a feline on the prowl. Without Brad looking into my eyes, I felt invisible, but now I had a new name and my heart was healing. My image, face framed by a red bandana, was slowly emerging like a reflection in a steamy mirror I still couldn't see clearly.

"Dieting is not the way to lose weight," Rachel said in the sanctimonious tone only someone with a high metabolism would use.

Poor Marie. She was the type who struggled to lose ten pounds only to put on fifteen as soon as she stopped dieting.

"So, what do you recommend, drugs?" I asked Rachel.

Ignoring her dirty look, I went to take a shower. The sign admonishing us to take a short shower was curling up at the edges and damp from humidity. When I returned to the living room, toweling off my damp hair, I couldn't help complain about my long stringy hair. It looked nothing like the model's thick glossy locks on the bottle of shampoo I had just used.

"I should just cut it off," I grumbled. "Whatever I do, it looks horrible."

Marie looked up from the letter she was writing. "I could cut it for you."

"What?"

"I went to beauty school, you know. Only I didn't have enough money to keep going and, anyway, hairdressers don't earn diddly squat back home. I do all my relatives' hair anyway."

She pulled me into the kitchen and shoved me onto a chair. "I like to give my clients a magazine to look through to choose a style." She looked around as though the old *Mad Magazines* and *Petersburg Pilots* lying around the house would suddenly morph into *Vogue* and *Seventeen*.

"You want to look like Alfred E. Neuman or Ole Olsen?" Deb asked helpfully.

Marie rummaged through the kitchen junk drawer—rubber bands, corks, old pens, a tide book, a fishing lure—until she found a pair of scissors. I watched as she felt the blunt edges and grimaced.

"Um, maybe we'll do this another time." I rose from the chair but Marie pushed me back.

"You'll never have big hair like Farah Fawcett and it isn't thick enough for a Dorothy Hamill wedge," she said, considering. "I'm guessing you won't take the time to curl it…"

"Definitely not. So, what does that leave?"

"A buzz cut?" Rachel offered.

"I know!" Marie announced brandishing the scissors.

"I feel like I'm facing the firing squad," I complained.

"Here, have a drink," Deb said, passing me the bottle.

"A blindfold?" Rachel offered.

"Oh, hush, you two," Marie said, getting irritated. "In fact, go in the other room."

Marie settled the towel around me. "Sit up," she commanded. "Face forward. Don't squirm."

I shut my eyes as she softly hummed in time to the snip of the scissors. My mother always said I wasn't a vain person, but she said it in a way that didn't sound complimentary, the same way she criticized my careless attitude about clothes and lack of artifice around boys. Still, I would prefer not to emerge from Marie's amateur haircut looking like some kind of ghoul who'd had her hair cut in a kitchen with rusty scissors.

When she released me from the towel, I ran to look in the bathroom mirror. Gazing back at me was someone I hadn't seen before. Someone with large, green eyes when I'd always thought mine were small and murky. Someone whose pixie cut made her look carefree and wanton, like someone I wanted to be. Maybe now that I was in Alaska with a new name and a new hairdo, never mind the red bandana, perhaps now I had become that woman.

NO ONE DRESSED UP FOR A night on the town, not in a fishing town like Petersburg anyway. But I wanted to look as spiffy as my new hairdo did—without being obvious. I pulled on a pair of black jeans and a lime green tee shirt that fit just a bit too snugly. I lingered in front of the dresser mirror, enjoying the way the green shirt brought out the green in my eyes and the way my beaded earrings dangled below the new short haircut.

"Where is everyone?" I asked Marie, who sat alone in the living room.

"Deb left to find Brian. Rachel just left," she answered. Rachel and Marie would never be good friends, but they managed to peacefully co-exist, for the most part.

"Well, then, time for us to go, too. Come on, I'll buy you a drink."

"You know I don't drink," Marie said primly.

"Oh, come on. They serve soda."

"Diet soda?"

"Club soda."

"Well, if you insist."

Marie was wearing a pink floral shirt I hadn't seen before and her long naturally curly hair cascaded loosely down her back. "I won't tell Danny," I said.

Jimmie waved us over to his table near the dance floor. The people there shifted their chairs to make room.

"Where's Bob?" I asked, looking around.

"Never comes."

"Why not?"

Jimmie shrugged. "Because he doesn't drink? Because he's a wet blanket?"

"Because he's engaged, silly," Marie said with finality.

"Guess that means no more fun," Jimmie said.

Marie punched his arm.

"I'll buy the first round," Jimmie laughed. "What'll you have?"

"Club soda," Marie said virtuously.

"*Mais non,*" I said. "We both want Miller Lites."

An arm I recognized reached from behind me to snag the ashtray. One of the guys—Rick, I think his name was—grabbed Rachel's wrist. "Wow, a tattoo! I've never seen one on a girl before."

"We *both* got tattoos in San Francisco last year," I announced quickly.

Rachel pretended to lose her balance and fell on Rick's lap. "We hitchhiked to San Francisco one morning," she said.

"And the next thing I knew, we were at Lyle Tuttle's Tattoo Parlor," I finished.

Rachel had pretended it was a spontaneous trip, but she already knew how to get there and what she wanted when we got there: the Hebrew L'chaim symbol tattooed on her upper arm. While she went under the needle, I flipped through binders of tattoo designs apparently irresistible to drunk sailors or hung-over gang members. Then, buried amid designs of flames, buxom mermaids, and skulls, I spotted a small red heart with one wing. Eureka!

Why one wing, Rachel asked afterward. I told her my heart was on the move, questing and not ready to settle down. I was thrilled with my daring, proof I was a free spirit, even though the proof was hidden on my hip where my mother couldn't see it.

Neither could young men in Saturday night bars.

Rick grabbed Rachel's arm and turned it gently back and forth. "So, what's it mean?"

"*L'chaim!* To life!" Rachel said. "The Nazis tattooed their prisoners even though the Torah forbids Jews to desecrate their bodies. My grandmother survived Auschwitz but never got hers removed, so as to never forget, she said. I got my tattoo to always remember." I looked at Rachel in amazement. It was a solemn speech for her. She broke the mood when she raised her beer, "L'chaim!"

"L'chaim," we responded,

Another record dropped in the jukebox. Another round of drinks appeared. Someone mentioned a rumor they'd heard about the next opening.

I couldn't let my new friends think Rachel was the only one with a cool tattoo. "Getting tattooed didn't hurt as much as I thought it would," I announced as though anyone cared.

"What is your tattoo?" Jimmie asked. "And *where?*"

I'd practically begged them to ask, and now I didn't know what to say. When I'd gotten the heart with one wing, I thought it a symbol of romantic freedom. My heart could fly anywhere but chose to alight on Brad. Now, I wouldn't be surprised to find my tattoo had a crack running through it, the wing scorched, the heart dented.

I was sad, but not sad enough—or drunk enough—to share *that* story. "Oh, that's strictly on a need-to-know basis," I answered airily. "And before you ask, you can only see it when I'm wearing a bikini—or nothing!"

I noticed with satisfaction the guys were busy imagining where it was and what it might look like, except for Rick, whose mind—and lips—were not on my tattoo, but Rachel's.

The bar lights dimmed; a live rock band started up. I lost count of how many beers I drank or dances I danced. The loud music fizzed in my blood like champagne and it was either dance or explode. Giddy with alcohol and innocent abandon, Rachel and I even danced together like we used to in Santa Cruz after a few beers, grinning and spinning and being silly together.

It was after midnight when I realized Marie was gone and Rachel nowhere to be seen. Most of the couples had drifted off and I didn't like how the remaining men looked at me. I rose unsteadily from the table, wet with spilled beer and cluttered with empty shot glasses, and slipped out the door. The misty night felt like a cool rag on my flushed face.

I started walking purposefully home, so anyone seeing me would know I had somewhere to go. When I passed the phone booth, I thought about calling home. I wouldn't care that Dad would call me Lizzie, and Mom would fuss about me being so far away. But it was late and I was drunk. Maybe I'd call Charlene instead. But, no, we'd never had that kind of it's-okay-to-call-in-the-middle-of-the-night kind of relationship. Call Brad? Now there was an idea. A very, very bad idea.

I'd had so much fun all night, I don't know why I was crying.

An Airmail Letter

WORK THIS WEEK WAS MUCH THE same as the week before. Marla watched us clock in, and ten hours later, watched us clock out. On Tuesday, she stopped me as I walked by. "We're a cannery. Not a post office. You get letters at the post office. You work at the cannery. Got it?"

"Got it."

She handed me a flimsy first class envelope, like Brad used when writing to me in France. It was even addressed to me in Brad's cramped handwriting. It had his name on the return address. Did he think Alaska was a foreign country?

In France, I had lived for those airmail letters, but I wasn't in France now and I didn't care about him anymore or what he had to say. I tore the letter in half.

Then I pieced the two sides together and read it.

He called me Lizzie…he'd transferred to UCLA …was living in Santa Monica…playing music on the weekend…living near Tom Hayden and his wife Jane Fonda. "Yes, Liz, *that* Jane Fonda"…and volunteering on Tom's political campaign. It was a mistake for us to break up, he said. He needed to see me again, he said, to ask for my forgiveness in person.

"P.S." he scrawled, "Distance is to love as wind is to fire. Blows out the little fires and fans the big ones. I'm burning for you, baby. Love, Brad."

Damn, I thought as I walked slowly back to the house. UCLA? Santa Monica? Forgiveness?

Burning for me?

Love?

I shoved the letter in my pocket and opened the front door to the sound of Helen Reddy blasting from the tape player. Deb was using her hairbrush as a microphone and Rachel was shimmying around the room waving a beer above her head with one hand and a joint in the other. The anthem was contagious and I joined in. "I am woman, hear me roar…" we sang as we danced around the living room.

Marie had been sitting on the couch reading a letter, but she suddenly burst into tears and ran into the bathroom.

I shrugged out of my jacket and the letter from Brad slipped to the floor.

"What's this?" Rachel asked, stooping to retrieve it.

Deb hurried to the bathroom door. "Marie, what's the matter?"

"Nothing. A letter from Brad." I snatched the letter back and hurried after Deb.

Rachel followed, a bloodhound in pursuit. "What's he want?"

I joined Deb at the bathroom door. "Hates East Coast winters," I said over my shoulder. "Transferred to UCLA, still playing music…"

"Shhhh…" Deb flapped her hands at us, irritated. "Marie, what's the matter?"

We could hear Marie sobbing on the other side of the door.

"Let us in," I tapped on the door. Rachel danced around trying to snatch the letter.

"Stop it!" I said, swatting Rachel's hand away.

"I can't stop it," Marie sobbed.

"I didn't mean you—"

"Who?" Deb asked confused.

"What else did he say?" Rachel demanded, not to be thrown off the scent.

"Hanging out with Tom Hayden and Jane Fonda," I hissed, my attention on the door.

"The radical running for Senate and Hanoi Jane?"

"Go away!" Deb commanded making shooing motions at us.

"You go away!" Marie's muffled voice responded.

"Yea, those guys," I continued. "He's working on Tom's political campaign…"

"Marie, what's the matter?" Deb addressed herself to the crack in the door.

"What's the schmuck want?" Rachel asked.

"He's not a schmuck," Marie wailed between hiccups.

"She means Brad," I said loudly. Turning back to Rachel, I whispered, "He wants to talk."

"About what?" Rachel demanded.

"Be quiet!" Deb commanded.

In the sudden silence, Marie muffled voice could be heard. "Maybe if you really love a man, you should forgive him. True love isn't always a smooth path." She hiccupped.

"You've been listening to too many country western songs," Rachel said scornfully to the closed door. "'Stand by your man…'" she warbled.

"And what would you know?" came Marie's angry voice. "You go to bed with one guy after another and they don't mean a thing to you—or you don't let them. What do you know about love? You act like commitment is a dirty word."

I stared in amazement at the door. I'd never heard Marie angry before.

"All I'm saying," she continued, "is that if the man you planned to spend the rest of your life with was unfaithful because you'd gone away for a while, well, maybe that's not such a big deal."

"Are we talking about Brad?" I asked.

"Yes," said Rachel.

"No," said Deb.

Marie threw open the door and stood before us. "All I know is that Melanie Price made a point of running into my sister at the Piggly Wiggly last week and said, all innocent, how she'd seen Danny on Friday night at the High Five dancing with Pricilla and did I know they'd been spending a lot of time together. And where I come from, 'spending time together' is code for sleeping together. And, I don't know, maybe it's my fault because I was the one who wanted a big wedding, even if it meant coming up here to earn the money for it. Danny said, as far as he was concerned, we should just elope. The important thing, he said, was to start spending the rest of our lives together." She took a deep, shuddering breath.

"But, no, I wanted a big fancy wedding. If I hadn't come up here to make money to pay for this big, fancy wedding, I'd be the one Danny was dancing with and 'spending time with,' not that stupid Pricilla bitch who probably didn't wait five minutes for me to leave town before she sank her claws into my boyfriend." With that, Marie shoved through us, went into her bedroom, and slammed the door.

Deb followed Marie into their room. Rachel and I returned to the living room.

"Well," Rachel demanded. "What else?"

Honestly, she could be relentless when she smelled blood. "Brad said that Boston girl was a mistake. He wants me to forgive him. He wants us to be together again."

His words coiled around my lonely core like intoxicating incense. Not like the cheap patchouli sticking out of the chipped jelly jar on the scarred coffee table. Brad's words were more like the seductive whisper of jazz late at night or the heady aroma of warm cognac. The glimpse of what life could be like for a young, progressive lawyer's wife in Santa Monica: getting gussied up in the morning and staying that way all day, working at some interesting and worthwhile career, drinking a California wine with friends after work while listening to live music. Brad's passionate arms around me at night.

"Maybe I should try harder to work things out," I said. Maybe there wasn't another fish in the sea, like my mom said. Maybe Brad was the one I let get away. "I'm tired of being alone."

"There are lots of men up here who'd love to be with you," Rachel pointed out.

"I don't want lots of men. One would do. Maybe Marie was right about letting bygones be bygones."

She rolled her eyes.

"Brad wants to come up here," I said.

I tried to imagine Brad in Petersburg with his trim haircut and California tan. Hands clean and soft. Drinking imported beer instead of Oly at the bar crowded with fishermen and loggers. Everyone would be nice, but it would be clear he didn't belong.

Still…

"He said he's burning for me," I told Rachel.

"Burn, baby, burn," Rachel said heartlessly. What the rioters had chanted when they burned Watts down.

The Dragon Bites

I ncoming!" Jimmie shouted as we clocked in the next morning. "Deck-loaded boat!"

On the boat out back, two crew members were knee-deep in humpies and shoveling them as quickly as possible into large plastic tubs which were hoisted into the cannery. Everyone was grinning and Allen was taking pictures. Then he looked around and saw us. "Get to work, ladies! We've got a shitload of humpies to process."

He herded us back into the cannery. "I'm speeding up the conveyor belt. Marla's calling for extra workers."

Harriet had told me that in the old days, all the women and older children in town dropped whatever they were doing when workers were needed in the cannery to process the fish their men worked so hard to catch. Now, so many college kids came to work for the season that most of the townspeople weren't needed. I couldn't tell if she thought this was good or bad.

I hurried to the slime line and concentrated on keeping up with the endless flow. Workers I didn't know joined the usual crew, there was more shouting and clanging of equipment than usual and the little fork lift constantly beeped as it maneuvered around the cannery hauling large plastic tubs of fish and boxes of cans. *Haste makes waste*, my mother warned, but I was sure she hadn't been referring to humpies going to waste.

The cacophony and extra workers provided a sense of urgency I found exciting after the usual old routine. Like on M*A*S*H when the helicopters came into the field hospital loaded with wounded, we all had our part to play in the unfolding drama.

Then, someone in the next room screamed. Machinery came to an abrupt halt and the silence left my ears ringing. I started to leave so I could find out what was going on, but one of the older women grabbed my arm. "Stay put until they give the all-clear."

Bob rushed by, escorting a worker with her hand wrapped in a towel. Everyone looked alike in raingear, but this one was wearing a pink sequined cap.

I got to the parking lot just in time to see Bob hustle Marie into his pickup truck and careen away. Deb and Rachel came up beside me.

"Mable called in sick today." Deb said miserably. "Allen told Marie to work the index machine instead."

We had been warned to give this machine a wide berth: the sharp blades that cut off the fish heads worked quickly. I chewed my cuticles while Deb and Rachel smoked. The cannery was silent. We were silent. Even the gulls' usually raucous cawing seemed muted.

Finally, Allen came up to us.

"Marie's going to be okay," he said. "But she's lost a finger. The doc said if we can rush it to the clinic, they might be able to reattach it. Get back there and look."

I swallowed the bile that rose in my throat. Back at my station, I looked around carefully, hoping—and not hoping—to find the finger.

"Can't find it," Allen announced. "We're starting back up."

That night, Deb, Rachel and I found the half-full bottle of Southern Comfort deemed too nasty to finish except in emergencies. This was an emergency.

"You don't suppose…?" Deb finally asked.

"What?" Rachel asked.

"That Marie hurt herself on purpose so she could go home and get married?"

I was shocked. "No way!"

"Well, she *was* afraid of losing Danny."

"But desperate enough to cut her finger off?"

"No way," Rachel said decisively. "She'd never have the guts."

It felt to me like the world had just tilted. Here I'd been living safe inside the castle, watching the summer glide by in a haze of work and play and rain and friends when all around me real danger lurked and bad things could happen. I'd been enjoying an exotic summer vacation oblivious to the fact that most of the people around me worked here because they had to. *It was too good to last*, my mother chided, as though I should have known better, as though my complacency had somehow brought about disaster, had caused the dragon, without warning, to lash out.

That night I dreamed of rows of fingers coming down the conveyor belt to stuff in cans like Vienna sausage.

Only the shrill alarm and the urgent need to pee and gulp aspirin got me out of bed the next morning, groggy and disoriented. I dressed, half asleep, and jostled my fellow zombies in the kitchen for hot coffee and cold cereal. Marie's absence was palpable; only now did I realize how much her cheerful banter had brightened our otherwise dreary mornings. I walked over to the cannery wrapped in a shroud of despondency.

The grim klunk of the time clock, formerly a source of pride, now mocked me with its heartless division of my day into hours and minutes, dollars and cents. I wondered if Marla would retrieve Marie's time card, still in its alphabetical slot, adding and subtracting its numbers until arriving at a final paycheck. Would the cost of what she'd lost be considered? How much was a finger worth, how many glasses of champagne, how much icing on the cake?

At least it wasn't her ring finger she'd lost.

Having lashed out yesterday, the cannery dragon today seemed not so much asleep as dead, and I, as mechanical as the cold metal that clattered and clanked around me, gutted like the carcasses I stuffed with numb fingers into an endless line of empty cans.

At break, I walked to a quiet spot on the dock away from the workers huddled around coffee cups and cigarettes. The feeble sunshine warmed my face, more wishful thinking than actual heat, and glittered on the water flowing by. Residual wisps of cloud ran playful fingers through the spruce boughs on the mountains across the Narrows. A lone eagle soared overhead, seeming contemptuous of the common gulls squabbling below.

How enticing the fishing boats looked as they passed by! I tried by force of will to transport myself aboard, longing to feel the wind in my hair, the surge and sway of the deck—the forward motion. When the cannery's shrill whistle ordered me back to work, I had to force myself to comply.

I did so only by vowing to find a job on a fishing boat as soon as I could, to leave behind the relentless drone of time clocks and monotonous cannery work. On a fishing boat, I was sure, I would I be free.

I told no one of my new-found determination, a desire so fragile I didn't dare reveal it to others for fear of having it disappear like strands of morning fog exposed to the heat of day.

Besides, in this desire I felt Rachel to be the competition. She would either scoff at my ambition, or beat me to it.

I started listening carefully to the fishermen's gossip, let drop a few hints I was looking for other work, and tried to figure out how I—young, inexperienced, and female—could make the leap from cannery to fishing boat.

It's a Parade

Two days later, Allen had told us to pack Marie's stuff up to mail to Seattle; she wouldn't be back. Her abrupt departure felt like a sudden death, the only trace she'd been here a few faded sheets of purple stationery tacked here and there, and a pink umbrella propped in the corner of the living room. The relics of a by-gone era.

With Marie gone, Deb, Rachel and I ricocheted around the house like pool balls without a positioning rack. Deb missed her friend and confidante. I missed her cheerfulness and sweet bossiness. Rachel, well, I think Rachel missed having someone to feel superior to.

Still, it was the Fourth of July and we had the day off. The whole town had the day off. I made as much noise as possible getting dressed while Rachel moaned and burrowed under her covers like a wounded animal refusing to leave its den.

"Parade starts at 10," I said, trying to channel Marie's bossy good cheer.

"I hate parades," came Rachel's muffled voice.

"We're leaving soon. Be there or be square!"

Deb, Rachel and I walked into town, joining other townspeople all headed in the same direction.

"Aliens called to the mother ship," Deb said.

"Rats following the Pied Piper?" Rachel sniffed.

Main street was barricaded from vehicles, the storefronts draped in red, white and blue bunting. The sidewalk was crowded with young mothers pushing baby carriages beside men carrying toddlers on their shoulders. Children with more energy than sense chased each other through the crowd or heckled their parents to buy snacks sold by youth clubs pushing their homemade treats from card tables shoved against the buildings.

"Have we wandered into a Norman Rockwell painting?" I asked.

"Haven't you been to a parade before?" asked Deb.

"Only the Rose Parade in Pasadena. There are so may cameras and celebrities there, it's easier to stay home and watch on TV. This is so…I don't know…so Hallmark."

"So, bullshit," Rachel said.

"More nice than not," I corrected.

Petersburg's only police car rolled slowly down the street, shooing the crowd onto the sidewalk. The people around me grew silent; hats came off, and a crying baby was quickly hushed. A Coast Guard honor guard marched to the nearby grandstand and stood at attention. After a teenager sang the National Anthem, the crowd joined in singing the Alaska Flag Song.

> *Eight stars of gold on a field of blue,*
> *Alaska's flag, may it mean to you,*
> *The blue of the sea, the evening sky,*
> *The mountain lakes and the flowers nearby,*
> *The gold of the early sourdough's dreams,*
> *The precious gold of the hills and streams,*
> *The brilliant stars in the northern sky,*
> *The "Bear," the "Dipper," and shining high,*
> *The great North Star with its steady light,*
> *O'er land and sea a beacon bright,*
> *Alaska's flag to Alaskans dear,*
> *The simple flag of a last frontier.*

By the last line, I was choked up.

"Does California even have a state song?" I whispered to Rachel.

"'California Dreaming'?" she responded. "I need a nap."

About twenty men of various ages brandishing small American flags walked casually behind a Veterans of Foreign Wars banner. Some were in old, too-tight military uniforms, while others wore a service hat or unbuttoned jacket. Two women in old-fashioned nurses' uniforms kept pace with an elderly, limping vet. A dozen men in their twenties strolled by sporting beards and long hair.

Rachel jabbed me in the ribs. "Vietnam Vets." She'd been an enthusiastic participant at anti-war protests in Berkeley and San Francisco, and I hoped she wasn't going to make a scene. A tall, good-looking guy in a worn combat jacket brought up the rear of the little contingent. He was pushing a man in a wheelchair who had an American flag draped over his lap. The two men talked quietly together, occasionally waving at someone in the crowd.

Back home, a crowd watching Vietnam veterans stroll past would not have been so friendly. Many would have jeered, called them "baby killers." Watching the crowd applaud as these men walked by, I wondered what drove some people to go to war while others took refuge in grad school.

The parade was only two blocks long. The mayor rode by in a vintage convertible with his family grinning and waving from the open car. Half a dozen decorated pickups inched by with commercial sponsor signs prominently displayed: Viking Insurance, Viking Travel, The Trading Union. Two dozen local day care kids straggled by in matching tie-dyed shirts. Baptists passed out pamphlets and Baha'i ladies in long flowing skirts tossed candy. The fire truck blared its siren, scaring some kids, delighting others. The ambulance cruised by, lights flashing. The Lion's Club men in bright yellow vests brought up the rear, sweeping up candy wrappers and empty soda cans with their brooms and dustpans.

The parade was followed by bike and trike races, an egg toss, and a husband calling contest. The winning caller was a heavy-set woman who hollered, "Harvey, you get out of the bar and come home for supper. Your lutefisk is waiting!"

"That's salted cod, pickled in lye," Jimmie explained as the crowd roared in delight. "A delicacy around here." He shuddered.

Bob and a couple of the other men took off their shirts for the pie eating contest, a sensible precaution given the berry pies lined up in front of them.

"I hope Bob spills pie on his chest and I get to lick it off," Rachel said, hardly bothering to lower her voice.

Men usually didn't withstand Rachel's interest, but so far Bob had. Which only seemed to whet her appetite. And pique my interest.

After that, the crowd moved to the harbor for the herring toss, where contestants threw a dead herring into a life ring floating on the water. The tote race consisted of participants crouching in a plastic tote the size of a bathtub and racing to the finish line using only one oar to paddle. One of the most popular competitions, judging by the excited crowd, was the log rolling contest with losing contestants tumbling into the cold water of the harbor to the jeers and cheers of the boisterous crowd.

I waited alongside Deb and Rachel for the final event: a tug-of-war between the fishermen and the loggers.

"Brian says fishermen think all loggers are dumb," Deb said. "And loggers think all fishermen are lazy."

"Well, I think they're all hot," said Rachel.

I couldn't peel my eyes away from the young men, shirts off, work gloves on, pulling with all their might to drag the opposing team across a line taped in the street. The only way to tell them apart was that the fishermen wore rubber boots, the loggers heavy work boots. Neither seemed advantageous on the pavement.

The crowd urged them on good-naturedly, cheering for their favorites and groaning every time the rope inched one way or the other.

"The fishermen have longer hair," Rachel observed. "Those loggers look like rednecks."

I looked closely at the men, admiring their bulging muscles and sweaty bodies. I recognized Bob, who looked grimly determined, and the tall man I'd seen marching in the parade.

"The question is," Rachel said, jabbing me in the ribs, "who do you think is hotter?"

"The fishermen," Deb responded loyally.

"Bob," declared Rachel.

I wasn't about to chase after an engaged man, much less someone my friend had her eye on. But if he chased me? What it would be like to be caught by his strong arms, swung around like a girl at a square dance, spirited away to a dark corner of the barn where the light was dim, the hay soft, Bob hard.

"Well?" demanded Rachel.

I tore my eyes away from Bob. "It's a tie."

A Picnic

EARLY THE NEXT MORNING, THE LOGGERS returned to work up in the mountains and the fishermen took to the sea. There was a big company picnic at Blind Slough for those of us left behind with nothing to do until the boats came back with fish to can. Or nothing to do that didn't cost money and/or involve sex, drugs or alcohol.

Bob drove the pickup truck and I made sure to sit between him and Jimmie in the cab. Rachel arrived at the last minute and wedged herself on Jimmie's lap. For once, I wasn't wearing rain gear and I pretended not to notice when Bob's arm brushed my breasts whenever he shifted gears. Nor did I lean away.

I was almost disappointed when the truck pulled into a parking lot and we tumbled out. Picnic tables were grouped under a wooden pavilion. Young people were setting food on the tables while others gathered around a campfire someone had started in a firepit. Bob hurried off to oversee the barbequing of the large salmon filets he'd brought.

After a feast of grilled salmon, potato salad, pot brownies and beer, Bob came up beside me and asked if I'd seen the fish ladder yet.

"I didn't know salmon could climb!" I joked nervously. "How do they do it, use their fins?"

"Come on, I'll show you." We walked down a dirt road to where a plank boardwalk meandered along the river. He helped me onto the boardwalk—not that I needed help—and kept hold of my hand as we walked toward the sound of a waterfall. His calloused hand engulfed mine, generating a warmth that radiated from my fingertips down past my pounding heart to a place between my legs I'd thought long dormant. We stopped at a viewing platform overlooking a small waterfall.

"There, that's the fish ladder." Bob pointed with his free hand toward a series of concrete stairs built into the riverbank. With water rushing over the latter, it appeared only marginally easier for the fish to swim up, but what do I know?

I did know it was a beautiful day and a guy I liked was standing beside me.

"More stairs than ladder," I observed. "No fish."

"No fish," Bob agreed. "More fish, and more bears, will be here later in the summer. Not just that one over there."

I was shocked to see a black bear ambling across the flats below us intent on whatever it is bears do on a peaceful afternoon in Alaska. I knew bears could be dangerous, but it was impossible to be alarmed on such a beautiful day. Gulls dove and squabbled at the tide's edge, and several bald eagles soared overhead. Tall lush grass whispered along the edge of the woods where giant, moss-covered spruce waved their boughs in the gentle breeze. The sun played peek-a-boo behind clouds that sailed regally overhead. Magenta flowers bloomed profusely on the edge of the forest and seemed to glow in the sunlight.

"Those purple flowers everywhere," I waved my hand in their general direction, more to have something to say than because I was curious. "What are they?"

"You mean these?" Bob took a few steps off the path, leaned down, and plucked a handful of the tall stalks. "Fireweed," he said, handing the bouquet to me with a flourish.

I buried my head in the fragrant blossoms, hoping I looked as good as I felt.

"Fireweed grows everywhere in Alaska," Bob said, watching me. "Here in Southeast, up north in the Interior, on the coast, everywhere. If you ask me, fireweed should be the state flower, not a forget-me-not."

"I've never seen a forget-me-not," I said.

"Exactly," Bob said, drawing me close. His face was inches from mine, his eyes held mine. I couldn't move. Could barely breathe.

"What about your fiancée?" I whispered.

"What about her?" he said, covering my lips in a kiss that sucked the breath from my lungs and all thought from my brain.

His husky voice, his strong arms, his hungry lips, his hard body. He drew desire from me like a parched plant soaking up a spring shower.

"Maddie! Bob! Where are you guys?" Rachel's voice carried over the sound of the rushing water.

We separated reluctantly. "Time to go," Bob said.

When we returned to the picnic hand in hand, I tried not to look smug. Bob had found *me* irresistible, even though I hadn't chased him. He wanted *me*, not one of the other girls, not Rachel.

Rachel looked at us impassively, then climbed into the back of the pickup with Jimmie and the others.

I sat close beside Bob in the cab during the return trip. When he wasn't using the shift stick, he tucked his hand between my thighs and I ran my hands up and down his arm.

"Will you come to the house tonight?" Bob asked hoarsely, eyes on the road.

"What about Jimmie?"

"Oh, he won't be there, I'll make sure!" He glanced over at me, eyes pleading.

"I need a shower," I said, catching a whiff of campfire smoke and bug dope clinging to my clothes.

"Come to my place after?"

The afternoon's buzz dissipated in the hot steamy shower. It was one thing to kiss a guy spontaneously by a waterfall on a beautiful summer day. It was another to have sex with an engaged man. But if he didn't care, why should I? I donned a fresh shirt and my woman-of-the-world persona.

"I was afraid you wouldn't come," Bob said when he answered the door.

"I almost didn't," I admitted.

Bob smelled of soap and shaving lotion and his hair was still damp. I ran my hands beneath his unbuttoned shirt, enjoying the delicious contrast between springy black chest hair and hard muscles. He pulled me into the small bedroom he shared with Jimmie and all but ripped my tee-shirt off. I was glad I hadn't bothered wearing a bra. His calloused hands caressing my breasts felt even better than I had imagined.

The sheets were clean but we wasted no time getting them rumpled. I wanted to feel his naked body against my stomach, along my legs, in my hands. I wanted to feel him inside me, and then he was. He thrust deep and then raised himself on his arms and withdrew slowly until all feeling was concentrated on that one tenuous link. I was pinned by desire. I moaned and grabbed his buttocks, desperate to draw him back into me. Even his butt was muscled.

"Wait, Maddie, don't move. I'm going to lose it." But he was already on the crest sliding down, down, down, thrusting inside me with increasing force until he shuddered and came. I tried but couldn't catch up. I'd missed the wave.

"It'll be better next time," he murmured as we shifted our bodies on the narrow bed trying to get comfortable. As soon as he fell asleep, I crept back to my own house, back to my own bed, and let my fingers quietly finish what Bob started.

Promotion

W HEN I CLOCKED IN AT WORK the next morning, Allen motioned me aside.

"Want to make a dollar an hour more? Work in a clean, dry place?"

"Mais oui! Bien sur!" I replied enthusiastically.

"Yes or no?" he asked impatiently.

"Yes."

Allen strode to a partitioned area in the cannery I'd barely noticed before. Ignoring the sign that said EGG ROOM, KEEP OUT, Allen led me inside past small wooden boxes and sacks of salt surrounded by dozens of plastic totes full of shiny salmon skeins bursting with eggs. No conveyor belt. No water or fish parts. No knife blades chopping off fish heads. No sharp-toothed dragon snapping at unwary fingers. An enclave of serenity in the heart of the dungeon's lair.

"The Japanese are in charge here," Allen said. "They pay good money for the roe—the fish eggs—to be packed and shipped to Asia. We make almost as much from the caviar as from the salmon."

He looked at me carefully. Was there a warning in his look? "The last girl got fired. They said she was lazy. They said they need someone who's careful and can work fast."

"Why not one of the more experienced workers, like Mable or Harriet?"

"Filipinos and Japanese don't mix."

"Mable's not Filipino."

"Mable and Mr. Tanaka don't mix. Look, Bob said you were the best one for the job. Do you want it or not?"

"I want it."

Allen jerked his head at a middle-aged Asian man approaching. "Mr. Tanaka will tell you what to do. Or rather, show you. Just watch what he does. It's more art than science. You're the artsy type. You'll be fine. Just don't piss him off."

The two men nodded at each other. "Mr. Tanaka, this is Maddie, your new worker."

Mr. Tanaka made an ever-so-slight bow toward Allen. His smile disappeared as soon as Allen did. At the steel table, he took one of the small wooden crates stamped with Japanese characters, carefully lifted skeins of salmon eggs from the basket, and layered them side by side in the box. When one row was done, he took a circular sieve that looked like a large tambourine, poured salt into it, and shook it quickly and evenly over the layer. "Not too much, not too little. This much."

He layered salmon skeins and salt in the box until it was full. Then he reverently placed it on a nearby scale and motioned me to look at the dial. "Ten kilos," he said with immense satisfaction. "Now you."

He hovered at my shoulder while I nervously tried to replicate his movements. He all but slapped my hands a few times while he rearranged my rows. "Very important to pack right!" he said crossly. "Very important. No pack good, no top dollar. Last girl no good. You be better."

Mr. Tanaka glowered when the scale read under the ten-kilo mark. He rearranged the top layer so he could add an additional skein while muttering what sounded like Japanese swear words.

I packed another crate. More salt! No, not that much. Lay the skeins side by side. No, overlap them more! I packed two more little boxes. He corrected them. By the fifth miniature crate, there was no difference I could see between how I'd packed the roe and how he wanted it done. No matter what I did, Mr. Tanaka criticized my work.

Finally, I lost my temper. "I'm trying my best. If I'm not doing it right, get someone else!"

There was a pause while I wondered if I would get demoted back to the slime line. At least there I knew what to do, knew how to goof around and gossip with my friends while our hands moved automatically at their tasks. It was lonely in the egg room. Just me and this grumpy old man. But a dollar an hour more, I reminded myself.

"I no understand," Mr. Tanaka said finally. He motioned for me to continue. He watched while I packed two more crates.

Finally, he left. When I couldn't wait any longer, I took a break, reminding myself this was a work place and not a torture chamber.

When I returned ten minutes later, Mr. Tanaka was waiting with two more tubs of roe. "Where you were?" he asked.

I started to apologize, then thought what the hell? "I needed a break."

"Next time need permission."

I took a deep breath. "Next time will be at lunch, and then at 3:00 p.m. Why not just give me permission now?'"

We locked eyes.

Mr. Tanaka broke first. He gave an infinitesimal nod and then pointed at the tubs. "Finish these. Tomorrow, I teach you pull eggs."

My housemates were in the kitchen eating Hamburger Helper when I finally got home that night. "How'd it go?" Deb asked.

"Well, I didn't get wet—"

"Lucky you."

"—but it was really boring and I was all alone in that room except for Mr. Tanaka, who is an ogre."

Rachel shrugged. "Who cares? A dollar an hour more!"

"Even with the raise, I'll be lucky to make it to Mexico. Everyone says it's a slow season."

Rachel rolled her eyes. "You're making more than I am."

I shrugged. I knew by now the real money was hauled in by the fishermen, not by the cannery workers.

As though reading my mind, Rachel said, "I wish I was earning the big bucks like the fishermen do. But what are the chances? Most of the women on boats are related to the skipper: wives on their husband's boat, a daughter on her dad's boat. They probably aren't even paid wages."

"It's a man's world," Deb agreed. "I guess you need a prick to work on a boat."

"Or, be one," Rachel added.

Ever since Marie's accident, my resolve to go fishing had strengthened. The chance to prove myself. Make more money. Be free. I didn't care what kind of boat, I just wanted to be on the ocean catching fish, not stuck on shore canning them.

Unfortunately, no one was willing to hire a woman, even if that woman wore a red bandana and knew her way around the cannery. They didn't care that I could swear in French and had a college degree. If anything, those accomplishments worked against me. They didn't care that I was a hard worker. No one would hire a woman.

BOB CAME BY THE HOUSE THAT night. "Let's take a walk and you can tell me about your first day in the egg room."

I walked with him to the darkened cannery. He unlocked the door and we slipped inside the eerily quiet building. Bob led me up to the dim canning room where we perched on a pile of flattened cartons. I started telling him about my day, but he was more interested in unbuttoning my shirt and fondling my breasts. I concentrated on the feel of his arms flexing around me, and not the edge of the cardboard digging into my hips. As his kisses got increasingly urgent, his hard-on pressed against my crotch and I was swept up in his desire. We yanked our pants down and I lay back on the stack of flattened boxes.

With a groan, Bob fell on me and we found our rhythm just as the stack of cardboard started sliding. There was no stopping Bob or the boxes. We rode the slippery cardboard down to the ground while I stifled laughter and Bob climaxed.

"Hello, anybody there?" a voice called out from below.

Bob put his hand over my mouth. "Shhh…the watchman."

Once again, I hadn't caught the wave. But, we didn't get caught either.

MY LIFE FELL INTO A PATTERN: days of monotonous work punctuated by snatches of intimacy with Bob. Or, maybe, intimacy was too tender a word for what went on between us. One time, we made love in a borrowed pickup truck and another time a quickie when Jimmie went to the bar. A slightly more acceptable coupling under the blankets at a "picnic" out the road. I told myself I didn't care, it was fun to be with Bob, the other cannery girls were envious, it was great to be desired. Still, I began to wish the sex included at least a glass of wine in a nice restaurant or a bed in a real house. But maybe that was me just romanticizing another time, another place, another person.

Tonight's encounter was par for the course. Jimmie had purposely taken his time leaving for the bar while Bob and I sat in their cramped kitchen making stilted conversation. Once Jimmie left, we stopped pretending and fell into Bob's cramped bed, the sheets none too clean, the love-making none too great.

When I returned to my own house, Deb was smoking at the kitchen table.

"What's going on?" Deb asked as I looked through the cupboard.

"You want some tea?" I asked.

"No"

"A beer?"

"Sure, and quit stalling."

I put water on to boil, handed her a beer.

Deb popped it open. "So, we're not talking about you and Bob?"

I shrugged. "What's to say?"

I hadn't talked about my…whatever it was, fling, affair, seduction (but by whom?)…with anyone, especially not with Rachel, whose studied nonchalance seemed more like jealousy than indifference.

My resolve to stay silent broke in the face of Deb's friendly detachment.

"I feel like I'm a toy Bob takes out to play with when he thinks no one's looking. Like I'm supposed to stay quietly on the shelf until playtime. Because, you know, he's a big boy and too old for toys."

"Not to mention too engaged," Deb added.

"Yeah, that too."

"And how do you feel about that?" Deb asked in her best pseudo-psychiatrist voice.

"I mind, and I don't mind," I said slowly. "I like the freedom of doing my own thing but the sneaking around is getting old. It's so juvenile. Like we're back in high school. Can't let the folks find out."

Although I still liked his hard body and his desire for me, the sex hadn't gotten much better. A few kisses, some hurried foreplay, awkward thrusts and grunts, and it was over. I worked hard to catch the wave, but too often he rode it without me. It would be fun to body surf with someone who didn't leave me high and dry.

"The earth never moves," I admitted. "Sometimes it barely trembles."

Deb took another puff and exhaled, trying to make a smoke ring.

"Not bad," I said.

"Rachel's teaching me. What about the fiancé?"

"One of the many things we don't talk about."

The front door opened and Rachel came into the kitchen. She spent a lot of time away from the house now, coming and going at all hours like a stray cat looking for handouts.

"What's up?" Rachel asked as she peered into the refrigerator.

I looked at Deb who busied herself blowing another smoke ring. I took a deep breath. "I was just saying I'm through with Bob."

I don't know what I expected her to do. Applaud? Ask why? Give a damn?

She took her time retrieving a beer from the fridge and popped it open. "Can I bum one?" she asked Deb, indicating her cigarettes.

Deb slid the pack toward her.

Rachel took a long drag and blew an almost perfect smoke ring. "I'm not surprised. Bob's a bore."

I guess she didn't remember she'd been licking her lips and flirting with Bob a few weeks earlier.

"A bore with a bod," Deb said.

That pretty much summarized it. I dumped the dregs of my tea into the sink and went to bed.

The Harbor Master's Office

I STARTED WANDERING THE DOCKS WHENEVER I had some free time, as though I might pass a fishing boat with a help wanted sign hanging in the window. Fat chance. One afternoon, I drifted into the harbor office. The work area with two desks and several file drawers was partitioned off from the entryway by a counter cluttered with maps and pamphlets. Large windows overlooked the busy harbor. Two folding chairs perched on either side of an old cabinet with a coffeemaker on top. Styrofoam cups, a box of sugar cubes and a jar of powered creamer made it clear visitors could help themselves. The smell of singed coffee made it easy for me to resist.

A battered bookcase with used paperbacks caught my eye. "Take one, leave one," read the faded handwritten sign. I picked up a battered copy of Jack London's *Call of the Wild*. 'Can Buck resist the lure of the wolves?' read the tag line. If the cover picture of two ferocious wolves fighting and snarling over a dog in the middle was any indication, I thought *lure* was not quite the right word. I returned it to the shelf.

Above the coffee pot hung a bulletin board with signs advertising everything from engine repair to local restaurants to taxis, of which there were only two. I spotted half a dozen help wanted signs. Pizza delivery. Maybe I could find a job while delivering pizza to hungry fishermen? Not likely. Petersburg Processors was looking for cannery hands, no experience needed. Tell me about it. Then, *voila*! The Nordic Adventurer was looking for a fisherman. Oh wait. An experienced halibut fisherman. I could handle a four-pound salmon, but how do you catch and subdue a four-hundred-pound halibut?

I picked up a well-thumbed copy of the current week's six-page *Petersburg Pilot*. Nothing pertinent in the small classified ad section, mostly boats and fishing gear for sale. I scanned the Police Blotter: reports of stolen bikes, bar fights, minor traffic violations, the theft of a fishing pole. Two juveniles were escorted home after curfew. A barking dog eluded capture. I wondered if I had stepped into an Andy Griffith show.

The man bending over the counter left and the harbor employee straightened up. He was over six foot tall with long dark brown hair. When he came around the counter, I saw he was wearing blue jeans and a denim work shirt. He smiled, and I realized it was the handsome Vietnam Vet I'd seen pushing the wheelchair in the parade.

"Can I help?" he asked.

"Just looking at the bulletin board," I said like I'd been caught doing something wrong.

"The help wanted ads?"

"Oh, I have a job now. It's just…" It's just that what I wanted sounded so stupid and hoping to find it on a bulletin board even more so.

"It's just that you want a job on a fishing boat and aren't finding one?" the stranger guessed.

I shrugged, embarrassed, and turned to go.

"Wait, don't go. Want a cup of coffee first?" I must have grimaced unintentionally because he added jokingly, "It was fresh only this morning."

A cup of that old coffee was not appealing. But the man offering it was. The same man I'd seen with his shirt off at the tug of war. I hoped I didn't blush.

"Sure, okay. Thanks."

He retrieved a white ceramic mug from the cabinet below the coffee pot.

"No Styrofoam cup for you. Only the best for special visitors!" he said with a flourish. He poured me a cup of coffee, then went to answer a phone ringing on his desk, something about a skiff left illegally on the beach. He gazed back at me making an obvious effort to cut the phone call short, saying, "Okay, thanks, I'll look into it," several times.

After he hung up, I put the coffee cup down. "I think I saw you in the parade," I said.

"Parades aren't my thing, but Barry wanted to go."

"Barry was in the wheelchair?" He was silent a moment and I wished I hadn't asked.

"We went through boot camp together," he finally said. "Barry tripped a land mine. I didn't."

I didn't know anyone who had gone to Vietnam, much less gotten so horribly injured.

"I'm sorry," I stammered.

He nodded, made an obvious attempt to change the subject.

"Anyway, I'm Anders."

"I'm Maddie, Maddie Maguire."

He nodded. "And you work at Processors."

"How do you know?"

"Oh, everyone knows everyone in this town."

A middle-aged man walked in, looked at the two of us, and scowled. He went around to the harbormaster's desk, grabbed a stack of papers, and dropped them on Anders's desk.

"I'm going to lunch now," he announced. "Are you on break or can you check out these boats? I'm not paying you to chat up every pretty girl who comes in here."

"Oh, not every pretty girl," Anders responded, grinning. "Just Maddie."

"Well, Just Maddie, you're distracting my assistant who's got work to do." With a pointed look at the clock above the door, he left, shaking his head.

"Guess I'd better leave," I said. "Where can I wash this out?"

"Here, I'll take it." Anders took my cup, opened the window, and threw the coffee out onto the damp rocks below. "Tide will be in shortly." He wrote "Maddie" with a black marker on the mug and ceremoniously put it in the cupboard below the coffee pot. "For next time?" he said, somewhere between a statement and a question.

"Okay. Yeah, sure. Well, thanks for the coffee."

"Hey, Maddie," he said as I was about to go out the door. "Meet me at The Can after I get off work? At five o'clock? I'll buy you a real drink."

The people I knew just drifted around, running into each other, or not. This was actually premeditated. Almost like a date.

"Okay, sure," I said, playing it cool. Not like I was excited.

I'd passed by the Salvation Army store many times, but had never entered. I don't think there was one where I grew up, or if there was, I'd never seen it. Boutiques and fashion stores, yes. Second-hand stores? No. But desperate times call for desperate measures. I wanted Anders to see me tonight in something other than work clothes and rubber boots.

Entering the store, I made my way past dusty bins of children's toys and boxes of jumbled hardware. Tucked away in the back was a rickety rack of women's clothes. Crammed among the polyester blouses and worn cardigans was a slinky short-sleeved white blouse with tiny faux pearl buttons up the front. When I held it up to me, the tailored forties vibe made me think of Ingrid Bergman and Katharine Hepburn. I was sure it would look just right when paired with jeans and my new tousled haircut. Sexy but not fancy. Maddie, not Lizzie.

Knock Knock

BACK AT THE HOUSE, I DABBED mascara on my eyelashes, just enough to make my eyes look bigger, but not enough for anyone to tell I was wearing makeup. Then I slid into the black lace underwear languishing in back of my drawer, a pair of black jeans, and the new blouse. I pawed through the debris on the dresser before finding my silver hoop earrings. All in all, I felt pretty good. Petersburg chic.

A knock at the door interrupted my self-admiration. A middle-aged man stood on the porch, finishing a cigarette.

"Whoa!" he exclaimed, throwing the cigarette away and looking me up and down. "I hope I've come to the right house and I hope you're the one looking for a job."

"Excuse me?"

"I'm Ron, skipper of the gillnet *Misty*. I need a deck hand and I heard there's a Processor chick who wants a fishing job. That you?"

I bristled at the word "chick" but figured this was no time to give him a language lesson. "Could be. I'm Maddie and I *am* looking for a fishing job."

"Great! I need to be in Goose Bay the day after tomorrow for an opening. You interested?" He ran a finger around the gold chain he wore like a noose around his neck. Not a good look unless you were trying to draw attention to the graying chest hair poking out of your open collar.

I wanted the job badly but what if he'd really come looking for Rachel? Well, 'chick' could apply to either of us and as my mother was fond of saying *opportunity knocks but once.*

"I'm interested!"

"Good! Room and board provided. You'll get a share of whatever we make.

My mouth felt dry. "Where and when?"

"I'm moored at the small boat harbor, slip C18. We'll leave about eight in the morning." He ran a finger through his hair. "Or nine. Stop by the Harbor later and I'll buy you a drink," he offered.

"No thanks. I've got some stuff to do. I'll be there in the morning."

I threw a few clothes and sundries into the red backpack and thought about what I needed to do before leaving. One: tell Bob, make a clean break. Two: tell Allen. Three: call my parents. Four: meet Anders.

I rehearsed exit lines as I walked over to Bob's house. *Hey Bob, I enjoy your naked body but can't help noticing your thinning hair when you take off your hat. Hey Bob, we don't have anything in common except sex and half the time I'm faking it. Bob, I like you but I don't love you and I'm tired of sneaking around. Hey Bob, who do you think about when we're together?*

Bob opened the door. "Hey, Maddie. What's up?" His hair was messy and his eyes sleepy. He must have been napping. It wasn't a bad look, actually. "Come in!" He looked more alert now. "Jim's gone into town."

The little house smelled of old cooking, mild dampness, and the incense Jimmie often burned. I smiled remembering the stupid Oriental accent he put on, claiming to be a Buddhist priest who needed to ward off the vengeful spirits of salmon who pursued him night and day from the cannery next door.

Seeing me smile, Bob pulled me toward him.

"Um, I can't stay," I pulled back nervously. "I'm on my way into town. To call my folks."

"Call them later." He slid his hands up my shirt. His hard body pressed up against me and—oh God, was I kissing him back? I forced myself to remember I was breaking up with him.

I pushed him away. "I need to let my folks know I got a fishing job! I'm leaving tomorrow."

"What?"

"I got a job on a gillnetter. I leave in the morning."

"You're going fishing?"

I nodded, busy keeping my body from swaying into his. Busy not noticing how the sleeves of his tee shirt stretched over his biceps.

"We can still hang out tonight." His hand had somehow slipped under my shirt while I was busy telling my rebellious body to knock it off. My lace bra chaffed deliciously as he rubbed his calloused hand over my breasts, my nipples growing hard of their own volition. Traitors.

I ordered my hormones to stand down and seized on the two words he'd used. "Hang out? Hang out? So, that's what we're doing? Hanging out?"

Bob looked confused. "What do you mean?"

"I wouldn't exactly call it *hanging out*. More like *having a fling. Creeping around.* Oh, I don't know. *Two-timing a fiancé?* Something like that."

He didn't like putting a name to it, whatever it was we were doing. It was easier to pretend it wasn't happening if it didn't have a name. Which I guess is why farm kids don't name the baby animals.

I took a shaky breath. "Bob, here's the thing. Whatever was going on between us, it's over."

"It doesn't feel over."

"Well, it is. No more…what did you call it? Oh yeah, no more *hanging out.*"

His hands fell to his sides and he looked dejected. "I didn't mean to hurt you. I just couldn't help myself."

"I'm not hurt," I said. "But that doesn't make it right. And I obviously liked *hanging out,* too. But, I'm ready to move on."

"Move on?" he repeated, like he tasted something bitter.

"Yeah, move on."

"Because you're going fishing. "

"Because I'm going fishing *and* I'm breaking up with you."

"You've told Allen?"

"It's none of his business!"

"That you're leaving the cannery."

"Oh, right," I said, embarrassed. "If I can't find him before I leave, will you let him know?"

"Tell him yourself," Bob said.

I thought I should feel sad or offended or something—but mostly I felt relief. Our bodies may have met, but not our minds. He'd never even seen my tattoo.

I did not want to be late for my not-a-date with Anders, so I hurried up the road to Allen's house. A woman with a toddler on her hip opened the door.

"Yes?" she asked through the screen.

"Is Allen here? I'm Maddie. I work at Processors."

"Allen's not home," she said, starting to close the door. "He's probably at the Harbor."

"Would you tell him I won't be at work for a few days? I have to leave town."

"If I remember," she said.

I went to the phone booth to call my folks. While waiting my turn, I pondered what to say. Not that Marie had her finger cut off by cannery equipment. Not that I had broken off my torrid affair with the engaged cannery foreman. I was going to tell them I'd been promoted from the slime line to the egg room, but that was before I'd gotten a job on a fishing boat. Somehow, I didn't think they'd be happy about either. What did that leave to talk about?

When my mom accepted the charges, I launched into a cheerful monologue about Pilot Bread and my new haircut before noticing she wasn't responding.

"Mom? You there?"

"Your father's in the hospital. We thought at first it was a heart attack, but it turns out he's got emphysema and couldn't breathe. I called the ambulance. He's okay but they're running more tests."

I slumped against the side of the booth, fighting panic. "Emphysema? What's that? How is he?"

"Elizabeth, he's okay. Or will be, if he follows the doctor's orders. His breathing hasn't been good for a while. I kept telling him to quit smoking, but he wouldn't listen to me. He'll have to listen to the doctors now."

"What happened?"

"What happened is that he ignored the signs. It was getting harder and harder for him to breathe. He was getting confused sometimes. I was afraid he was getting senile, so I'm actually relieved it's something treatable. If you had called home before this, I could have told you sooner."

"I'm sorry, Mom, the cannery's been so busy." I wiped my eyes on my jacket sleeve. "Is he really okay? Can I talk to him?"

"They're keeping him in the hospital overnight. I'm headed back there now. If all goes well, he'll be discharged tomorrow and you can call him at home then."

"Well, the thing is, I just got a job on a fishing boat. We're supposed to leave tomorrow. Unless I should come home. I can find Ron, he's the skipper, tell him I can't go. I'll get home as soon as I can…" Words couldn't squeeze by the lump in my throat.

"Don't come home," my mother interrupted. "Your dad and I already talked it over. There's no point rushing down here just to sit around watching him recuperate."

I tried to decipher the sigh traveling through the phone wire. Exhaustion? Exasperation?

"He thinks you're still working in the cannery," she continued. "I am *not* going to tell him about this new job of yours. Off on a fishing boat, Elizabeth? Really? He worries enough about you in that darned cannery."

I listened to the static hissing down the line. Maybe that's what nonverbal guilt and recrimination sound like.

"I'll call again as soon as I can," I choked out. "Tell Dad I love him…And, you, too."

She hung up so quickly, I wasn't sure she heard. Is there another frequency for love?

Cognac in the Can

I WALKED SLOWLY TO THE CAN, THINKING things over. Turns out being mature and independent means having to make a lot of choices. Was I making the right ones, severing ties with the cannery and with Bob, staying up here instead of going home?

Did I love Bob? *Non.* Was he engaged? *Oui.* Then breaking up with him was the right thing to do.

Was I going to work in the cannery tomorrow? *Non.* Was getting a message to Allen the right thing? *Oui.*

So, two for two.

Was Dad sick? *Oui.* Did my parents want me to come home? *Non.*

Okay, three for three.

I pushed open the door to The Can with a slightly lighter heart.

"Hey, babe, buy you a drink?" a male voice asked. I bristled at the standard pickup line until I saw Anders grinning at me from the bar. He motioned me over and pulled out the stool next to him.

"Well, that's a surprise," I blurted.

"Surprise? I thought we agreed to meet."

"No, not that. I'm surprised you're drinking cognac. No one around here drinks cognac. They do in France, of course, but not around here." Stop babbling, I commanded myself.

"Sit down and I'll buy you one," he said.

"Well, I do have something to celebrate. Well, two things. One, my dad is doing well after having some kind of emphysema attack a couple days ago."

"He's okay?"

"Yep, Mom said it was scary, but he's okay and I'm not to come home. And two, I got a job on a fishing boat!"

Anders grin faltered. "We just met and now you're telling me you're leaving? I'm not sure that's cause to celebrate, but we'll drink to it anyway." He told the bartender to bring me a cognac. "Tell me about the job."

"Let's see. The skipper's name is Ron and he needs someone on the boat with him for the opening at Goose Bay."

"What's his last name?" Anders frowned.

"Sanders? Sandberg? Something like that."

"You don't know?"

I felt idiotic. "His gillnetter is the *Misty*."

"I know most of the boats around here. I've never heard of a Ron Something-or-other *or* the *Misty*. I'll check at the office Monday."

"We're leaving tomorrow.'"

He put his glass down. "Maybe that's not such a good idea."

"Maybe that's none of your business," I snapped.

My cognac arrived in a cold glass, not a warm snifter. I took a sip.

"You're right, I hardly know you," he said.

"Ron fishes out of Juneau," I said with more assurance than I felt. "So, so that's probably why you haven't heard of him."

"Right," Anders said. "Let's start over. Tell me all about yourself and quickly, since you're leaving in the morning. None of that horoscope crap. Can you do it in twenty words?"

I took another sip, playing for time. "Okay, here goes." I counted off on my fingers. "*California born and raised. Bachelor's degree in French Lit from UC Santa Cruz.* I'm counting that as one word."

He nodded.

"*One year studying in France.*"

"Four left."

"*Ran away to Alaska!*"

He raised his glass in a salute and we toasted.

"Your turn!" I said.

Anders thought for a minute.

"*Grew up in Petersburg. Norwegian parents. Dad fishes. Marines. Vietnam. Graduate school in Fairbanks. Environmental engineering.*"

"That's fifteen."

"Sixteen, but who's counting? So, four left." He took a deep breath. "*I'm-Libra-and-like-long-walks-on-the-beach-at-sunset,*" he said running the words together.

"Hey, that's more than twenty! And you're a Libra? I think that's a deal killer for a Leo."

I liked his self-deprecating laugh and his quiet confidence, the fact he was going to grad school and was here, drinking cognac in The Cannery Bar. Alcohol buzzed and zinged in my blood while Anders looked at me intently. It was not the stare of a predator watching its prey, or the gaze of a friendly dog wanting a pet. Anders looked at me with a look I only vaguely remembered, or had maybe never seen before.

"So, what brings you to my little corner of the world?" Anders asked.

"I wish I could say it was something important or dramatic, but the truth is I just didn't know what else to do. Everyone had an opinion about what I should do after graduation, but I didn't want to do any of it."

Anders nodded his head sympathetically. "I know what it's like when everyone tells you what to do."

"You do?"

He laughed ironically. "Well, I did spend three years in the Marines."

"While you were in Vietnam, I was at Santa Cruz protesting," I admitted. "The riot police scared me."

"The protestors scared *me*," Anders responded. "Civilians saw a guy in uniform, they'd spit on you, treat you like shit. I re-upped for a second tour figuring it was better to be in 'Nam than back home wearing a uniform. At least there you could shoot back."

I was shocked.

"Maddie, I'm kidding. I was a mechanic. I carried a wrench more than a gun."

"Yeah, right," I said but let it go.

"It was a bad time, all around," Anders said. "I was in country when Hanoi Jane had her photo taken a few hundred yards from where our POWs were being tortured. Fucking Jane Fonda," he said bitterly.

Now my ex-boyfriend was working on her husband's political campaign in Santa Monica. I wasn't ready to go there. I swirled the cognac in my glass instead.

"Forget 'Nam," Anders said. "How did we get on this topic anyway?"

"The cognac, I think."

"You're really leaving tomorrow?" Anders asked.

I nodded. "Just for a few days…I think."

"Well then," he said. "You should come have dinner with Bear and me."

"What?"

"Bear, that's my dad. His real name is Bjorn. I guess that was too hard for Americans to pronounce so everyone calls him Bear, which is what Bjorn means in Norwegian. Or maybe because he resembles one."

"Because he's big and hairy? Mean and ornery?" I teased.

Anders slid off the bar stool without answering. "You will come back to the house, won't you? I always eat dinner with him when I'm home, and he gets grumpy if he's not fed by six o'clock."

Before I could answer, Rachel and a couple of her friends were at my shoulder ordering drinks. The lights were dimmer, the music louder. Another Friday night in The Can had commenced.

Rachel looked at Anders with her hungry predatory look. "Hi, I'm Rachel, an old friend of Maddie's."

"Hi, I'm Anders, a new friend."

"Want to join us?" she asked. "We've got a table down by the dance floor." I swear Rachel was licking her lips again.

"No, thanks, we're leaving. At least I am." Anders turned to me. "You coming, Maddie? Meet Dad and have dinner with us?"

"Meet the bear in his lair? Sure, that'd be great."

Before Rachel could go, I grabbed her arm. "Hey, guess what? I got a job on a gillnetter, starting tomorrow."

"Great," Rachel said, but not like she really meant it.

As we walked up the hill, Anders pointed out places where he had played as a kid, gardens he had raided, the large spruce tree he climbed and rode down as it was felled. "Once my dad made sure I was okay, he just about killed me. I've still got the scars to prove it. From the tree, not from my dad," he added, seeing my alarmed face.

I followed Anders up the porch stairs of a tidy two-story white house, removed my boots in the entry, and followed Anders into the living room.

"Hey, Dad, we have company for dinner!"

"Is Darlene here?" a raspy voice asked, sounding pleased.

"No, not Darlene," Anders said dismissively. "Dad, this is Maddie. Maddie, my dad. Call him Bear."

A man in his late sixties sat in a large overstuffed chair, smoking a cigarette and playing a game of solitaire on a TV tray. His gray hair was shaved in a crewcut, his eyes were faded blue, and his face weathered. He didn't look as tall as Anders, but even sitting I noticed his powerful build. He sipped amber liquid from a jelly jar dwarfed by his huge hands.

"Not Darlene?" the old man said querulously. "Karn told me Darlene might drop by." The old man squinted at me. He did resemble a bear.

Anders rolled his eyes. "No, not Darlene, Dad. This is Maddie. She's having dinner with us."

"Well, I'm not sure there's enough ribs to go around," the old man said in a distinct Norwegian accent.

"There's always enough," Anders replied easily. "I'll make extra potatoes."

The glowing TV provided the only illumination in the room. Various community announcements flashed by while Muzak played in the background. Rummage sale in the Lutheran church basement Saturday. Petersburg Vikings versus the Wrangell Werewolves at the ball field tonight. Canned peaches on sale at the Trading Union.

"You do know we also have a broadcast channel, right?" Anders teased his father as he went around the room turning on lights. "Except everything on it is broadcast two days late," he said to me, "Unless the plane doesn't make it in. Then it's even older."

"I've never been in someone's home in Petersburg before," I said gazing around the room. I'd been oblivious to the fact that the cute town wasn't just the backdrop for a summer adventure, that people lived and worked here year-round. "Everyone in California is always moving around. More going than staying."

"More staying than changing around here," Anders surprised me by saying. He closed the living room curtains.

Bear stubbed out his cigarette. "Where's Darlene?"

"Darlene's not here. Maddie is," Anders said exasperated. "I'm putting on the potatoes."

Anders went in the kitchen and I heard pots banging around.

"Don't forget to peel the potatoes," Bear called out.

I followed Anders into the kitchen. "Should I ask who Darlene is?" I asked cautiously.

"An old family friend," Anders said dismissively. "She likes to think I was her boyfriend, once upon a time. Dad likes to think I still am."

Sounded like past history to me.

"Potatoes won't take long," he said now. "You like venison?"

"I've never had wild game of any kind. Where I grew up, meat comes from the supermarket."

"Here, meat comes from four-legged creatures we go out in the woods to hunt."

"I'm sure I'll like it," I said. "Is there somewhere I can wash up?"

"There's a bathroom through the living room and up the stairs."

I walked slowly around the living room on my way to the stairs. The furniture was old but serviceable, the carpet worn and clean. Faded photos of stern-looking ancestors gazed from the wall, and yellowing lace doilies covered the tables. I paused at the bookshelf. A lot of the books were about Alaska, and some had titles in Norwegian, including a small Bible. Well-thumbed Louis L'Amour books were stacked on the middle shelf. I bent closer to examine a large, framed photo of a handsome young man posed formally beside a heavy-set woman in a dark taffeta dress.

"Me and Astrid," Bear volunteered, watching me. "Our wedding picture."

The photo beside it showed three young girls in matching dresses and a little boy in a sailor suit with big ears, a crew cut, and a gap-toothed smile. Bear motioned me to bring it over.

"Oline, Jennie, Karn and Anders," he pointed to each child in turn.

"I thought all Norwegians were blond," I said.

"The blonds are Swedes," Bear said dismissively.

I climbed the wooden stairs to the second floor. On the left was a large room with three beds, the walls plastered with the remnants of girlhood. To the right, a smaller bedroom contained two nightstands and a large bed. The temperature upstairs was just cool enough to make me wonder what it would feel like to snuggle under the fluffy quilt with Anders. Then I reminded myself I was leaving in the morning.

"Salted venison ribs, potatoes, peas," Anders announced as he set plates down on the yellow Formica table.

Once Bear had made a dent in his dinner and was maybe in a better mood, I asked what had brought him to Petersburg.

"I needed a job."

He resumed stabbing peas with his fork in his right hand, the European way.

"In Norway, the older brother inherits the farm," Anders elaborated. "That keeps the farms intact, but if you weren't the eldest son, you had to move away, learn a trade, maybe become a pastor."

"Or marry a girl who was inheriting her father's farm," Bear added with a twinkle in his eye. "Weren't too many of them around. I know. I looked. So, the farmer next to ours said he'd sell me his farm when I saved up enough money. We shook hands and I came here to work. Lived in a warehouse with no heat, worked from a wooden dory hauling nets by hand, and saved up enough money to buy the farm." He flexed his hand reflectively, lost in thought.

"Except by the time you got back," Anders prompted, "the farmer had died and his children reneged on the deal."

"Said they'd sell me the farm, but not the tools," said Bear in disgust. "What good's a farm without a hoe or a tractor?"

We contemplated that question in silence until Bear finally said, "Anyway, I'd met Astrid by then. I came back here, got married, and bought a halibut boat instead of a farm."

"Probably just as well," Anders reminded his old man.

"Ya, so it is."

"And Astrid?" I asked.

"Mom was the oldest of ten children." Anders said. "Her mom didn't survive the eleventh but the baby lived. So, then Astrid had to raise her younger siblings and help take care of the farm. One day, her father disappeared without a word and returned a week later with a young bride barely older than Astrid. The stepmother treated her like a servant, and as soon as she could, she fled to an aunt's house in Ketchikan. Dad met her there and the rest, as they say, is history."

Take Me Out to the Ball Game

I WASHED THE DISHES WHILE ANDERS PUT the leftovers away. We kept bumping into each other in the small kitchen, his body exerting an almost magnetic pull. Most of the guys I knew were either coming on to me or not interested. I couldn't tell with Anders.

"Okay, time to go!" Anders announced when the kitchen was clean. "If we hurry, we can catch the last few innings."

He turned to his father and spoke loudly, "Dad, you coming?"

"Is Erik playing?" The old man briefly considered, then shook his head. "Nah, not tonight. Next time, get here earlier so we go can watch the whole game."

"Go where?" I asked. "What game?"

"The high school ball game. My nephew Erik is pitching against their cross-town rivals. Or should I say, *cross-straits*." He chuckled at his lame joke. "Come on, Maddie. It'll be fun. It's what we do if we don't want to sit around watching old movies all night."

I glanced at the TV and saw Bear had changed the channel. He was now watching Humphry Bogart say goodbye to Ingrid Bergman at a foggy airport in Morocco.

"We must have seen Casablanca twenty times by now," Anders said, following my gaze.

"You watch old movies?" He didn't seem the type.

"I grew up in a house with three older sisters, remember? I know Frank Sinatra and Elvis songs by heart, can tell you the signs of the zodiac, interpret Tarot cards, and read the I-Ching. I went hunting and fishing up Petersburg Creek as often as possible to escape."

While Anders was saying this, he took Bear's overflowing ashtray and dumped the ashes into the kitchen trash. "You really should stop smoking, Dad," he said. Bear ignored him and dealt out another hand of solitaire.

Anders shrugged. "You going to be warm enough?" he asked me.

"Maybe. Barely. It wasn't this cold when I left the house. I should be getting home anyway. I'm leaving tomorrow," I remembered.

"There's only an hour left in the game. Didn't you say you were all ready to go?"

"Well, yes…"

Anders looked at the grandfather clock. "It's only eight o'clock."

"Well, okay. Then I really have to go."

"You'll be home by ten, I promise."

Anders rummaged through the front closet until he found a wool jacket approximately my size. "I don't know who this belongs to. One of my sisters must have left it."

He held the jacket out for me to slip into and I was taken off guard by his good manners. "I'll be sure to return it," I stammered.

"That way I know I'll see you again," he said casually.

I poked my head back in the living room. "Thanks for the dinner and stories, Bear."

He heaved himself out of his chair. "What?"

"Thanks for dinner," I repeated loudly.

"Ya, sure," Bear said dismissively as he brushed by me to sit on the porch glider.

"Guess Dad's going to see who comes and goes from the game!" joked Anders. He grabbed an Afghan from the couch and tossed it over his father's lap.

When we reached the street, Anders put his arm around my shoulders to steer me to the right and matched his pace to mine.

"I hope you didn't mind dinner…or Dad," Anders said

"I liked them both."

"And he really liked you."

"How can you tell?"

"He's not usually so chatty."

"Once he got over the fact I wasn't Darlene," I teased.

"Yeah, well, I think he just wants to see me settled down."

"With Darlene?"

"Darlene and I went to school together. Of course, everyone in town went to school together. I spent most of my free time hunting or fishing, but once in a while she'd talk me into going to the movies or a party. She asked me to the prom and I didn't know how to say no."

I didn't say anything, so he added, "When I left for college, I made it pretty clear I wasn't coming back. Darlene stayed, got pregnant, got married, got divorced—in that order. Typical around here."

"And you?" I asked.

"Went to California, supposedly to go to college. I bought a used convertible and drove on as many roads as I could as fast as I could." He turned to look at me. "I was a seventeen-year-old boy from an island with only one road." He shook his head. "A couple months later, the car engine blew out, which probably saved my life, but not before I was failing my classes."

We cut across the muddy street and I could see the school at the end of the road. "Then what?" I asked.

"Then I joined the Marines before I got drafted." His eyes got a far-away look but came back into focus as I nudged his arm. "Afterwards, I went back to school on the GI bill, graduated, enrolled in grad school in Fairbanks. And here we are!"

The crack of a bat and the sounds of cheering indicated a ball game in progress. "I've never been to a high school baseball game before," I confessed. "I went to one high school football game, mostly to make fun of the jocks and cheerleaders while smoking pot under the bleachers."

"If you weren't a jock or a cheerleader, what were you?" Anders asked curiously.

"A nobody," I said. "Just a nowhere girl. There were over three thousand kids in my high school. I knew maybe twenty."

"Less than twenty graduates in mine and I knew them all. *And* their sisters and brothers and mothers and fathers. You'll see most of them at the game tonight."

"A baseball diamond hacked into the bog!" I exclaimed as we walked around in back of the school.

"Muskeg."

"What?"

"The ground is called muskeg, not bog."

People were streaming out of the bleachers as we neared.

"Is the game over?"

"Nah, seventh inning stretch."

Kids ran everywhere while the adults greeted one another with hugs or slaps on the shoulder. Almost everyone knew Anders, many coming up to greet him and eyeing me curiously. Several youngsters ran up and he swung them in the air, laughing as they screamed and begged for more.

"My nieces and nephews, I forget their names," Anders joked. "But this is the best of the bunch." He one-arm hugged a pretty teenager who had come up beside him. "Meet Greta. Greta, this is Maddie." She nodded at me shyly, then pulled his head down and whispered something in his ear.

Anders squeezed her shoulder and said, "We'll talk later, okay?" Greta drifted off and Anders shrugged. "Teenage angst. I wouldn't be her age again for a million dollars."

Just then a large woman came up to Anders and hugged him. When he got free, he introduced me to his big sister Karn, "Mother of baseball superstar Erik and the lovely Greta, among others."

Karn swatted her brother and looked me over from head to toe. Oh no, was I wearing her jacket? How embarrassing. Then another woman about Anders' age came up. There was an awkward pause until Anders said, "Maddie, meet Darlene. Darlene, Maddie."

I had imagined her plump and matronly. I was disappointed to see she had a slim build, artificially streaked blond hair, and carefully-applied make-up.

"So, you're one of the cannery girls?" Darlene asked, appraising me back.

"Well, actually, I'm going gillnetting in the morning. What do you do?"

"Oh, I work as a stylist in the hair salon. You probably don't know it. Most seasonal workers don't bother with their appearance."

My hands flew unbidden to my hair, which I knew was messy and windblown. I wanted to explain it usually looked better than this, except it didn't. Anders saved me from responding by taking my arm. "We're off to get popcorn. See you later."

He greeted the volunteers at the concession stand by name and they were all keen to help him and look me over. Before we left, he quietly left a twenty-dollar bill in the tip jar for the booster club. I was glad we had to squeeze together in the bleachers to watch the rest of the game.

"There's Erik, pitching. Go, Erik!" he yelled. There was almost as much cheering for the out-of-town team, which lost, as for the home team, which won by two runs.

"You know why Erik pitches so well?" Anders asked as we made our way out. "Because yours truly spends hours playing catch with him while his dad is away fishing all summer. I give him pointers, kind of like I'm his coach," Anders bragged with exaggerated false modesty. "I plan to be his agent when he makes the big time."

"Did you play baseball, too?" I asked.

"Hoops were my thing. Our high school sports teams travel to away games via ferry. No other way to get around. You'd think all those teenagers on the ferry would be wild, but we got kicked off the team pronto if we didn't behave. So, we did, most of the time. Or, made sure not to get caught."

Although the cognac buzz had long faded, my head was still spinning. Anders was so different from the other people I knew. My California friends and I boomeranged around each other like we had no past and weren't thinking about the future. Anders was so grounded. Not grounded as in stranded or beached. Grounded as in having his feet on the ground and knowing his place in the world. He was part of a large family and loved them, warts and all. In fact, the entire town was like one huge extended family. I thought about my own small nuclear family existing in the midst of a large anonymous city. It seemed like a pretty lonely way to live.

We rounded a corner of the school, and Anders tugged me gently down a covered walkway. "I used to sneak out this way when I cut school so I could go hunting or fishing before dinner. I didn't get serious about school until after 'Nam. I bet you were a straight A student."

I started to say "As and Bs" but Anders wasn't listening, he was pulling me toward him, and I was happy to let him, expecting a kiss, wanting a kiss. He stopped when our faces were just inches apart, examining me as though he'd never seen me before. Or as though he'd known me years before and was now trying to ascertain if I was the same person.

His eyes were blue, like the clean, clear turquoise of a swimming pool on a hot summer day. I felt like I did when teetering on the high dive, that delicious moment just after you lean over the edge but haven't yet succumbed to gravity.

Anders pulled back. "This probably isn't a good idea."

"I think it's a great idea."

"We just met. You're leaving."

"We're here now. Let's just go with the flow." More like a flood tide.

Anders uttered something between a groan and a laugh. "Jesus, Maddie. I'm afraid if I start kissing you, I'll never stop."

"So, don't," I said, pulling his head down so I could fall into his kisses. Can you fall up? And then all I knew was how good his lips felt, how soft his moustache was, how being all bundled up made my exposed parts extra sensitive: my eyelids, my earlobes, my neck. His eyelashes tickled my cheek

When I came up for air, my brain slowly creaked back into gear, as though all the oxygen had rushed to my heart. Or lower.

"Okay, maybe you were right," I said shakily. "I'm sorry. I do have to get back."

"Don't go. Not yet." He pulled me close and kissed me again.

Finally, I pulled away. "I really do have to go."

I started walking away before I could change my mind.

"How did you get this gillnet job anyway?" Anders asked, catching up to me.

"Ron came to the door; said he'd heard someone at the house was looking for work on a fishing boat."

"Jesus, Maddie. Doesn't that seem a little …"

"Lucky?"

"Suspicious. Like too good to be true."

I bristled. "I'll be fine."

I softened my voice. "I want to see you when I get back."

Except I realized I hadn't asked Ron when that would be. I hadn't asked him much of anything. Earlier in the day, I had assumed I was in control of my life. Now I realized that going with the flow was taking me into unfamiliar waters. Or down the drain.

I shivered and hugged the borrowed jacket. When we reached the white house, I turned to Anders, wanting to bring the evening back to its previous delicious intimacy.

He leaned over as if to kiss me but instead turned up the collar of my borrowed jacket and gave me a gentle shove. "Off with you then, matey! Anchors away and all that! Ho, ho, ho and a bottle of rum!"

In a surprisingly nice baritone, he sang an old sea chanty as he walked away:

"When I was a little boy, my mother always told me,

that if I did not kiss the girls, my lips would grow all moldy!"

That night, I dreamed about trout fishing with my dad on a lake. We were sitting in a skiff as it swung on its anchor in a gentle arc, free to ride the swells and respond to the wind but not come unmoored.

The Misty

The next morning, I found the 30-foot *Misty* tied up in the harbor where Ron said it would be. It looked like what I would call a regular boat, with the addition of a large metal drum mounted horizontally in the stern. Ron was perched on the rail drinking coffee, looking hung over.

I dropped my gear on deck and jumped nonchalantly over the transom, stumbling and landing hard. *Look before you leap,* I heard my mom's voice admonish.

"*Merde,*" I swore.

"What?"

"Um, nothing." I limped across the small deck in my wrinkled jeans and wool jacket, noticing his white polo shirt and khaki pants. A red sweater was tied casually around his neck. More GQ than Alaska Magazine. "You look awfully clean to be going fishing," I blurted.

"You look awfully pretty to be going fishing," he said, "So, let's not!" He laughed and tossed the residue of his coffee overboard. "Well, I guess we should. When the engine's warmed up, you can cast off."

I stared at the early morning town, full of people going about their business oblivious to my departure. I wished I had time to call home and make sure my dad was okay. I wished I could see Anders again, but the harbor office was dark. A little part of me wished I wasn't going but the flow already had me in its grasp.

"Okay, you can cast off now," Ron called.

The town quickly shrank as we left the protected waters of the Narrows and entered the broad expanse of Frederick Sound which separated Southeast Alaska from British Columbia. Here, the powerful current clashed with the outgoing tide in a relentless battle for supremacy, one that could make an unwary boat just a piece of collateral damage. A cold wind rushed down the towering mountains to join the fray, not on any particular side, just enjoying the chaos.

I usually loved being on boats. Sailing on my cousin's yacht to Catalina Island, my heart leapt as we left the harbor's breakwater for the unprotected Santa Barbara Channel. As the sailboat gained speed and heeled to one side, I would cling to the mast enjoying the thrust and plunge, the wind ravishing my hair and throwing salt spray all around like sharp, cold confetti. On calmer days, I hung over the railing, watching the sleek gray torpedo-shaped dolphins race along the bow. What would it be like to be them—looking upward into this world instead of down into theirs?

Being on the *Misty* in Frederick Sound was completely different. Here, the water was hostile and grim, the coastal mountains standing like stoic sentinels guarding the border, their jagged peaks stabbing the clouds, forbidding access. Thoroughly chilled and barely able to stand on the bucking deck, I grabbed my gear and went inside.

"There you are!" Ron called jovially. "I was afraid you'd fallen overboard."

He was perched on a raised captain's chair in front of a large semi-circle of windows, surrounded by an array of navigation and steering equipment. A small sink, refrigerator and stove were built into one wall of the cabin, while a table and bench seats took up the remaining space. Behind the interior door, I glimpsed two steps leading to a dim area below the bow, and at the bottom of the stairs off to the side, a tiny bathroom.

Before I could investigate further, Ron swiveled in the chair. "Wouldn't do to lose my first mate when we've barely left port."

"I've been admiring the view," I said politely. "I haven't been out in the Sound before. Can you show me on the map where we are?"

"It's called a chart, honey, not a map," Ron chuckled. "We're here," he pointed to a spot on the chart. "We're headed north to Taku Inlet, south of Juneau. We'll anchor in a nearby cove for the night. Be on the fishing grounds tomorrow."

Leaning over the chart, I saw a complex maze of squiggly lines, numbers, names, and abbreviations superimposed over a blue, green and yellow color scheme. I had no idea how to match the one-dimensional map with the water, bays, mountains and island outside the window.

Seeing my confusion, Ron grinned. "Reading the chart is easy. Stay in the white, avoid the green, and for God's sake, don't hit the yellow!"

He waved a hand at the mountain range across the Sound. "You see that landmark peak sticking up?"

"I've seen it from Petersburg on a clear day."

"It's called Devil's Thumb. I think it's really God giving us the finger," he laughed. "You want something to drink? You're not seasick, are you?"

"I'm fine," I said.

"It's rough out today. I'll teach you to steer when it settles down."

I gradually relaxed and watched the world pass slowly by: mountains and water and sky in an ever-changing motion picture. Boats of all sizes traveled north with an occasional maverick headed south. The large seiners charged down the middle of the Sound while the smaller boats, like ours, stayed closer to shore.

Around noon, Ron fiddled with navigational dials. "Okay, I'm taking a break. Iron Mike will take over."

"Who?"

He snickered. "Not who. What. The auto pilot. Call me if we're going to run into anything."

Once the cabin door shut behind Ron, I set my hands lightly on the wheel, just enough to feel like I was steering, but not enough to interfere with the automatic controls. Nothing to it. I was working on a fishing boat! If only my friends could see me now.

Back inside, Ron rummaged in the galley and returned with a box of crackers, sliced cheese, beef jerky and two beers. "Lunchtime!"

I nibbled on the cheese and crackers but didn't drink the beer. Ron consumed the beer but not much else.

"There's Coke in the fridge and rum to go with it, if you want," he offered.

"Maybe later," I said. "Tell me about gillnetting."

"You know a gillnet hangs in the water, right?

That's about all I did know.

"The gillnet on this boat runs off the drum in the stern, so it's a stern-picker." He looked at me with exaggerated attention. "If the net is set off the bow, it's called a…"

"Bow-picker!"

"Pretty *and* smart!" He took another swig of beer. "The bottom of the net is weighted down by leads, the top floats on the surface by the cork line. The net soaks for a few hours while fish swim in and get caught by their gills. Then it's reeled back on board so the fish can be picked out."

"What's my job?"

"Keeping me company," he winked.

Seeing my expression, he laughed. "Just kidding. You'll cook, help pick fish when we bring the net in. If the fish are running, there'll be plenty to do."

And if not? I wondered.

Late afternoon, we pulled into a small bay. Ron released the anchor, which rattled overboard, then caught. The boat swung around into the wind and Ron turned off the engine.

"Just relax tonight," he said. "Tomorrow you can take over the cooking."

I got a book out of my pack. Ron poured a hefty slug of scotch into his coffee cup and put the bottle and a glass down in front of me. "Help yourself."

When I declined, he got out a jug of Gallo. "You like wine better?"

Feeling it would be churlish to keep refusing, I let him pour some into the plastic cup and took a cautious sip. The sky outside was darkening, like a heavy blanket thrown over the boat.

Ron chose a cassette from a small stack by the tape player and was soon humming along to the sounds of Frank Sinatra. My mother loved Frank Sinatra and only stopped playing his records when Charlene and I declared him simply too square to be tolerated. How old was Ron, anyway, I wondered?

I peered over the top of my book as he put a package of chicken on the counter and got out a paring knife. The rasp of the blade across a whetstone drowned out the tinny music.

Suddenly, he spun around brandishing the knife. My heart lurched. My book fell to the floor.

"You like Chow Mein?" he asked.

I leaned over to retrieve my book, chiding myself for over-reacting. "It's okay," I mumbled.

Ron threw the chicken pieces, skin and all, into the hot skillet. Hot grease and chicken blood splattered over the stovetop.

"What happened to the last deckhand, anyway?" I asked.

"She left," he said.

He opened two cans of chow mien while the chicken scorched unattended in the skillet.

"Why?" I asked.

There was a silence.

"She was…unreliable," he finally answered, prying the lid off the can.

Before I could ask what that meant, Ron dumped the canned glop into the skillet. "What kind of wine goes with Chinese food anyway? Maybe I should have brought sake."

"That's Japanese."

"Ahh, pretty *and* cultured. You're a real keeper."

He poured more Scotch into his cup and more Gallo into mine. "Drink up! You like Roy Orbison?"

"Not really," I said as he turned up the music. "Who told you I was looking for a fishing job?"

He got two plates out of a cupboard. "What?"

"How did you know I wanted a job on a fishing boat?"

"Someone at the Harbor Bar," Ron shrugged and busied himself spooning glops of chow mien on our plates.

As he put the plates down on the table, I thought of all the questions I should have asked, but hadn't, the biggest one being whether he'd been looking for Rachel when he came to our door. I wished I hadn't been so quick to open it.

I pushed the mess of meat and noodles around my plate while Ron ate and drank with gusto. When he was done, I jumped up to do the dishes, happy to have something to do. The cabin stank of burnt food and grease. When I looked out the little window above the sink, the night was pitch black and all I could see was my own reflection. Condensation like sweat dripped down my anxious image. The idyllic cove where we had moored now felt menacing and desolate. Unease rose in my throat tasting of cheap wine and grease.

Just as I turned from the sink, Ron imprisoned me in an awkward embrace.

"Come on, baby, it's time to dance," he crooned. His arms clamped around me vice-like and, with his body pressed tight against mine, he swayed in time to the music. His breath stank of booze, his body of sweat.

"Stop it! Let go!" I struggled against him, but it was no use. His face loomed up against mine, so close I could see oily perspiration shining on his stubble. When he thrust his tongue in my mouth, I almost gagged. I wish I had.

"You like it," he said, laughing and pressing me up against the sink. "I know your type."

He twisted both my arms behind my back and grabbed my wrists with one beefy hand. He slid his other hand down my bra and roughly fondled my breasts while thrusting his pelvis against mine.

"Yeah, you want it and I'm going to give it to you."

My efforts to free myself were getting him more excited, like a cat seeing the twitches of a dying mouse. I stopped struggling and sagged against the counter.

"Not here," I choked out. "The bed."

"Now, you're talking."

I squirmed from his arms and bolted down the two stairs to the bathroom. To my dismay, there was only a flimsy accordion door to shut. It would stop someone from entering for all of ten seconds.

I heard Ron go outside and piss over the side of the boat. He knew there was nowhere to run, nowhere to hide. Perhaps he considered this foreplay. Perhaps he was enjoying himself. The thought made me mad.

I returned to the galley and snatched the paring knife from the drainboard. I wedged myself on the bench between the table and the wall. I was shaking so badly, I had to brace the knife between my knees, blade pointing up and out.

Ron stumbled back into the dim cabin, zipping his fly.

"Maddie? You ready?" He started through the galley, but stopped when he saw me.

"There you are," he said.

He reached out to grab me, but I moved the knife just enough so his hand encountered the blade instead of me.

"What the…?" he yelled.

We both watched in surprise as blood dripped onto his white polo shirt.

He angrily grabbed a dishtowel and wrapped it around his hand. "You bitch! You cut me!"

"Come near me again and see what else I cut." My shaking voice didn't sound as threatening as I wanted, but he got the idea.

"Jesus, bitch, we were just having fun."

"I wasn't."

"I should throw you overboard."

"Just try it." We watched each other for a long moment, like in the documentary I watched where a wounded bear watches a cornered wolverine, trying to decide if it was worth another injury to get his prey.

I tried to look fierce and determined. Inside, I was quaking, wondering if I could really slash Ron and what would happen after that.

Finally, Ron shook his head, grabbed the bottle of scotch, and staggered down to his bunk. In the film, you could see the wolverine shaking long after the bear had gone.

I spent the night crouched behind the cabin table, drifting in and out of sleep. I could hear Ron snoring on his bed. Toward dawn, I dreamed my mother was pulling me out of a cactus bush. *You never learn, you never learn*, she said over and over. Pins and needles ran up and down my cramped legs while I wondered what it was I was supposed to learn. That being a good girl isn't always enough? That things aren't necessarily what they seem?

Life isn't always fair, Elizabeth, my mother retorted. *Be smart.*

I hated how my mother always had to have the last word.

When daylight had seeped into the cabin, I tucked the paring knife in my sleeve. I contemplated using it to slice Ron's throat, or worse— slice the part of him he pressed into my crotch. But I was stuck—he was the only one who could work the boat and get us back to town. I hated how vulnerable I felt.

Ron woke and stumbled on deck without a word, as though nothing had happened. But something *had* happened, damn it. When he came back in the galley, I took a deep breath. "I want off this boat. As soon as possible."

Ron shrugged. "Why'd you come, then?"

I pressed the knife's handle, willing myself not to cry. "Not to be assaulted."

He took a seat in the captain's chair and swiveled away from me.

"We'll be in Juneau by noon. You can get back from there."

Once I was safely on the southbound ferry, I gave in to tears. I had been assaulted, almost raped, and had cut a man with a knife. I wanted to feel totally wronged but a tiny part of me squirmed. Why had I ignored Ron's gold chain and sleezy clothes, the shmaltzy music and cheap wine? Why hadn't I even asked his last name? Why didn't I know there was only one bed on a gillnetter?

When I was fifteen and learning to drive, I had taken the steep curves down Mulholland Drive a little too fast. "Slow down," my normally unflappable father yelled. "Can't you see the signs?"

"Yes, but I thought they were just suggestions," I'd replied sheepishly.

"Well, they were damned good suggestions! Don't ignore the signs, Elizabeth."

It could have gone either way. I had ignored the signs and it had gone badly. But it could have been worse. The only thing that really hurt was my pride, having to slink back to Petersburg with nothing to show for my trouble except a paring knife hidden in my pocket. I wondered how my friends would react. Of course, Deb and Jimmie would be happy to see me. I'd buy pizza for dinner and it would be like nothing had happened. Rachel was another matter.

The Pirate

I WALKED FROM THE FERRY TERMINAL TO the brightly lit house with my metaphorical tail between my legs. Creedence blared out the windows. I knocked, then entered.

"My God, back already?" Deb exclaimed.

"The fishing job didn't work out." I mumbled. I wanted to say more, but half a dozen people I didn't know were sprawled around the room, smoking a joint. "Where's Rachel?"

Deb shrugged. "Out."

"You guys working tomorrow?"

"Yep."

The room reeked of patchouli from a joss stick burning on a chipped plate, the ash curling behind it like discarded skin. I waved my hand theatrically in front of my face to clear the air. "Partying on a work night? Tsk, tsk. What would Marie say?"

"That things have gone to heck in a handbasket, is what Marie would say."

Indeed, the list of house rules had cigarette burns where Marie's heart-shaped exclamation marks used to be.

I swam up from a deep sleep when I heard the alarm clock go off, happy to find myself in my own bed. When I pried open my eyes, Rachel was combing her hair. Her dark eyes met mine in the mirror.

"Madeline Maguire," she said. "What are you doing here?"

I was so happy to be here and not on the *Misty*, I ignored her hostile tone. "Rach, it was horrible. The skipper got drunk and tried to rape me. I cut him with a paring knife. He passed out. I made him take me to Juneau this morning so I could catch the ferry back." Tears leaked from my eyes.

Rachel came over to my bed, speechless for once.

I sat up and took the hair brush out of her hand. "Sit down. I'll braid your hair."

"You really cut him?" she asked.

I nodded.

"So, no more fishing boats?"

I shrugged. "No more gillnetters anyway," I said. "Did you know they only have one bunk?"

What I really wanted to know is if she'd been the one Ron had been looking for when I answered the door but I couldn't make myself ask. I slipped a rubber band over the end of her braid.

"You going to report him?" she asked.

"Nah, it's just his word against mine. I'll go over later and ask Allen if I can have my old job back."

She narrowed her eyes at me. "I'm in the egg room now."

"I mean, go back to the slime line."

Rachel nodded and tied a batik scarf over her braid.

I snorted. "Rosie the Riveter meets Pocahontas."

Rachel studied her reflection in the mirror. "More Indian princess than cannery worker, though, don't you think?" She blew her reflection a kiss and hurried out, late as usual.

Marla glanced up when I entered the cannery office. "Madeline Maguire. We heard you quit. No clocking in until Allen says otherwise."

Good to see you, too. "Is he around?"

"Out back."

I went through the busy cannery to the dock. Allen stood with one leg propped on an overturned crate, sipping a cup of coffee and talking intently with an older man. The stranger was about fifty years old with a chiseled face, watery blue eyes, and close-cropped gray hair. He wore a faded blue mariner's cap with gold braid and an anchor on the brim. Captain Ahab, I presumed.

Allen looked over and gave an exaggerated start. "Maddie, why aren't you inside working? Oh yeah, right. You got a fishing job."

I hadn't told his wife I was going fishing, only that I'd be gone a few days. Small town gossip at work.

"What are you doing here?" he asked.

I cast about for something to say that didn't sound pathetic. "The gillnetter didn't work out. Skipper was a jerk." I took a deep breath. "I'm hoping for my old job back."

Allen didn't respond, he just raised an eyebrow and looked at the older man. The man shrugged and said, "Your call."

Allen straightened decisively and waved his coffee cup in our general direction. "Roger, meet Maddie. Maddie, Roger."

Roger tapped his cap and nodded.

I thought about shaking hands, but decided that was too corporate. "Hello," I mumbled.

"You want to go out on a boat, right?" Allen asked.

"Depends," I replied cautiously. "Which boat?"

"This boat," Allen gestured at a 75-foot boat tied up at the dock. It looked like a seiner except it didn't have a bulky seine net or power skiff on the deck.

"Which skipper…?"

"This skipper." He gestured at Roger. "The *Silver Bandit's* a tender. Roger's the skipper. He needs a deckhand to go with him to Point Baker so the gillnetters can off-load tonight."

"Point Baker's south, not north, right?"

They nodded.

"You tendered before?" Roger asked without much hope.

"No, I've been working at the cannery."

"You said you were out on a gillnetter?"

I nodded.

He raised one bushy eyebrow. "And…?"

I didn't want to say I'd almost been raped. I felt ashamed, like Ron's assault was my fault or I was being overly dramatic. A cry-baby. "Turns out the skipper was more interested in catching me than catching fish." I mumbled.

He nodded, like he wasn't surprised. "All you have to do on the *Bandit* is work hard and do your job. Can you do that?"

"Anyone else on board?" I asked.

"No. You can have your pick of bunks."

My index finger worried at a torn cuticle on my thumb. "What happened to the last deckhand?"

"Wasn't one," Allen replied. "We just now got the *Bandit* repaired so we can send her out." Then he understood what I was really asking. "You'll be okay."

The *Bandit* remained tied up at the dock while Roger and I spent the afternoon getting groceries and diesel. I wanted to see Anders, but I was pretty sure running off to see someone would not endear me to my new boss. Besides, I had no idea what I'd say to Anders when I did see him again. Maybe it would be better to wait until I had something positive to say, besides that he was right when he said I shouldn't go out on the *Misty*.

"What happens after we reach the grounds?" I asked.

"They'll be ready to off-load what they've caught and get back to fishing."

"How will they know we're there?"

He pointed to a radio that had been crackling softly in the background. "The VHF is on channel 16 all the time. Once a boat has contacted us, we'll switch to another channel on the CB."

"CB radio like what the truckers use in the movies?" I asked.

"CB radio like what the fishermen use in real life," he replied dryly.

He fiddled with some knobs and I heard a voice over the radio say, "*Sea Fly. Sea Fly.* This is the *Charles T.* Do you read me?'

After a pause, "This is the *Charles T.* calling the *Sea Fly.* Do you read me?"

"Copy, *Charles T.* This is the *Sea Fly.*"

"Switch to channel eight?"

"Switching to eight. *Sea Fly* out."

"*Charles T.* out."

Roger switched to channel eight.

"Are we going to eavesdrop?" I asked, thrilled and uneasy.

"I'm going to teach you that nothing said on a radio is ever private," he replied unapologetically.

"Hey, Tom, how's Aunt Sue?"

"She's okay, but Cousin Harvey is sick."

"Sorry to hear that. I'll be back in touch."

"*Sea Fly* out."

"*Charles T.* out."

"They're just talking about their family," I said, disappointed.

"No, they're not. None of the boats want the others to know how they're doing, so they use codes they only share with the tender or cannery, or with their fishing buddies. Aunt Sue may mean the humpies are running, or maybe it means they're not. Cousin Harvey being sick may mean the water is rough, or maybe it means the water's calm. It may even mean Harvey really is sick."

He laughed. "I remember one time someone was talking to his wife. Said to make sure she paid the mortgage on time. She let out a huge cheer and so then we all knew their code for a large run."

"We listen to the radio for weather reports, Fish and Game announcements, whatever keeps us awake on wheel watch. Sometimes on calm nights, we get CB operators around the world and even music from Toyoko or somewhere. Sometimes those Coasties stuck on lighthouses for months on end talk so dirty with their wives, it scorches the airwaves. One time I heard some guy talking that way with his wife, and then he turned around and said the same thing to another lady!"

"Remember," he said, "If you're ever on the radio, keep it short and remember nothing you say is ever private."

I listened carefully to the garbled voices reaching us as though from a faraway portal. I couldn't understand them, but Roger was fluent in this alien language.

Even though it was technically still daylight when we finally left the dock, the sun had eased behind the tall mountains, and the long, slow Alaska summer twilight was underway. As we headed down the Narrows. I studied the complex web of numbers and contour lines on the maritime chart beside Roger.

"Other places aren't as complicated as Southeast," he said. "Here, you've got hundreds, maybe thousands of islands. Reefs that are buried at high tide but exposed when it's low. Huge boulders and spits of land jut out into the water, most of them surrounded by shallows. The tide surges back and forth through these narrow channels every twelve hours."

"No wonder everyone studies the charts so closely," I said, tracing our path through the maze of data.

"That's not all," Roger said, gesturing out the window. "There's equally important stuff that's not on the chart. You need to know which way the wind is blowing and the current running. What's the tide doing? You have to watch out for submerged logs, sleeping whales, icebergs with most of their mass underwater. Storms can blow in without warning. Commercial fishing in Alaska is a hazardous business."

"Death by drowning?" I asked, glad I knew how to swim.

"Hypothermia first. You have less than five minutes in these waters before your limbs stop working. If it's any consolation, as many people die from fires and explosions on boats as going in the water."

"No consolation," I said, shivering. "What I don't understand is how you know where the boat is on this chart?" I had spent my entire life on roads and freeways littered with signs but there were none on the water.

"You learn the landmarks. Nearby mountains. Familiar bays. There are a few lighthouses and buoys. The compass tells you what direction you're headed and the knotmeter how fast you're going. You've got to pay attention, put it all together. Here, you try it."

The boat veered first one way, then the other as I tried to keep the *Bandit* on the exact heading.

"You're not threading a needle," he said. "You're herding an old boat through the water. Use a light touch to guide it in the general direction."

When he was satisfied, Roger pointed to our location on the chart. "We're here. Keep the red buoy lights to port and the green to starboard. You do know port from starboard?"

"Port, left. Starboard, right. I learned the alphabet using semaphore flags in Girl Scouts, too," I boasted.

He laughed. "Great. If our radio fails, you're on."

Roger watched for a few minutes, then announced he was taking a break. "Steady as she goes," he said as he left the wheelhouse.

Steering the boat was a heady experience. That I, so small, could control such a mighty beast made me feel powerful, too. I tracked our progress by comparing the buoys we passed with those on the chart, counting two red and one green so far. Red to port and green to starboard.

The radio crackled with annoying static, so I turned it down and allowed the boat to find its way through the Narrows like a trusty steed picking its way through the scrub. I thought about how my mother always admonished me to follow the straight and narrow. But maybe most things made better progress when allowed a little leeway.

Was that three green and three red buoys now, or had we passed four on the right? And where was Roger? Unease niggled at the edges of my earlier smugness.

Pride comes before a fall, my mother admonished.

Zip it, I told her.

I lost track of how long Roger was gone or where we were. I wiped my sweaty palms on my wool jacket—actually Anders' sister's wool jacket—feeling the paring knife in my pocket. A lot of good that would do me. I needed Roger to be here, not fight him off.

"Roger?" I called. "Roger!"

No answer. I called again, more loudly. What were my options? I could keep going until the boat ran aground. I could leave the helm to look for Roger and have the boat run aground. I could shut the engine off and be carried aground. I slowed the boat down as much as I dared and hurried down to the galley.

One light bulb swayed gently above the table where I found Roger—face down in the potato salad with a mostly empty pint of whiskey beside him.

Heart pounding, I leaned over him and said firmly, "Roger, Roger, wake up!" His eyes fluttered and I ran back up to the wheelhouse. I corrected course so the *Bandit* was equal distance between the red and green buoys ahead. Something bumped the boat and slid along the hull.

I ran back down and found Roger passed out again. This time, I forced myself to do something polite girls in California never do.

I slapped him.

Roger's eyes opened, then shut. I leaned into his face and said very loudly and slowly, "Roger. Wake. Up."

"Huh?"

"You passed out. You need to wake up."

He sat up and rubbed his face. "Who's steering?"

"No one."

That got his attention.

"Oh, God, I'll be right up."

I made sure he was on his feet before running back to the pilot house. Roger, his face and hair dripping with water, appeared a few minutes later.

He checked the instruments, peered at the chart and tapped up the speed. "Damn, we missed the turn into Tugboat Channel." He shook his head like that would help clear it.

"What do we do now?"

"Keep going in the main channel."

We passed two more buoys.

"How long was I asleep?" he asked.

"You weren't asleep. You were passed out. Drunk."

He ran a hand through his wet hair. Turned up the volume on the VHF and fiddled with one of the knobs to reduce the static. I heard someone calling the *Silver Bandit*.

Roger took the mike. "This is the *Silver Bandit*. Over."

"Switch to our working channel, *Bandit*."

"Roger," said Roger. He yanked his head at me. "Go make me coffee."

I left, then paused out of sight.

"Roger, this is Allen."

"I read you."

"Where are you?"

"Coming down main channel."

"Not the Tug channel?"

Roger hesitated. "No."

"What the …?" There was another pause. "Why aren't you at Point Baker?"

Another pause before Roger said, "We'll be there shortly."

"What's going on?" Allen asked suspiciously.

"I didn't feel well. I fell asleep," Roger enunciated. "Maddie was at the wheel. Won't happen again."

There was a long pause.

"Make sure it doesn't," Allen said disgustedly and signed off.

When I returned bearing two cups of coffee, Roger gazed steadily out the windows. "Keep the coffee coming, mate, it's going to be a long night. We start taking on fish as soon as we arrive."

As we neared Point Baker, Roger grew more sober and more anxious. The next time I filled up my coffee mug, I topped it off with the dregs of the whiskey for courage. "Dutch courage," I'd heard it called. Maybe it should be called "Maddie's courage."

"Get on your warm clothes and rain gear. You'll be icing fish while I run the hydraulics. There's a box of giant rubber bands down there somewhere. Put them on the outside of your rain pants around your ankles so the ice doesn't get up your pants. Then come back."

After I'd done as ordered, Roger said, "The boat crew will already have their brailler bag loaded…"

"Brailler bag?"

"The cargo net that carries fish from their boat to ours. The boom on the *Bandit* has a scale on it that they'll hook up the brailler. After reading the brailler weight, I'll bring it over to our boat, we double-check and record the weight, then you jump down into the hold…"

"How far?"

"Oh, maybe a five-foot drop. Duck under the deck so when the hoist lowers the brailler bag you don't get caught under it. Release the hook attached to the scales on top of the bag and attach it to the other side so when I lift it up, the bag dumps the fish out. I'll show you how the first time and I'll tell you which section of the hold to use. There's a separate compartment for each species, although they're mostly catching coho right now."

"Layer the fish in the proper section," he continued. "Shovel some ice on them, then start another layer. The gillnetter will keep loading the fish into brailler bags and I'll keep weighing and dumping them in the hold. In between, you ice them down. Once you get the hang of it, we should be able to off-load five or six bags in fifteen minutes. Do it quickly, so they can get back to fishing. We don't want them selling to another cannery, so work fast and don't waste their time."

Then don't get drunk, I thought.

The *Bandit* turned into the bay and slowed as a gillnetter approached. They tied the smaller boat onto ours and both boats turned on their harsh stern lights, making it as bright as day on deck. Roger and I lifted the hatch cover off the hold and my stomach lurched at the darkness below.

"There's a Maglite in the galley," Roger directed, "Use one of them rubber bands to attach it to your cap and hurry!"

Roger showed me the tag line that I would detach from the scale on the boom and attach to the line that would drop the bag with its load of fish into the hold.

"In you go!" Roger said quietly, like he didn't want the gillnetter to know how inexperienced I was. "Yell when the bag is resting on the ice so you can reach the tag line."

I swung my legs over the edge and let myself drop about six feet, landing on a mound of flake ice. The hold was dim and spooky. I ignored the dark nooks and crannies in favor of watching Roger lower the first bag full of fish down into the hold. It bumped me on the head before I remembered to duck under the deck. I yelled, the bag stopped, I found and switched the tag line, yelled again, and it rose, spilling dozens of salmon at my feet. I started grabbing slimy fish and laying them in the post aft compartment like I'd been told. Five loads later, I heard the gillnetter roar off. While I was icing down the fish already in the hold, I heard another boat tie up and soon more fish tumbled into the tender's hold.

Seven boats off-loaded that night before Roger peered at me from the deck above. He shone the flashlight around.

"Finish icing the fish, then you can take a break while we head back to town."

Five hours later, Petersburg was in sight.

"Get the first Trayco ready to off-load," Roger said when I stuck my head in the pilot house.

"Trayco?"

"Those large plastic totes on deck, size of a bathtub. Don't need to weigh the fish again. The cannery boys will take care of things on their end. You just keep loading fish into the Traycos."

"By hand?"

"No, by magic," he replied sarcastically. "Wear gloves."

I didn't want to admit how tired I was. My back hurt, my legs hurt, and my stomach roiled from too much bad coffee and not enough food. None of which overrode my euphoria at having successfully completed a trip on a commercial fishing boat. I envisioned myself doing this the rest of the summer: days in town alternating with days on the fishing grounds, a fairly comfortable boat, a fairly decent skipper—when he was sober. Now that I knew what to expect in that department, I'd keep a sharper eye out for his little disappearing act.

The cannery was expecting us. We pulled up alongside the dock and, after a brief wave to acknowledge my readiness, the boom was dropped into the Pirate's hold for me to hook the first loaded Trayco onto. I no sooner got one Trayco loaded and lifted off the boat, than an empty one appeared waiting to be filled. I would have fallen behind except one of the cannery workers, I didn't know who, jumped in the hold and, cheerfully but silently, worked beside me to get the fish unloaded.

In the bowels of the cannery, I knew my friends would be sliming and packing these same fish. But I wasn't working in the cannery, I was working on a boat!

After off-loading the fish, I hosed down the hold and climbed wearily onto the deck where Allen was talking heatedly to Roger. Roger nodded a few times and I heard him say, "Sorry, boss, it won't happen again."

I was shocked when Allen yelled, "You're damn right it won't happen again because you're fired." Then in a calmer tone, "You're never taking one of my boats out again."

"Just give me another chance…"

"I'm done giving you second chances. Just leave. I've got someone coming to move the boat."

Roger's shoulders slumped and he brushed by me without a word.

Allen motioned me over. "So…Roger got drunk on the way to Point Baker."

I didn't know what to say. I wanted to be loyal to Roger who—when sober—was a good boss, but the image of what might have gone wrong haunted me.

"No one could raise the *Bandit*." Allen continued. "Gillnetters were waiting at Point Baker to off-load. Waiting," he repeated. "Not fishing."

I nodded miserably.

"Roger's fired."

"Me, too?"

"Look, Maddie, I'm sorry."

I thought Allen meant he was sorry for firing me.

"I told you it would be okay, and it wasn't," he continued. "I ignored the signs. Jesus Christ, enough shit happens when the skipper is sober. If you weren't so green, I'd be pissed at you, too. Roger said none of it was your fault. You can have your job back in the cannery. Get your stuff off the boat before you leave. Marla has your tendering check in the office." He turned to go, then snapped his fingers and turned back. "Marla said something about a message for you."

I STUFFED MY CLOTHES IN THE PACK and my sleeping bag in its sack. So much for tendering the rest of the summer. It was back to the slime line for me. But first, I needed to call home.

The cannery office was humming. Marla was talking on the phone and typing on a big electric typewriter when I poked my head inside her domain. Her usual forbidding countenance softened when I entered. She put a hand over the receiver. "Your mother called yesterday," she said. "You need to call home. Use the office phone on that empty desk. Reverse the charges."

"What's the matter?" I asked.

She shrugged and returned to her phone conversation. I dialed the operator with shaking hands. The phone rang ten times.

My sister finally answered. "Maguire residence. Charlene speaking."

"Char? It's Maddie."

There was a pause and then Charlene responded in her normal snotty tone. "About time. Dad had a heart attack two days ago."

The blood rushed from my face and my mind went blank.

"But he's okay," Charlene added.

My heart resumed beating. "What happened?"

"A blocked artery ruptured is what happened, which you would know if we had been able to contact you. All we had was that stupid general delivery address. I finally dug up the name of the cannery where you're working." She paused a beat. "Oh, but guess what? You're not working there any longer." Another pause. "They said you were out fishing." An even longer pause. "What the hell?"

I finally found my voice. "I called as soon as I could." It sounded lame and defensive even to my ear. "Where are mom and dad?"

"At the hospital. Where I'm headed after I pick up a few things for Dad."

"But, he's okay?"

"He is now. It was touch and go for a while."

Guilt and relief washed over me. What if he had died? I started crying.

"I said I'd come home when we talked before," I blubbered, "Mom said not to." Maybe I should have. Maybe my mother had been wrong.

"That was emphysema. This was a heart attack."

We listened to me cry for a while.

"For goodness' sake," Charlene finally said. "I said he was okay."

I found the red bandana in my pocket and blew my nose. Took a couple of deep breaths.

"Should I come home?" I asked shakily.

Char was silent a moment. "You'll have to make up your own mind."

Static cackled over the phone line like messages coming from far away in a frequency I couldn't understand, no matter how hard I tried.

"I'll see how soon I can get a flight," I finally said, hoping I had interpreted the signals and signs correctly.

I wanted so badly to see Anders. It seemed like weeks since we'd said goodbye, not days. But first I had to make arrangements to go home.

I went to the Viking Travel Agency and asked about flights to Los Angeles. Turns out the plane ticket was going to cost more than I had earned so far all summer. Luckily, the clerk said I could use Mom's credit card number. All I had to do was go to the airport the next day.

I went to the bank to liquidate my meager account. When I reached the front of the line, the teller smiled at me with practiced good cheer. "Hello! How may I help you.?" Then she saw the name on my withdrawal slip and peered over her reading glasses. "Oh. It's you."

I glanced at the nameplate. "Hi Karn. Pleased to see you," I lied.

"Closing out your account? Going home?" she asked with a satisfied air. I thought about telling her my dad was in the hospital except it was none of her business.

"Weren't here long, were you?" she said, stamping the withdrawal slip like it needed knocking out, might otherwise flop around the counter and get away.

"How's Bear?" I asked instead.

"Bear? You mean my father? Dad is well, thank you. We're having a special dinner with Darlene tonight to celebrate his birthday—and maybe Darlene and Anders will finally make the big announcement. Engagements are so exciting, don't you think!" Karn slid the cash and receipt to me with a satisfied air.

She looked over my shoulder. "Next!"

Since I was leaving Petersburg, it didn't matter that Anders was getting engaged—except it did. I guess I was just another seasonal worker to him, someone to pass the time with while he played hard to get with the local women—with overgroomed, hair-sprayed, man-hungry, divorcees named Darlene, to be exact.

I returned to the empty white house to pack. Since most of my clothes were dirty, I decided I might as well go to the laundromat before taking them home. Wouldn't want to contaminate my mom's washer.

The laundromat was fairly empty; the fishermen busy fishing and the cannery workers canning. An old man mumbled to himself in the corner and several young mothers flipped through magazines as they chatted among themselves. Children tumbled around their feet, tottering on chairs and scribbling in the magazines. One of the women picked up a child who had fallen, cuddled him before he could cry, then passed him to another woman who fed him a cookie. A pregnant woman rocked a sleeping baby in its buggy.

The scene reminded me of how I chatted with my girlfriends around the kitchen table, except we were always in a hurry, always rushing to get ready or rushing to leave, not wanting to miss the next joint, the next drink, the next romance.

I didn't want to be like these women, but something about the slow rhythm of the morning was so soothing: the clean smell of detergent, the swish of washing machines, the thump of driers, the children's sticky hands and the way the moms welcomed their chocolate kisses. It was all so sweet and sad I wanted to curl up in a pile of warm clothes all day, hide away from the haste and menace of the cannery, from nasty skippers and scary waters, from the reality of ailing parents and broken hearts, the guilt of being here and not there.

I folded my dried clothes as neatly as I could, wondering if my mother would suggest throwing them out when I got home. I knew she'd be happy to buy me new ones and, in fact, I couldn't see wearing my jeans and wool shirts in Southern California. Still, I wasn't ready to acknowledge I was never coming back. I pushed that thought to the back along with my flannel shirt and the slinky blouse.

One thing for sure, I wasn't going to tell my mother I'd heard her voice in my head the whole time I'd been gone. I would tell Dad about the fishing in Alaska and how we should come back someday and catch big feisty salmon instead of wimpy California trout. Oh my God, what if he couldn't go fishing anymore, or eat chocolate ice cream? A fat teardrop fell on my dry underwear and I blew my nose quickly before any more of my clothes got wet.

The Pity Party

WHEN I WALKED BY THE CAN on my way home, it seemed like a good idea to go inside.

The bottles behind the bar glittered, a country-western singer crooned on the juke box and Jerry, the bartender, greeted me warmly. "A pretty girl on a dreary afternoon! What's up?

"I just found out my dad had a heart attack. I'm on my way home tomorrow."

"Sorry to hear that," Jerry said perfunctorily. "Want one of my special Margaritas for people who've had bad news?"

The downpour outside provided no incentive to leave. I asked Jerry to forget about the margarita and just bring me a shot of tequila with a slice of lemon. I downed it in one gulp. Jerry brought me another.

"So, you like tequila?" a voice behind me asked.

My heart leapt as I heard Anders, until I remembered he was engaged and I was leaving town.

"Not especially," I said, not turning around. "But my dad's had a heart attack and I'm going home in the morning. If that doesn't call for tequila, I don't know what does."

"God, Maddie, that's awful!" Anders slid onto the stool beside me. "Is he going to be okay?"

"They think so."

I concentrated on the complicated process of licking salt from my finger and swallowing the shot of tequila. The lemon slice I quickly sucked on was so sour, it brought tears to my eyes.

Anders passed me a wad of cocktail napkins and I wiped my eyes. Took a shaky breath. "Mom said he's recuperating, but I think I should go home anyway. Nothing is working out for me here."

"The gillnetter?"

"It was horrible. I had to defend myself from the skipper with a knife. You were right, I shouldn't have gone on that damn boat." When I glanced up, his eyes were full of concern, not I-told-you-so. I took a deep breath and plunged on.

"Then, as soon as I got back, Allen threw me on a company tender. He said Roger, the skipper, would be okay. Except he wasn't. He got drunk and passed out, leaving me to steer the boat in the dark. I was terrified we'd run aground or sink. I finally had to slap him to get him to wake up. Allen fired him when we got back."

"He had it coming."

"Yeah, well, I'm out of a job, too." I took a shaky breath. "People think it's bad luck to have a woman on board, but it's really the men who are the problem."

Anders didn't disagree.

"Then I called home and found out about my dad." Somehow there was another shot in front of me, which I dispatched. "How'd you know I was in town anyway?"

"Karn said she saw you in the bank," Anders motioned for Jerry to bring him a beer and me a glass of water.

I snorted and then tried to turn it into a cough.

"Was she a bitch?" he asked.

"No. Not really. She just made sure I know you're engaged." I ran my tongue around the empty jigger, in case there was still any booze lurking in it. There wasn't.

Anders cupped my chin in his hand and gently turned my face until I had no choice but to meet his gaze. "I made it clear to Darlene once and for all that there is not now and never will be anything between us." He enunciated like the words would sink in better that way. "She left in a huff."

"So…you're not engaged?"

He shook his head. "Then, I thought I might as well tell Dad I was never going to take over his halibut boat either. I expected a big argument, but I guess deep inside he already knew."

"Wow, you really burned some bridges."

He thought about that while he took a swallow of beer. "Not burning bridges so much as discarding stuff you don't need. Easier to move forward that way."

My heart thumped at the way he said it, or maybe the way he looked at me. I wished I hadn't had so much to drink. I wished I looked better and didn't need a breath mint. Then I remembered it didn't matter.

"I need to call my folks and tell them I'm coming home. I can call them at the hospital during visiting hours."

I started to get off the stool but it wobbled, or I did. "I think I might have drunk too much," I said like it would be news to Anders. "Be right back."

I got up and attempted to walk majestically to the bathroom, but some of the chairs and tables got in the way. When I came out, Anders was waiting.

"Come on," he said, "you can call from my house."

When we got to Anders' house, I slumped on the couch while he brewed a pot of coffee and brought me a box of Kleenex. I knew I looked a mess: my face mottled, my eyes red, my nose runny. I curled under the afghan like a sea anemone after being poked.

"Do you have the hospital number?" he asked.

I extended my arm from under the blanket. I hadn't had any paper when I talked to Char, only a ball-point pen.

He twisted my ink-stained arm this way and that. "Good thing the ink didn't come off."

When he waved a cup of coffee near my nose, I cautiously poked my head out of my cocoon.

Two cups of coffee, three aspirin, cold water on my face, and a piece of toast later, I sat at Anders' kitchen table while he dialed the number transcribed from my arm. He pushed a pen and a pad of paper toward me and left the room.

"Ken Maguire's room."

"Mom, it's me. How's Dad?"

"Elizabeth! Charlene said you finally called the house."

"Mom. How's Dad?"

"Weak, but they say he'll be okay."

I took a deep breath. "I'm coming home tomorrow. The airlines said you can give them your credit card number to pay for the ticket. Okay?"

"Yes, of course, but…here…your father wants to talk to you."

Dad's voice came on the line, frail but unmistakable. "Mizzie."

"Dad. How are you?"

"I've been better."

"I'm coming home tomorrow."

"No, you're not."

"What?"

"You're not coming home."

I started to say something but he interrupted. "Hush, I can't talk long. I've had a scare but the doc gave me a bunch of meds and put me on a new diet. Made me promise to exercise more. Your mother and Charlene fuss over me like you wouldn't believe."

"Dad, I'm coming home to take care of you, too."

"Hold on." I heard him talking to my mom, suggesting she grab a cup of coffee. Then he came back on line. "When I was a young man, I planned to travel and see the world before I settled down. Then World War II broke out and I saw some South Pacific Islands from the deck of a ship and that was about it. When I got discharged, I took off from San Diego, planning to hitchhike across the country. I made it as far as Los Angeles when I met your mom. Stopped me in my tracks."

He took several deep breaths while I gripped the receiver so tightly, I thought I might wring the black off. "We got married, bought a house, started our family. It's been a great life. I have no regrets. Only sometimes

I wonder what it would be like to see New Orleans, the Mississippi, New York. You were ten before I got as far as the Grand Canyon."

"Oh, Dad, …"

"What I'm saying is, it's okay to take some time to find yourself. Isn't that what all you young people say nowadays, 'find yourself?' When I was your age, I found myself on a destroyer in the Pacific. It was enough just to stay alive."

In the background, I heard my mother return and say, "Oh Ken, don't tire yourself."

He kept going. "Maddie, you're fortunate enough to have options so you might as well take the time to find out what will make you happy. Learn stuff that's not in a book. Go places you want to explore. That's all I'm saying."

Tears ran down my face and I heard Mom's voice in the background saying, "That's enough now, Ken."

"We're agreed, Maddie?" he asked, his voice stronger. "No coming home tomorrow?"

I nodded, then realized he couldn't see me. "If you're sure. Daddy, I love you."

I heard only static whispering its inarticulate messages on the line, but this time I knew it was Dad saying he loved me back.

The coffee and aspirin had temporarily held my hangover at bay, but as soon as I hung up, exhaustion and nausea came crashing back. I told Anders my dad wanted me to stay here, not go home, but all I could manage in way of explanation were incoherent phrases like new meds, no ice cream, a destroyer in the South Pacific, never seeing New York.

He must have picked up the gist because he nodded once, slung my pack over one arm and held me up with the other as he walked me home. The rain had stopped but in its aftermath the town was quiet, the normal street sounds muffled. His bulk beside me was a silent but comforting presence.

"So, you're not going home?" He asked as we neared the house.

I shook my head gingerly. "Dad said I should figure things out first. Figure out what I want to do. He said it's pretty clear that means not going home right now."

"Smart man," Anders said.

We walked down the boardwalk to the house.

"So, tell me Maddie. What is it you really want to do?"

A fog horn sounded its plaintive warning out in the Narrows. I thought back to the day after Marie lost her finger. How I'd stood on the dock longing to feel the wind in my hair, the surge and sway of a boat deck, the forward motion.

"I want to go fishing."

"Seriously?"

"Seriously."

"Because that's worked out really well for you so far?"

"Because, I don't know. Because if I don't, I'll always regret it." I peered into his eyes, now gray and inscrutable. "What is it *you* really want?"

He looked at me a moment, then shook his head. "I'll tell you what I really want when you're in a condition to do something about it. Which is not right now."

He helped me into my room, pulled off my boots, and pulled the blanket up over me.

The Job Interview

THE FIRST THING I SAW WHEN I pried my dry eyes open the next morning was an index card propped on the table beside me. It had a hole in one corner like it had been pinned up on a bulletin board. I brought it up to my eyes and read: SEINER COOK AND DECKHAND NEEDED ASAP ON THE *MISS CORA*. BERTH E25.

I showered quickly and found a box of muffin mix and a small bowl of fresh blueberries in the fridge. An hour later, I hurried to the harbor with the still-warm muffins wrapped in foil.

I paused at the top of the ramp and looked down at all the boats. I could now tell the difference between types of fishing boats. The large seiners were unmistakable, their decks piled high with seine net and their heavy skiffs riding on top. I spotted the *Miss Cora* at the end of arm E. Problem was, two other boats were tied between the dock and the boat. I stopped at the high gunwale of the first seiner, unsure what to do.

"Just climb over," a voice directed. A man hopped casually over the gunwale of one boat, crossed the deck, and hopped over the next until he was beside me on the dock. The boats were so heavy, they didn't rock a bit when he crossed.

"Are you sure I won't be trespassing?"

"Nah, that's how it's done. When space is limited, the boats raft up. Only way to go back and forth is across the decks. But don't go inside without permission."

"You're not the *Miss Cora's* skipper, are you?"

"Hardly. Joe's probably aboard drinking coffee." With a friendly wave, he strode away.

I crossed the boats one by one, pausing when I reached the *Miss Cora*. The smell of coffee wafted out of the open galley door.

I knocked on the door frame and peered inside. "Hello. Anybody home?"

"Yeah, what?" A large, middle-aged man turned from the stove, coffee pot in one hand, the ubiquitous white porcelain mug in the other.

"Hello. Hi, I'm Maddie. Maddie Maguire. I heard the *Miss Cora* is looking for a cook and deckhand. Are you the skipper?"

"Yeah, I'm Joe Stefanović. Come aboard." Joe was somewhere between forty and sixty, with a clean-shaven face and short, salt-and-pepper hair. His name sounded Slavic, but he had the swarthy features of the Tlingit Indians who lived in Southeast.

I held out the bag of muffins. "I made muffins this morning. Kind of like a resume, you know?"

"Coffee?" he asked, waving me to a seat at the galley table.

"Thanks."

Joe slid onto the other bench seat and added several heaping tablespoons of sugar into his cup. "You ever seined before?"

"I've been on a gillnetter and a tender, but I really want to work on a seiner," I replied carefully.

He looked disappointed but cheered up when he bit into a muffin. "Tastes like you can cook. What else can you make besides muffins?"

"Spaghetti. Meat loaf. Pot roast. Chicken." I learned to cook as a teenager thanks to my mom, the kitchen having by tacit agreement been declared neutral ground in our endless mother-daughter battles. Cooking became the one arena in which I found her advice encouraging rather than judgmental "Oatmeal. Pancakes. Cookies. Muffins, obviously."

"You ever cooked three meals a day for five hungry people?"

"Not exactly. But it's not a problem. It's like cooking for myself, only times five." I hoped he would laugh, and he did.

"Cooking's the *easy* part. You'd also have to work on deck."

"How, exactly?" I asked.

"Slinging leads."

He looked at my uncomprehending face and sighed. "Slinging leads means you help bring in the net by gathering the steel rings along the bottom and slinging them onto a metal arm." He spoke slowly like I was an idiot. "Rings used to be made out of lead, so it's called the lead line. Ever done that before?" he asked without much hope.

"No, but I'm a fast learner and I can start right away."

I drank my coffee while Joe gave me the rundown.

"Room and board are provided. You'll get a crew share at the end of the season." He looked at me. "That's a percentage of whatever the boat earns all season. Minus the boat share, the skipper's share, the cost of fuel, food and other expenses. And, of course, you'll split the crew share four ways, since there are four of you. The cook–that's you—doesn't have to ice the fish in the hold or do chores on deck because you'll be busy cooking. When we're hauling in the net, you'll handle the lead line."

I nodded.

"If there are fish, we work as long as we can. Grab a nap when the net is setting or if we're running to another spot. We may or may not fish at night. The openings are only a day or two but sometimes Fish and Game extends it if they get the escapement they want. All depends."

Joe poured himself more coffee and bit into another muffin.

"I'll put your crew share in the bank until you leave or the season ends. You can have a hundred-dollar advance whenever we go to town. No pot. No booze. No beer. None of that on my boat, you hear?"

Three weeks ago, I would have been bummed at such a stringent regime. Three weeks ago, I hadn't been assaulted by a drunk skipper and almost shipwrecked by another. "No problem," I said with relief.

"Well, I'm over a barrel. I'll hire you for this next opening, and we'll see how it goes. When the opening is over, we off-load in Ketchikan."

"Ketchikan?"

"Yep, that's where I live."

"Not Petersburg?"

"Nope. Ketchikan. That a problem?"

I knew nothing about Ketchikan except it was even rainier than Petersburg. All my friends were in Petersburg. Anders was in Petersburg. Had I gotten a reprieve from returning to California only to be stuck in Ketchikan the rest of the season? But still. It was a real fishing job on a real fishing boat.

"Ketchikan's fine," I lied. "What happened to the last cook?"

"Appendicitis. Petersburg was the nearest town with a clinic."

"How do I get mail and can my folks call in an emergency?"

"Send mail in care of the *Miss Cora*, Ketchikan, Alaska. If someone needs to contact you, they can dial the marine operator and ask to talk ship-to-shore. Their phone, our radio. Only in an emergency," he emphasized.

"Right. Thanks."

"Hey, Marilyn!" he yelled toward a dark opening that led below deck. "Come meet the new cook."

A tall, skinny girl with her hair in two shoulder-length braids emerged. I was so relieved another woman was on board I could have kissed her.

"We're going to try Maddie for the next opening," Joe said.

"Hi," she said, looking me over. "Hope you're a better cook than the last one."

I held out the muffins. She bit into one and smiled.

"Dennis and JJ are in town. I'm off, too. See ya." She grabbed another muffin and disappeared out the door.

"Come down to the boat Friday morning with your gear," Joe directed. "If you're not here by 7:00 a.m. we leave without you."

"What about groceries?"

Joe nodded in approval. "We already have most everything we need. I'll pick up some fresh bread and a few other things before we go. You want anything in particular?"

I thought for a moment. "Filet Mignon? Lobster?"

"Ha. Ha. More like meat and potatoes."

"How about garlic salt? Onion soup mix for pot roast. Fresh or frozen veggies, I hope. Not canned."

"Canned veggies are a staple. This is a boat, not a damned café."

I shrugged. "Chocolate chips?"

"They're a staple."

Cutthroat Fishing

I HURRIED TO THE HARBOR OFFICE AFTER leaving the *Miss Cora* but Anders wasn't there. I wandered to the coffee pot thinking I could nurse a cup of coffee until he returned. Inside the thick mug with my name on it was an envelope addressed to me.

> Maddie, I'll be gone all day retrieving a skiff drifting in Frederick's Sound, but I have tomorrow off. Would you go cutthroat fishing with me? If so, be here at 7:00 a.m. to catch the tide. Anders.

I pocketed the envelope and returned the mug to the shelf, pleased at the creative way he'd found to contact me and even more pleased he still wanted to see me after the previous night. It was a strange feeling to have the whole day ahead of me with nothing in particular to do and everyone else I knew working. I wandered down the main street looking in the windows I had previously just hurried by. Entering the town's one nice gift shop, I perused the display of beautifully engraved silver jewelry.

"May I help you?" The saleswoman was dressed up for Petersburg in slacks and a nice Norwegian sweater but she had too much hair spray on her bouffant hairdo for my taste. Darlene must do her hair.

"I'm admiring this beautiful jewelry," I said, twirling the display.

"The Tlingit tribe is known for their intricate carvings of spirit animals on everything from totem poles to jewelry." She jangled her wrist to show off four pretty bracelets. "The silver bracelets are a sign of wealth, power and prestige," she smiled. "You should have one."

"Probably, but not now. I'll come back later." Or so I hoped.

I bought groceries, wine, and, on impulse, a bouquet of only slightly wilted carnations. I tacked a note on Bob and Jimmie's door inviting them to dinner.

Dirty dishes in the sink indicated my housemates had come and gone for lunch. I washed the dishes, swept the floor and even cleaned the bathroom. Then I made lasagna for dinner and set aside a portion without meat for Rachel.

At dinnertime, Deb and Rachel piled into the kitchen and introduced the new girl, Leslie. She'd been working at a shrimp cannery near Kodiak, but hated peeling shrimp twelve hours a day in cold water, and wanted to see a different part of Alaska. She seemed nice enough.

Jimmie came in, took my hand and placed it over his heart. "Lovely lady, you have returned to us! To what do we owe this great honor?" He bowed and kissed my hand.

I curtseyed back with matching ceremony, "Now that, kind sir, is a tale worthy of a glass of mead. Come, partake of a beverage while I tell you of the many trials and tribulations—and the ultimate triumph—I have experienced since last I saw you."

I was relieved Bob was a no show. While my friends ate hungrily, I told them about my experiences on the gillnetter and the tender, and how excited I was to be going out on the *Miss Cora.* I offered to do the dishes after dinner. "You guys have to work tomorrow. I'm going fishing with Anders."

"Good for you!" Deb exclaimed.

"Not very romantic," Rachel observed.

"I disagree," Jimmie said. "If you want to sleep with someone, you meet her at the bar. If you want to get to know her, you take her fishing."

Early the next morning, I walked into a town washed clean by the previous night's rain. The rising sun sparkled like diamonds on the water and the air smelled of spruce and salt water. My high spirits evaporated when I found the harbor office dark and empty. Then I saw Anders bounding up the ramp from the small boat harbor.

"I was afraid you wouldn't come," he said.

"I was afraid you wouldn't be here!"

"I was taking a load down to the skiff." He looked at me expectantly. "Well?"

"Well, what?" I teased.

"Well, did you get the job on the *Miss Cora?*"

"Yep!" I said smugly. "We leave tomorrow morning."

His grin faltered. "Well, good for you. We've got to get going now or we'll miss the tide. A few groceries first. Then we're off."

"Um, wait, Anders."

He stopped. "What?"

His eyes had been smoky gray in the bar, then deep blue when we'd kissed after the ball game. This morning, they were such an intense sea-green, I had to look away. "About last night. I mean, the night before. At the bar…"

"What about it?"

I took a deep breath. "I don't usually drink tequila like that."

"How do you usually drink it?" he asked.

I slapped him playfully on the chest. "I don't usually drink tequila at all and I wish I hadn't."

I took a breath. "Thanks for listening to me rant and helping me call my folks. And giving me the notice about the *Miss Cora*."

Anders starred at me intently. "Listen, I've cried in my beer more than once. It's allowed. I'm just glad your dad is okay and you don't have to go home. And maybe don't thank me for getting you that seine job just yet. What if it's another bust? Have you thought about that?"

"Yes, of course, I've thought about that," I bristled. "There's another female deck hand and we all sleep in bunks below deck and no booze or pot allowed. The skipper seems decent enough. Decent *and* terrifying."

Anders nodded. "Sig says Joe used to be a real hell raiser. Can't handle the booze, or the anger. His daughter died, his wife left, and he bottomed out. It got so bad no one would work with him. Then he found Jesus, got married again, and now he runs a tight ship."

"Wow, you vetted him for me."

"Well, I don't know what he was doing in Petersburg. Sig says he usually gets his crew from Ketchikan."

"The cook got appendicitis and they had to rush her to the clinic here. And he needs to get out again for the next opening." I was proud that this time I knew what I was getting into.

"Maybe no one would sign on with him in Ketchikan. Maybe he had to come to Petersburg to find a cook," he teased.

I jabbed him in the ribs.

"Ouch!" he said, batting my hand away. "All right, apology accepted, warning issued, let's go cutthroat fishing."

"What's that?"

"Cutthroat fishing. Dad loves trout."

When I still looked blank, he sighed. "Cutthroat are a type of trout, named for their red gills." He jabbed his hand at his neck where his gills would be if he had them. "High tide is in an hour. We've got to ride it up the creek and come back down when it ebbs."

"I thought it might be called cutthroat fishing because we have to fight for space on the riverbank."

"Hardly. I bet we're the only people up there. Come on!"

We hurried to the grocery store, open early for fishermen and cannery workers. "What kind of beer do you want?" Anders asked.

"I don't much like beer," I admitted.

"Tequila? Cognac?" he teased.

I made a face. "How about a wine cooler?"

"We should take candy bars, too."

I wrinkled my nose at the Mr. Goodbar he chose. "I don't like peanuts."

"Wait, let me guess! Any girl who likes cognac likes dark chocolate. Am I right? I'm right!" he crowed as I chose a dark chocolate bar with almonds.

I felt ridiculously happy as we walked to his 16-foot skiff. He handed me a float vest and a cut-down plastic jug. I bailed rainwater out while he hooked the gas hose onto the outboard and cranked the starter. The smell of diesel, oil, salt water, and fresh air made me feel as high as if I'd just smoked a joint. I admired the way his arms flexed when he pulled on the starter, his easy confidence, his competence as he went about readying the skiff. A seal poked its head above water not fifteen feet away and examined us with dark, round eyes.

"Look who's curious!" I exclaimed delightedly.

Anders sighted along his arm until it was pointing at the seal and pulled the mock trigger. The seal dove and was gone. "Got it!" Anders said, satisfied.

"You killed it," I said, shocked. Of course, he hadn't, but his intention was clear.

He looked at me curiously. "That bother you?"

I shrugged, embarrassed.

"You know my dad was a long-line halibut fisherman, right?"

"What does that have to do with killing that poor innocent animal?" I demanded, only half kidding. "Next, you'll be clubbing baby seals."

Instead of taking offense, he sighed. "Long-lining means you anchor a heavy line hundreds of feet down in the ocean with bait clipped onto it at intervals. It soaks in the water for hours while you set another line somewhere else. Then you return to the first set, reel the first line back on board, and if you're lucky there are halibut on some of the hooks. Then you bait and set the line again, go get the second line, and so on, day after day."

"So…?"

"So, it's hard and dangerous work" Ander continued. "Large hooks and sharp knives are always around. Men get tangled up in the lines and go overboard. Not to mention how a three- or four-hundred-pound halibut thrashes when it's brought onboard."

"And that has to do with seals, how?"

"Seals steal the bait off the hooks—and the halibut, too. All that work for nothing. One of the few jobs I liked as a kid working on the boat was sitting in the stern with an old lever-action .22 to shoot the damn thieves. Of course, you can't do that anymore. They're protected." He sounded regretful.

"That seal did look kind of crafty, now that you mention it," I said.

"It's a different world up here," Anders agreed. "But we're not shooting seals today. Let's go slay trout!"

I turned my back to the bow so the brunt of the cold wind hit my back and watched Anders steer the skiff away from the dock and into the Narrows. He had one hand on the tiller and the other tucked into his jacket pocket. His grin snatched my breath away.

After traveling along the shore for about twenty minutes, he turned the skiff into a cove where a large river ran into the slough.

"Five Mile Creek," Anders announced proprietarily.

The skeleton of a large dilapidated cabin guarded the entrance, having long ago given up its fight against the elements. What remained now was little more now than a pile of boards providing support for the fireweed and spruce that sprang out of the cabin's carcass. Weathered fence posts and outbuildings stuck up at odd angles, like ancient soldiers three sheets to the wind.

"Who used to live there?"I asked.

"A family with high hopes or great desperation, I guess. Free land, plenty of fish and game, berries, some root crops—pretty nice in summer. Then winter came. Babies came. Isolation, probably hunger." Anders shrugged. "They left. The land stayed."

Something shifted inside me like the tumblers of a lock clicking into place: the realization that two extremes could exist side by side, the presence of danger making the promise of peace that much sweeter.

We took our gear ashore and then Anders pulled his hip boots up and walked the skiff ahead of him into the slough. When he'd gone as far as he could, he shoved the skiff out into the deep water and watched the bowline play out. Then he jerked the line so the anchor fell overboard and caught on the river bottom.

"There," Anders said with satisfaction as he tied the end of the bowline around a nearby spruce. "The skiff will still be in the river channel when we get back instead of up on shore when the tide goes out."

We walked up the slippery grass to where the salt water gave way to the fresh water creek. Now that we were out of the open boat and walking on shore, I warmed up enough to take off my sweatshirt and tie it around my waist.

"When I was a kid, maybe twelve years old," Anders reminisced, "My buddy Hafter and I came up here one summer evening to fish. We lost track of time and when we returned to the slough, it was low tide and the skiff was high and dry, much too heavy to haul over the beach to the water."

"Oh no, what'd you do?"

"I knew we'd be in trouble when we didn't return in time for supper, but there was nothing to do. Sure enough, we saw Bear's big halibut boat nosing into the bay at dusk. We jumped up and down hollering from the beach so he'd know we were okay."

Anders stepped over a slippery log and paused to make sure I made it over, too.

"So, your dad came and got you?" I asked.

"Not exactly. When Bear saw we were safe and the skiff was high and dry on the beach, he turned his boat around and went back to town."

"What? He didn't rescue you?" I asked in disbelief.

"There was nothing he could do. The water was too shallow for his boat to come any further into the bay and he could see we were safe. Besides, he wanted to teach us a lesson."

"What did you do?"

"Built a fire, roasted some trout on a stick, waited overnight for the tide to change. I never forgot about the tide after that!" He laughed at the memory and then looked at me. "Although getting stranded here all night with you might not be so bad!"

Stranded in a bed might be better, I thought.

"I can't imagine a life where your kids take a boat to go fishing and get stranded," I said.

"I can't imagine a childhood where you have to drive everywhere and kids aren't safe on the streets."

"*Touché.*"

We put our picnic food down on a stump in a small meadow and Anders opened up his tackle box. Hoping to impress him, I started stringing up one of the fishing poles.

"You know how?" he asked.

"Yes, I know how to use a fishing pole," I said with exaggerated patience. "My dad took us camping in the Sierras every summer. My mom and sister hated the bugs and dirt, but Dad and I loved being in the mountains. If we were lucky, we'd catch a couple small rainbow trout and consider ourselves quite the fishermen."

"My old man likes them pan-sized. Makes a nice change from all those huge halibut and salmon we usually catch," he grinned.

I rummaged through the tackle box and held up a small red and white lure I recognized. "What about this Super Duper?" I asked.

A flicker of admiration crossed his face and he nodded. I'd heard the old adage that the way to a man's heart was through his stomach, but I thought maybe knowing how to fish was the way to Anders'.

I enjoyed splashing up the creek in my rain boots, casting the little red and white lure into the quiet water beside logs or boulders. When my line grew taut and danced at my gentle pull, I reeled in an eight-inch trout with bright red gills. Anders watched with approval from where he fished about twenty feet upriver. I took the fish off the hook and strung it onto a nylon stringer.

After a while I'd caught three more trout and wandered back to the meadow where our drinks were cooling in the stream. Anders continued to move slowly upriver, absorbed in casting and catching. Finally, he strode back holding a forked stick on which five trout were skewered. He popped open a Budweiser. "Here's to a great dinner for us!"

I opened the box of crackers and sliced the cheese with the little paring knife I now carried with me everywhere. Anders stretched out on the grass, his arms propping up his back as he watched. I started to hand a cracker to him but then I leaned over and brought it to his mouth. Never taking my eyes off his, I placed the cracker gently on his tongue. I thought about making a wisecrack about feeding a baby bird, but it didn't feel like that at all. It felt more like a sacrament.

Anders sat up and pulled me to him. Our lips met like a pair of magnets leaping together. His kiss tasted of cheddar and beer, of sun and desire. He leaned back, taking me with him, and I let myself fall the length of his body. The sound of my name murmured between kisses sounded like the breeze whispering through cedar branches.

We rolled over so he was looking down into my eyes: his, two blue pools of desire sucking me up into him.

A sharp rock jabbed my butt. I shifted away.

"Tide's going out," Anders said shakily. "Go back or stay?"

I knew I had only to shuck off my jeans and then I would be able to feel him inside me as well as on top. It was so tempting. Except maybe the rock was a sign to slow down.

"Well…" I said, sitting up and pretending to weigh the options with my hands. "Stay. Go. Stay. Go."

When I said "stay," I thought how making love right then might turn out to be just one more stolen moment in an awkward place, one more casual coupling with mosquito bites lasting longer than kisses.

When I said go, I thought of the tide already ebbing and a seiner that wouldn't wait for me in the morning.

Staying meant I could lose myself, at least temporarily.

Going meant I might find myself, perhaps permanently.

"Go," I said reluctantly.

Anders drained his beer, crushed the can and put our picnic debris back in the bag. "I guess I won't get to see the black underwear I glimpsed last night."

"Sorry, it's white cotton today," I said shakily.

"I could be appeased by seeing that cute little tattoo." He was teasing now.

"And it wants to see you, too, but the tide's going out."

"Then we'd better get going now, too, before the skiff gets carried away, or I do. You are coming to the house for dinner, aren't you?"

"Well, I have to go back to my house first…"

"Yeah, yeah, I know," Anders said glumly. "You're leaving tomorrow. You will come over for dinner though?"

"That'd be great. Do you think I could store a box up at your place while I'm gone? Stuff I won't need on the boat. I've been evicted from the cannery house and I don't know what else to do."

"That's fine. You can leave it in my sisters' old room. Then I know you'll be coming back."

Back in town, Anders kissed me at the top of the ramp, making me wish we had stayed up the creek. He broke away first. "Whoa, Maddie, if this is how you kiss in public, I can't wait to do more in private."

Looking around, I was embarrassed to see several people watching with obvious enjoyment. One fisherman even gave Anders a thumbs up, which he returned with a happy wave.

After the angst and agony of loving and losing Brad, Anders' admiration was a balm to my battered self-esteem. After Bob's furtive embraces and our guilty coupling in cramped spaces, kissing Anders in sunshine and laughter was like plunging into a clear pool on a hot day.

Maybe passion didn't need to be stimulated by pot or fueled by alcohol, maybe love could be something I didn't need to be ashamed of or hide. Maybe loving someone in broad daylight could feel as good as groping in the dark. Maybe better.

Surprise!

I PACKED WHAT I NEEDED TO GO seining and boxed up what was left—a handful of books and cassette tapes, some spare clothes, a souvenir shot glass. I started to put the paring knife I'd been carrying around since the *Misty* in the kitchen drawer. Then I hesitated. The knife was more symbolic than useful when it came to self-defense and no help at all when navigating a boat in the dark. Maybe on the *Miss Cora* I would actually use it to peel potatoes

With no one bugging me to use the bathroom, I stepped out of the shower, wiped the mirror, and studied the image that slowly emerged from the steam. I'd lost weight, pilot bread not being the same temptation to overindulge that croissants had been in France. All that walking and manual labor had replaced stubborn baby fat and teenage flab with muscle. Striking a body builder pose, I noted with satisfaction the slight bulge in my biceps. My calves flexed when I pointed my toes. My stomach was flat and my breasts weren't. The haircut Marie had given me had grown out a bit, but my short hair still fluffed around my face and made my eyes appear larger than they were. I stood tall with my shoulders back like my mother always nagged me to do. Peering down at my tattoo, I thought *let 'er fly!* It was time for someone to see my heart, and I knew just who.

I finished dressing when there was a knock at the door.

"Surprise!"

I didn't realize until that moment that blood could literally rush from one's head. "Brad! What are you doing here?"

His grin faltered. "What do you mean, what am I doing here? I wrote and said I was coming."

"You wrote and said you *might* come. And I wrote back not to."

"Yeah, well, I thought I should come up in person to plead my case. Seeing as I'm almost a lawyer now."

"I've got a job on a fishing boat leaving tomorrow." I sputtered. "You shouldn't have come."

"Look," he said, trying again. "I came a long way to talk to you, to ask your forgiveness. At least go to dinner with me. Please? After I use the bathroom."

Brad dropped his gear in the living room and disappeared down the hallway. I looked at his backpack a long moment, remembering how he had proudly brought it back from REI and propped it against the bedroom wall like he was ready to hit the road at any moment. The aluminum struts were still shiny, the turquoise nylon bag unblemished. I guess he never had.

Another knock at the front door.

Who could it be this time? Another ghost from my past? My indignant mother? A vengeful Ron?

Before I could open the door again, Anders poked his head inside. His eyes lit up when he saw me. "Permission to come aboard?" he asked, and stepped inside.

Before I could respond, Brad came in from the hallway. "Hey, Liz, you ready to grab some dinner?"

He stopped when he saw Anders, whose grin had evaporated, who now held himself completely still.

"Who's Liz?" Anders asked, watching Brad.

I cleared my throat nervously. "Uh, my given name. I changed it to Maddie last year. Long story. Anders, this is Brad, a friend from back home. Brad, Anders."

The two men nodded but didn't shake hands.

Brad was the first to speak. "Liz and I go way back. I'm on a break from law school at UCLA. Came to see what she's up to."

"Maddie and I just met," Anders responded. "I'm on summer break from grad school in Fairbanks. Maddie is leaving on a seine boat tomorrow is what she's up to." The light in Anders' eyes had dimmed. They were now hard gray like the bay on a cold winter day.

"Yes, well, I thought she might be tired of the cannery by now," Brad said. "I thought maybe she'd be ready to come back home."

My eyes ping-ponged back and forth, taken aback to hear myself referred to in the third person, like I wasn't there. But when I opened my mouth to speak, nothing came out. The silence stretched awkwardly in the room like someone had farted.

Anders broke the silence. "You coming to dinner, Maddie? Dad's waiting. I'm sorry we didn't catch enough trout for you, too," he told Brad insincerely.

"Did you two have plans tonight?" Brad asked. "I didn't mean to barge in."

"And yet, here you are." Anders said.

"Please, Lizzie, let me take you to dinner," Brad said, turning to me. "We need to talk."

I stood frozen like one of those icebergs floating in the water. The part of me they could see looked like the girl they thought they knew, but underneath the surface lurked a mass of thoughts and feelings invisible to the naked eye. Those icebergs looked so free sailing majestically down the Narrows, only now I realized their options were limited: either a slow thaw as they were carried out to sea, or a quick melt stranded on a beach at low tide. Either way, it would not end well.

I took a breath. "Brad's come a long way. We need to talk."

Anders looked at me, but I couldn't tell what was going on behind those icy eyes.

"You still want to store that box at Dad's?" he finally asked.

"Yes, please. I'll be back for it when I can."

Anders gestured toward Brad. "That GI jacket you're wearing? Were you in the Army?"

"What? God, no. Army-Navy surplus."

"Well, I wouldn't wear it around here if I were you. People might get the wrong idea, might think you actually served." Anders hoisted the box onto his shoulder, opened the door, and shut it firmly behind him.

In the sudden silence, I could hear the ticking of the kitchen clock. Brad was the first to speak. "Lizzie, I'm sorry to drop in like this. I thought it would be a nice surprise."

"Surprise? Yes. But nice? I'm not so sure."

Brad cleared his throat and tried again. "Is something going on between you and that Andrew guy?"

"Anders."

"Whatever."

Brad wore a white oxford shirt and the blue jeans I'd patched for him two years ago and embroidered with bright daisies. A frisson of… what? Memory? Desire? Habit? ran through me.

"I'm not surprised you're cold," Brad said, seeing me shiver. "It hasn't stopped raining since I got here." He raised his hand to brush the bangs away from my face in an old familiar gesture, then dropped it without touching me. "Look, can we at least talk? I'm not an idiot. I know it can't be like before. I don't want it to be like before. I want it to be better."

His words felt like a band-aid being pulled off an old wound that still hadn't entirely healed. Perhaps exposing the past to fresh air would be the antiseptic needed to heal my broken heart. Maybe then one wing would be strong enough to carry a healed heart forward.

"So, talk," I said, crossing my arms over my chest. And when we're done, I thought, maybe this time I can find my own exit line instead of using someone else's words to say I no longer give a damn.

"Can we eat, too? I'm starving. I saw a seafood place on the way here."

"It's expensive."

"I'll buy."

I went in the bathroom and pressed a cool washcloth over my face. When I came out, Brad had exchanged the GI jacket for a soft denim shirt I remembered from our Berkeley days. I reached for my own jacket, then realized it was the one Anders had loaned me. I took my turquoise raincoat instead.

Sigrid's Galley perched on a hill above the ferry dock. It was close to the house but off limits to a cannery worker trying to save her money. Inside, an effort had been made to decorate the space so it didn't look like the upstairs of a strip mall. Fishing nets interspersed with glass floats hung from the ceiling. The tables were covered with cloth tablecloths, and starched napkins were folded like origami into the water glasses. The chairs were like those in an upscale meeting room, padded and functional. Each table boasted an imitation ship's lantern with a tea candle inside. Muzak played softly in the background.

If Brad said one wrong word, if he pretended like nothing had happened or that things were like they were before, I was going to walk out. Instead, he took wire-rimmed granny glasses out of his pocket I'd never seen before to read the menu. When I said I was sick of salmon, we both ordered halibut. He requested a bottle of Sauvignon Blanc, using the proper pronunciation. The waiter was impressed even if I wasn't.

Brad lined up his silverware as though marshaling his arguments and when he was satisfied, he said, "Liz…"

"My name is Maddie. I'm not Liz anymore."

"…Maddie…I'm so sorry if I hurt you."

"If? There is no if about it. I loved you. I thought you loved me. You didn't have to go to school back east."

"I was about to get drafted! What was I supposed to do?"

"You didn't have to fall in love with someone else."

"You didn't have to go to France."

Our recriminations landed on each other like blows to the heart until finally we stopped to catch our breath, like boxers between rounds. Sipping wine but tasting vinegar.

Brad moved his fork a millimeter to the left and entered the fray again. "Maddie, you're right about one thing. I acted like a jerk. That's not me, that's not who I am. I am so sorry."

He picked up the fork and absentmindedly stabbed the prongs into the tablecloth. "I'm not sure what I thought would happen when I got to Greece." He set the fork down. "When you threw me out, when I found my pack outside the room and the door locked, I don't know. I guess my heart broke, too. I'm sorry it took me so long to figure that out."

I felt a tiny glow of satisfaction at hearing his apology at long last, and ignored the twinge of guilt nibbling around the edges.

He tilted his glass toward mine. "A toast, to us."

"There is no 'us.'"

"Well, then, to new beginnings?"

"You can't just waltz in here and act like nothing happened!"

He stopped smoothing the tablecloth with the back of his spoon and looked at me earnestly. "I know a lot has happened. I wish we could erase the past and start over. Even when I was with someone else, I never stopped thinking about you. About how well you know me. How well we go together. I made a big mistake last year and now I'm here to apologize. I never meant to hurt you."

"But you did, damn it. You broke my heart."

"It will never happen again, I swear."

"Oh yeah? What about what's-her-name? I'm supposed to forget you were 'in love' with someone else?" I added air quotes for effect. "Is she still in the picture? Or someone else? How could I ever trust you again?"

Several nearby diners turned toward my raised voice.

Brad leaned across the table and spoke softly, deliberately. "There is no one else. Not now. Not ever. It's you I want. We're supposed to be together always, I see that now. Please forgive me so we can move on."

His words hovered in the air between us like the faint scent of an old campfire: smokey and sweet and scorched all at once. I leaned back as the waiter placed two salads down in front of us: small plates containing droopy iceberg lettuce, two black olives, and slices of canned beets bleeding red onto the plate.

"I hate canned beets," I said.

"I'll trade you my olives for your beets," Brad said.

I used to think it was so romantic when we shared food. Now my stomach clenched when he stabbed the beets with his fork and brought them, dripping with red juice, to his mouth. I knew it wasn't just the beets making me queasy, it was a guilty conscience.

"Brad, since we broke up, I've blamed you for what went wrong. Now I know it wasn't all your fault. We were so young, and we were apart so much. I think over time, I made you into someone you weren't."

He started to speak but I plunged on. "No, listen. I'd been in love with you since high school. We had a great year in Berkeley. When you went to Boston and I went to France, I thought our love would last. By then, I'd constructed such a fantasy of who you were that other guys didn't stand a chance. You were a dream boyfriend, not a real one."

"Back then I wasn't ready to be the man of your dreams. But I am now. You're the woman of mine."

I snorted. "Wow, I'd forgotten how good you are with words. You still writing songs?"

He waved away my question. "Please don't throw us away."

"You did."

"I came back. So can you. We can decide where we go next together, okay?"

I was saved from answering when the waiter brought our dinners. Brad took a few cautious bites, then attacked his meal ravenously. I didn't have much appetite, just a big knot in my stomach that only wine seemed able to slide past.

I watched the rain splatter against the window, refracting the harbor lights into a kaleidoscope of wavering beams. An instrumental version of *California Dreaming* played softly in the background. I wondered if fresh cutthroat tastes better than halibut and whether a cranky Bear was telling Anders he was better off without me.

"That is the best halibut I've ever had." Brad motioned for the waiter to take our plates and poured more wine into our glasses. "Lizzie, I mean, Maddie. What's going on? Do you really want to stay up here, waste your degree? Run away from home and never come back?"

"You sound like my mother."

"Would that be so bad?"

"What? Sounding like my mother or going back?"

"Look, I can understand wanting to get away from your childhood home, from your folks, from Encino. That's part of the reason I went up to Berkeley and then back East. What you've done here, the trip you're on, I don't know, is it a boomerang that will bring you back, or a sling shot catapulting you away?"

"God, you're speaking in lyrics again. Should I grab a pen?"

He smiled wryly. "Perhaps not. The napkins here are linen, not paper."

I took another breath. "Look, Brad, when I was in France, I compared every man I met to an idealized version of you, and they fell short. I realize now I didn't really know you."

"I compared every woman I was with to the real you, and *they* fell short. Give me a chance to make your dreams come true."

"Brad, my dreams have changed. God, I sound like I'm in a rom-com."

He picked up his spoon and peered in it a moment like his reflection might hold the answer. Then set it down like he didn't like what he saw. "What *are* your dreams now?"

Brad, Anders, even my dad, they were all asking the same question. "I'm not sure—but I do know they don't involve settling down with a particular man. Not you. Not anyone." I thought of Anders and wondered if that was true. "My dream right now is to go on that fishing boat tomorrow morning."

Brad shook his head ruefully. "And after that?"

"I'm not sure. Maybe go to grad school. Maybe do something with my French degree. Maybe go back to California. Definitely go to Mexico with Rachel this winter."

An instrumental version of *Leaving on a Jet Plane* played in the background, anthem of my teenaged longing to leave California. I guess I'd gone and done it after all, only I'd taken a ferry instead of a plane.

Brad took my hand from the wine glass and held it, turning it this way and that. "You've stopped biting your nails."

I tried to pull my hand away. "I've got calluses now."

"They look good on you. Everything looks good on you." He kissed my palm and gave me back my hand. "I want a life. I want a steady lady. I like the scene in Santa Monica. You will, too. Tom Hayden and Jane Fonda live only a mile away, did I tell you? He's going to run for Senate and I'm going to work on the campaign. You could help."

"What, come back and stuff envelopes?"

"I didn't mean that. You can go to grad school, get a job, do nothing, I don't care. Just come back."

"All I know right now is I'm leaving on that fishing boat in the morning."

He smiled sadly. "All I know is I want you back in my life. It was good, wasn't it?"

I gazed out the window but all I could see was my own reflection. "I don't know. I remember a lot of absences and arguments. Where to go. What to do. What we should feel."

Brad swallowed the last of his wine. "I came at a bad time; I see that now. But I'm no good at writing letters. Only songs." He smiled wryly. "If I'd brought my guitar, I'd play you a song. You'd like that, wouldn't you? That's what I'll do, I'll write you a song."

"Brad, I'm tired," I said. I pushed back my chair. "I need to go to sleep. I don't care what you do. Crash on the couch or get a hotel room."

He opened his mouth, but then shut it, took out his wallet, and paid the bill.

"If it's okay with you, I'll crash at your house tonight," Brad said. "Figure out what to do in the morning."

I shrugged. "Sorry you came all this way for nothing," I said, although I wasn't sure I meant it. I felt like I had finally finished something that had started years ago, freeing me up to move on.

"Just think about what I said," Brad said. "You don't have to decide anything tonight." He took my arm as we left the restaurant and leaned forward to kiss me.

The French say that in affairs of the heart there is always one who kisses and one who offers the cheek. I offered my cheek.

Back at the house, Rachel, Deb, the new girl and several guys, including Brian, were sprawled in the living room listening to music. Brian had his head in Deb's lap playing air guitar. Deb had told us more than once Brian was in a bluegrass band back in Portland. The smell of incense smoldering in an ashtray did little to disguise the smell of pot and tobacco. Several smashed cans leaked beer onto the coffee table. Good thing Marie was not around.

"Brad, what are you doing here?" Rachel exclaimed when she saw us. "And Maddie? I thought you were with Anders tonight."

"Surprise," I replied shortly. "I'm leaving in the morning. I told Brad he could crash on the couch tonight."

"I thought you were going out with Anders tonight." Rachel repeated.

"And yet, here I am," I muttered.

Deb intervened. "Hey, Brad, why don't you pick out a tape? I'll grab you a beer. Maddie, you want one?"

I shook my head and went into the bedroom, emerging with my old banjo. Thrusting it at Brian, I said, "Here, Brian, a gift. You'll need to get new strings and tune it, but it'll be good company when you're out trolling."

Brian sat up and took it eagerly. "Really? You're giving it to me?"

"Yep, I'm leaving on a seiner in the morning. It's time to get rid of things I don't need any more." I purposely did not look at Brad as I slipped out the door.

I walked slowly to Anders's house. I had no idea what to say, or how he would react. I only knew I had to see him before I left. Make sure he knew I was through with Brad. Because I was. Wasn't I?

Creeping up the front steps, I heard the TV blaring in the living room. *Nothing ventured, nothing gained.* Wait. Was that mom's voice or my own? I knocked softly. No response. I forced myself to knock harder. The door opened.

"Maddie," Anders said flatly. "Or, should I say Lizzie?"

"Can we talk?"

"Go ahead."

"Can I come in?"

"Well, you can but it's probably quieter out here."

He shut the door and stood on the porch with his arms crossed. "Where's your California boyfriend?"

"My *ex*-boyfriend, a ghost from the past."

"We all have ghosts, Maddie. Are you sure you don't want this one resurrected? Because it kind of looked that way to me."

"I didn't know he was coming!" I tried not to remember the letter. "I never meant to hurt you."

"I'm a big boy. I can take care of myself." He cocked an eyebrow. "Can you? Or are you trying too hard to please everyone around you?"

I tried to think of an answer.

"Never mind," Anders finally said. "It's late. You're leaving in the morning. I'll walk you home."

"You don't have to," I said defensively. "I can walk back on my own."

"I know you *can*. But I want to. If that's okay?"

We walked down the steps in silence. The drizzle, my imminent departure, the sense of lost opportunity engulfed me.

"You know in the movie *Casablanca*?" I blurted. "When Ilsa has to leave Rick?"

"Jesus, Maddie, this isn't a movie."

"I know!" I said, stung. "I mean the rain, the sense of departure—"

"Ilsa sleeping with her long-lost lover?"

"No, not that!" I struggled not to cry. "I'm not sleeping with Brad."

We were silent a moment.

"Well, it was foggy there, too," Anders conceded. Then, he took a deep breath. "You know, you really bummed me out tonight. I'm not like some old box you can shove in a closet for later. You need to decide what you want. I've made it pretty clear what I want."

"I want to see you, too," I said in a rush. "When I get back."

He gazed at me thoughtfully, like he hadn't heard.

"Why does that heart tattoo of yours have only one wing? Does it fly in circles and never land?"

I was flabbergasted. I'd never thought of it that way. I was still casting around for an answer when we arrived at my house.

Anders pulled me to him and said in his best Bogart imitation, "Of all the harbor offices in all the towns in all the world, you had to walk into mine." He kissed me hard and left.

Damn. Now that's a great exit line.

I tiptoed into the house, ignoring the music and laughter coming from the living room. I brushed my teeth, set my trusty alarm clock to 5:00 a.m., and crawled into bed.

"I thought I saw you sneak in," Rachel said as she came in and perched on the edge of the bed "Don't worry, no one else noticed." She offered me the joint she was smoking. "Guess you were surprised to see Brad?"

"You could say that!" I took the joint like it was a peace pipe and took a long drag.

"You guys back together?"

I blew the smoke out. "No, not hardly."

"Did you tell him to take a hike?"

I took another hit while I thought about my answer. "You know, it's funny. For a long time, all I wanted was to have Brad back. Now that I can, I don't think I want him."

"I thought you had the hots for Anders," Rachel said.

"I did. I do. But he's about had it with me."

"Gee, I wonder why." Rachel said sarcastically. Then after a moment, "Geeze, Maddie, are you crying?"

I shook my head. "It's the smoke."

She handed me a Kleenex and I wiped my eyes.

"The hell with men," I said. "Instead of a wild hot sendoff, I'm crying myself to sleep."

"Maddie, you don't have to be alone. There are at least two guys I know who'd love to be with you right now."

"And yet, here I am."

"They use saltpeter in the navy so the sailors don't get horny," Rachel said. "Maybe it's the same on fishing boats. Did you ask?"

"I don't think we'll be gone that long." I looked down at the fraying sheet. "Rach, are you mad at me?"

"For what?" she asked cautiously.

"Well, for starters, are you mad about Bob? I thought maybe you were, I don't know, interested in him?"

"Maybe I was, at first. But then I realized he's not my type." She laughed at my astonishment. "Yes, Maddie, I'm learning to have a 'type.'"

"You mean, besides two arms, two legs, and a you-know-what between them?"

"More like, in addition to all that."

"So, what is your type?" I asked.

"Not a cowboy from Montana!"

"Yeah, not mine either."

"My type might be a Fish and Game intern named Reed. You would not believe it when he comes into town all hot and horny from wherever the Forest Service sent him that week."

"Wow, you've been together, what, four weeks? That's a record."

"If we're still together in September, we're going Outside together."

I sat up in alarm. "What about Mexico?"

"Relax, amigo. Reed's going back to school this winter."

I was building up my courage to ask her about Ron when she snuffed out the stub of the joint and rose to leave. Coward that I was, I let her.

The Miss Cora

I WAS RELIEVED WHEN THE ALARM GAVE me permission to stop my restless dreams. In the living room, I skirted the detritus of last night's party and watched Brad asleep on the couch. I thought about waking him to say goodbye, but didn't. The front door clicked softly behind me like a sigh of relief.

I felt like an old hand as I climbed over the two other seiners to reach the *Miss Cora*, but then I hesitated in front of the closed galley door. I had wanted to turn around instead of boarding the *Misty* a few weeks ago and, in retrospect, I should have. But now, I clenched my fist around the wrapped paring knife, knocked, and stepped inside.

"Hey, Cookie," Joe turned from the stove. "Right on time. Stow your gear in the fo'c'sle and I'll help you fix breakfast, this time."

I climbed down the ladder to the crew quarters and peered around in the dim light. I made out sleeping forms in three of the bunks so I piled my gear quietly on the empty one and went back to the galley.

Joe nodded toward the table. "Some guy left that for you last night."

He indicated a white porcelain mug with an envelope tucked inside. When I snatched it up, I saw my name on it in Anders's neat script written there the day we met.

I started to rip open the envelope, and then noticed Joe leaning against the counter watching me like a cat waits for the mouse to twitch before pouncing.

I thought of how hard I'd struggled to get here, to this job, to this moment on the *Miss Cora.* I didn't want to act like a lovesick girl eager to open an airmail letter from her boyfriend. I was not the same girl who had run away to Alaska because she didn't know what she wanted to do next; nor the lonely girl who had jumped in the sack with the first man since Brad who beckoned. I was no longer the Maddie who had almost gotten raped on a gillnetter and who had piloted a tender in the dark because she was too afraid to wake the drunk skipper.

Not just my name and my hairdo were different. I was different, and I didn't want to blow it now.

I put the envelope in my pocket and poured coffee into the mug, inhaling its steamy warmth like the aftermath of a kiss.

"As soon as I start the engine, the crew will be up," Joe said. "You can fix bacon and pancakes this morning. There won't be time once we're out on the grounds."

Joe slid onto the bench around the galley table and continued directing. "Butter, eggs and bacon are in the fridge. Syrup and pancake mix in the cupboard. Griddles and fry pan over the stove. Plates down there. Make sure the coffee pot is full at all times."

"What about garbage?"

"Anything fish will eat goes overboard. Paper and plastic go back to the town in garbage bags."

I nodded and got to work under Joe's watchful eye. Thirty minutes later, I had fried a pound of bacon, stacked pancakes on a large platter, and set orange juice, butter, and syrup on the table. Joe took his own plate up to the pilot house and started the ship's engine.

Like a gun had gone off, Marilyn and two guys rushed up from their bunks. There was a flurry of activity, everyone pouring coffee and piling their plates with food.

With his mouth full, the youngest deck hand waved his fork at me. "You the new cook? I'm Dennis." He looked to be about eighteen and had dishwater blond hair and brown eyes.

The other deckhand was a few years older and looked Tlingit. "I'm JJ."

"Joe's nephew," said Dennis in a tone somewhere between envy and warning.

Marilyn took another pancake. "Thank God, we don't have to eat Joe's cooking anymore. He's a better captain than cook." She looked at me. "Joe can be a real hard ass, but he knows his stuff. I'm learning all I can so I can be the first woman seining captain. You ever slung leads before?"

I shook my head.

"I was afraid of that," she said frowning.

"There's nothing to it," Dennis said between mouthfuls.

"As long as you don't mind jellies raining down on you," Marilyn said with relish.

"Jellies?" I asked.

"Jellyfish." JJ clarified. "There are three kinds up here: red, lion's main, and moon jellies. Red's the most common, and the worst."

"I hate them all," Dennis said glumly. "There can be hundred, thousands of them drifting around with the salmon. Doesn't matter if they're dead or alive. They still sting."

"Jellyfish aren't so bad," JJ said. "The only kind that will really kill you is the box jelly in Australia."

"Easy for you to say," Dennis said resentfully. "You're in the skiff."

"I've paid my dues." JJ looked at me. "You know what they call a group of geese?"

"Sure. A gaggle."

"A bunch of eagles?" he continued.

"A convention? No, wait…a convocation!"

He nodded. "A bunch of jellyfish?"

"There's a word for a bunch of jellyfish?" I asked incredulously.

JJ nodded. "A smack!"

My crewmates wolfed down the last of their breakfast and rushed outside. They pulled in the bumpers protecting the *Miss Cora* from the *Suzanna*, whose crew was doing the same so both boats could leave. Dennis and JJ exchanged good-natured insults with the other crew as Joe steered the *Miss Cora* away from the dock.

"Make sure Joe stays in the wheelhouse," Marilyn warned. "If he has to yell out the window or, worse yet, come on deck, someone's in trouble."

"Which means we all are," added Dennis glumly.

Since I knew more about handling a skillet than a boat, I was glad to stay in the galley. What was the worst I could do, burn the pancakes? I peeked out the galley door as we left town, but the harbor office was dark.

The galley was a tidy but functional space. The cabinets had latches to keep from falling open and the shelves were lined with plastic non-slip liners. Every heavy white porcelain plate and stainless-steel pot had its place. The only appliance left out when the boat was underway was the coffeepot, which could be secured to the stove top with a small bungee cord. I was drying the coffee mugs and hanging them on their hooks under the cabinet when JJ came by.

He quickly turned them around. "Always hang them facing down so water runs out.

"Out of the cup?"

"Out of the boat."

"A superstition?"

"Well, we haven't sunk yet."

Wedged behind the sink was a bottle of antacids. Marilyn noticed me swallowing four.

"Seasick?" she asked without a dollop of sympathy.

"Nervous."

"You'll be fine." She poured a cup of coffee on the way to the wheelhouse. "Do what Joe wants, the way he wants, when he wants, and don't get him mad or we'll *all* get mad at you." I wondered if Joe was really the tyrant Marilyn made him out to be, or if she was just trying to rattle me. If so, it was working.

The crackle of radio static and snatches of conversation drifted down from the pilot house. Garbled voices said inane things about the weather and the price of eggs. I knew now they were talking in code so only the person on the other end knew exactly where they planned to fish or what the conditions were like.

Joe entered the tidy galley and looked around with approval. "We'll be running all day. That means sandwiches at noon, fruit, cookies, whatever doesn't need heating. When we're working, make sure there's hot soup at lunch. You can fry up some pork chops for dinner. Okay?"

I nodded, only slightly terrified.

"Tomorrow, we'll practice setting the net. Opening starts Sunday at 6:00 a.m."

Then I was totally terrified.

Alone in the galley, I sat down at the table and ripped opened Anders' envelope. A pretty silver bracelet fell out. His note read: *Here's looking at you kid.*

I had seen silver bracelets clanking and sparkling on the arms of women around town, a sign of wealth and prestige according to the woman in the gift store. This one had two silver birds whose copper heads overlapped. The bird's red eye gleamed. Had Anders remembered I was a Leo, which meant a ruby birthstone?

JJ came up silently behind me and leaned over to examine the bracelet. "Do you know what those are?"

"Birds?"

"A raven and an eagle. Tlingits are born into one clan or the other. You have to marry outside your clan. Your bracelet depicts one of each. So, lovebirds."

I slipped the bracelet on my wrist and admired it.

"This was a gift?" JJ asked.

I nodded.

"You and your boyfriend must be pretty serious."

"We're not, he's not…I don't know…we're…just friends," I stammered.

"Just friends," JJ repeated dryly. "Does he know that?"

I thought about what Anders' gift and message might mean, like trying to decipher a radio conversation conveyed on an open channel. The words said one thing but might mean something else.

"Probably more a token of what might have been than a souvenir of what was," I finally said.

But JJ was already gone.

Marilyn took one look at the bracelet and said, "Don't wear jewelry on the boat. Too dangerous if it gets caught on something. Take those earrings off, too."

My hands flew to the gold posts in my ears. "Right."

Down at my bunk, I opened my pack to tuck the jewelry away.

On top was a note Brad must have left for me last night, a quote I remembered from the book he'd given me: *Hemingway says you can't get away from yourself by moving from place to place. I say, come home to me and find yourself.*

Great. Now that I had decided I didn't need a man in my life, I had two. One wanted me to return to California. The other thought I should forge a new path forward. Ironic they thought they knew what was best for me when I didn't know myself.

I put the bracelet from Anders in the right-side pocket of my pack and the note from Brad in the left one. I didn't want them comparing notes, but if they could, I wondered what they would say.

While we ran south, I explored the boat by first venturing up to the wheelhouse where Joe perched on a raised captain's chair. Marilyn squeezed over to make room for me, making it clear I didn't belong. Joe was clearly in his element here, watching out the windows, keeping a large hand on the steering wheel, monitoring the various instruments, and listening to the radio.

Joe nodded. "Great view, huh?"

"It's beautiful."

"You'll get to enjoy it from the deck," Marilyn said pointedly. "The cook doesn't have to stand wheel watch."

I took the hint. Back down in the foc's'le where we slept, I opened a small door past the bunks and was assaulted by the smell of diesel and oil and the racket of a large noisy engine. I quickly shut the door. Having seen all there was to see inside, I went out on deck. Dennis was perched on the rail smoking a cigarette and gazing out at the water. He nodded when I approached.

"Cigarette?" he offered.

"No, thanks, I don't smoke."

"I never used to either, except it's the one vice Joe allows." Dennis took a long drag and expelled slowly. "As long as we smoke outside. When there's nothing else that needs to be done. Which is hardly ever." He threw the cigarette butt overboard and we watched it disappear in the boat's wake. "Don't even try smoking pot on board," he added glumly.

"That's probably a good thing not to do on a boat."

He shrugged.

I clambered up the neatly stacked seine net occupying the entire stern so I could peek inside the large skiff on top. Out of sight and protected from the wind, JJ hunkered down reading a large, battered book.

"Busted," he said, looking up.

"Sorry, I didn't mean to intrude. What are you reading?"

He showed me the cover.

"Wow." I was impressed.

"I know, you don't expect an Indian to be studying *Grey's Anatomy*," he said with a slight smile that took the sting out of his words.

"I don't expect *anyone* to be studying *Grey's Anatomy*."

He gazed at me impassively. "They've published over twenty-five editions since it first came out. This one's from 1952."

"The year I was born."

"The blink of an eye in terms of human evolution. Not a lot changes in the human body, only in our understanding of it."

We contemplated that wisdom for a few minutes. At least, that's what I did. It was hard to know what was going on in JJ's mind.

"Seining helps pay my tuition." He opened up the book again.

"I'll leave you to it," I said.

Next, I went around the port side of the boat, hugging the wall so I didn't tumble over the side. A space the size of a tiny broom closet contained a toilet and I took advantage of it to do my business. When finished, I reached for the handle to flush. There was no handle. The toilet drained directly into the ocean and a bucket of saltwater with a rope attached made it clear how the toilet was flushed.

Realizing I shouldn't leave the bucket empty for the next person, I squeezed out the door and looked over the side at the water racing by. Afraid of losing the bucket overboard, I wrapped the line around my wrist and was just about to throw it overboard when Marilyn yelled, "Stop!"

She unwrapped the line from my wrist. "That's a good way to lose your arm," she said disdainfully. "Do it like this."

She tied the end of the line around the rail and tossed the bucket backwards into the water so the current didn't run directly into it. "Remember, empty buckets go upside down on a boat, otherwise it's bad luck."

I waited for her to laugh but she didn't. I set the full bucket next to the toilet and latched the door on the outside so it didn't blow open.

I crossed over the bow, carefully avoiding the neat mess of ropes, buoys, winches, and other nautical paraphernalia, and returned to the stern. This was it, my new home. I took a moment to savor the wind rushing through my hair, the sight of the vast coast dotted with islands, the gulls ignoring us as they flew by. I had done it. I was working on a fishing boat.

Dry Run

THE ALARM UNDER MY PILLOW RANG at 5:00 a.m. and I slipped quietly out of my top bunk. My crewmates didn't stir—or if they did it was only to roll over. My jeans were warm from having spent the night shoved inside my sleeping bag, but my rubber boots on the floor were ice-cold.

As soon as I started making coffee in the quiet galley, Joe climbed down from the pilot house where he slept on a narrow bunk opposite the wheel. "Oatmeal. Bacon. Toast. Orange juice," he grunted on his way out the door.

"Good morning, to you, too," I chirped to his back.

When he came back inside and started up the ship's engine, my crewmates appeared like mushrooms popping up after an overnight rainfall.

"We'll do a dry run after breakfast," Joe ordered. "I don't want you guys screwing up when we have fish to catch. Dennis can work the skiff."

Dennis grinned. JJ didn't.

After washing the dishes, I donned rain pants, rain jacket, rain boots, and tied my red bandana around my head.

"That won't do," JJ said on his way by. "Put on this old sou'wester." He tossed me an ugly yellow hat that tied under the chin and had a brim longer in the back than the front. Since it wasn't raining, I didn't know why. Joe started the engine from the pilot house and then came down to operate the power block from the controls mounted on deck.

Dennis climbed aboard the seine skiff before it was hoisted down to the water. When I saw the weighty lines running from the heavy net to the skiff, I understood why it needed to be more massive than regular skiffs. More Clydesdale than quarter horse.

At a signal from Joe, Dennis tried to start the skiff engine. It sputtered a few times but didn't catch. After several more attempts, a disgusted Joe motioned for JJ to take Dennis' place.

"Engine floods if you don't know what you're doing," JJ whispered to me in passing. "Especially if someone left the choke on."

A dejected Dennis came back on board.

JJ quickly started the skiff and towed the seine net in a circle off the side of the seiner. It uncoiled and slithered over the deck and into the water like a powerful anaconda.

"If something goes wrong now and the net gets snagged, there'll be hell to pay," Dennis warned.

"Don't get tangled in the gear either," Marilyn added with ghoulish satisfaction. "If you do, you won't be brought back up alive."

After twenty minutes, a line of yellow corks bobbed in a circle off to one side of the boat, while the lead line kept the bottom of the net deep in the water. Fish were supposed to swim into the net and mill around until Joe gave the signal to close or "purse" the bottom to prevent them from escaping.

"Okay, party time!" Marilyn announced. "I supervise bringing in the net."

"You do what Joe tells you," corrected Dennis crossly.

"Joe doesn't need to tell me much anymore," Marilyn replied airily. "Maddie, you stand over by the lead line. I'll handle the cork line and Dennis takes the middle."

I stood on the starboard side as instructed. The low gunwale barely reached above my knees and there was no rail. I was shaken by how easy it would be tumble overboard.

"Okay, girls, here she comes!" shouted Joe and the wet, heavy net rose to the top of the power block high on the mast. "Maddie, when the steel rings come at you, feed them onto the metal arm there and pile your part of the net on deck. If you don't stack the rings in order, we can't fix it later and the net won't feed out properly the next time."

"The last time that happened, he fired the deckhand," Dennis said beside me.

"Joe was so mad, I thought he would bust a gut," added Marilyn. "Glen was lucky he didn't get thrown overboard."

"He probably wished he had been by the time Joe got through with him."

As if I hadn't been nervous enough before.

The seine net rose through the power block above us and started its slow descent, swinging back and forth while dripping water and kelp on top of our heads. The elongated brim of my hat funneled water down the outside of my jacket so it didn't flow down my neck into my clothes. Hence, the rain hat's weird design.

Marilyn, as deck boss, tried to make sure the net was piled evenly across the deck. If too much was mounded in the back, the boat would be stern heavy. If too much was in front, there'd be no room to walk around the cabin.

I slowly got the hang of it. My left hand grabbed the lead line while I tossed the steel rings onto a horizontal bar and piled net with my right hand.

I looked up occasionally to watch the net coming down through the block until a deluge of red-tinged gelatinous jellyfish started raining down on us in disgusting plops and gooey strings. Everything I touched stung. Yet the net kept coming. Jellyfish kept oozing down. And I had to keep slinging the lead rings onto the bar and pile the net on deck. There was no escape. My aching arms and shoulders were nothing compared to my burning hands.

Marilyn and Dennis glanced over occasionally to see how I was taking it. I bit my lip, kept my head down, and kept working.

"Go faster!" Joe yelled. Then, a few minutes later, "Slow down! There's too much net in the back! No, too much in front. Pile it more evenly!"

While we hauled the net on board, the *Miss Cora* idled in neutral and was carried toward the mouth of the bay by the outgoing tide. The swells increased until I grabbed handfuls of net as much to keep my footing on the swaying deck as to guide the net. I almost missed throwing one of the rings when the boat lurched.

Joe stopped the power winch while the bottom of the net was still in the water. All of us, including Joe, peered over the rail to see what was caught in the "purse." What we'd caught was a small writhing mass of kelp and miscellaneous marine life.

"No salmon!" I exclaimed in disappointment as the purse was opened in the water and the goo disgorged back into the sea.

Marilyn shot me a superior gaze. "It's illegal to catch fish before the opening."

"But not illegal to see if there are any!" Joe said cheerfully.

"Once more," he yelled after we'd brought in the net and powered back up the bay. "Do it right this time!"

JJ pulled away in the skiff, dragging the seine net behind him. Once again, the net was hitched onto the power winch and brought back to the ship. We piled the net on the deck while Joe operated the winch. Once again, the net was stopped to examine the purse full of sea debris. Again, the gunk was released back into the sea, the remainder of the net piled on board, and again, Joe screamed at us and at JJ who couldn't hear him. Joe's verbal abuse was like a shotgun, splattering everywhere. Then in the next moment, he'd be all jovial.

"Okay, girls, that's it for now," Joe announced. Dennis scowled. Joe turned toward me with a grin. "How'd you like those jellies?"

Never let a bully smell your fear, or you're really in for it. "Now I know why it's called a smack of jellyfish," I replied.

He roared with laughter. "That's right, you're learning! Don't rub your eyes or you'll go blind."

"No, you won't," JJ said as he came up beside me. "But you may feel like it."

He filled a bucket with salt water and set it on deck. "Stick your hands in there to cool off."

JJ turned the hose on his raingear. "Some people wear gloves when the jellies are bad."

"Like me," said Dennis.

"Yeah, but you're a wimp," JJ said. "Maddie's not."

For Real

THE SUN PEEKED OVER THE MOUNTAINS at 5:30 a.m. as we pulled anchor and Joe steered the boat into the fishing grounds. By 5:45, JJ was in the skiff warming up the motor and Dennis was standing on deck smoking. Marilyn scanned the water for the telltale flip of a fin while Joe maneuvered the boat into position among the other boats, all of them equally determined to set their net in the best spot. I watched from my position outside the galley door.

At six o'clock sharp, Joe yelled, "Let 'er rip!" and JJ roared away, pulling the net behind the skiff in a giant arc. The other boats were all doing the same. The coffee in my stomach roiled in rhythm with the gentle swells.

With a self-important air, Marilyn took a twenty-foot pole with a plunger on one end and began jabbing it into the water where the net was still open to the sea.

"What's that?" I asked.

"That thing that looks like a plunger?" Dennis asked.

I nodded.

"A plunger," Dennis said.

I stuck my tongue out at him and he laughed. "Some people think the noise scares the fish from swimming out the opening, keeps 'em inside the net instead of escaping."

I watched Marilyn plunge and retrieve the pole, plunge and retrieve.

"Other people just like having something to do," he said.

"How long until we pull in the net?" I asked Dennis.

"About twenty minutes, give or take. Joe will read the signs, watch the other boats, do his mojo." He wiggled his fingers as though casting a spell. "If the net stays out longer than twenty minutes, another boat has the right to set their net in front of yours. That way you can't hog the good spot."

We watched for a few moments.

You ever heard of corking?" Dennis asked.

"As in opening a bottle of wine?"

"As in setting your net in front of another, so you scoop up the fish before they do. Very bad. No one does it anymore. Nowadays, most boats respect the twenty-minute limit."

Joe hollered from the pilot house for JJ to bring the skiff full circle to the boat. That was my cue to work beside Marilyn and Dennis to haul in the net.

Suddenly, Joe stopped the winch. "Get that log out! Don't rip the net! Don't let the fish escape!"

We had surrounded a drifting log along with the salmon.

Marilyn used a long pike pole with a hook on the end to lever the waterlogged tree trunk close to the boat while Dennis and I hung over the railing to force it over the cork line. I fully expected the stubborn log to thrash around like an angry alligator but it remained subdued.

When the log was free, Joe finished bringing the purse net on board. Soon, bright salmon cascaded onto the deck like silver dollars tumbling from a slot machine.

Jackpot!

Joe and the others weren't as impressed. My crewmembers shoveled the fish into the hold while Joe maneuvered the *Miss Cora* to another spot in the bay. I made a fresh pot of coffee and handed mugs and slices of cold toast to the grateful crew. Then we did the whole operation all over again. And again. And again. In between sets, I made sandwiches and more coffee.

It was nine o'clock when we set the net for the last time, a disappointing haul confirming Joe's inclination to call it quits for the night. Joe motored over to a nearby tender and, while we waiting our turn to offload, I started dinner, grateful to be in the warm, dry galley and not down in the hold with the others. When the stew was bubbling, I went outside to watch them finish.

One of the tender crew saw me and handed a six pack over the rail. "What's this?" I asked.

"You must be new," he said. "Standard operating procedure. Every boat gets a six-pack after they off-load."

"Not on my boat!" Joe roared from his position near the open hatch.

I quickly thrust the six-pack away as though scorched. "I didn't know!"

The tender skipper came out on deck and handed me a box of frozen ice cream bars. "Never mind, my guy is new, too. Joe always gets ice cream from us, not beer."

While we finished dinner, I could see some of the boats still working, their powerful deck lights like a spotlight in the otherwise dark night. "Some of the boats are still setting," I commented.

"There are old fishermen and there are bold fishermen," Joe said, yawning ferociously. "But there are no old, bold fishermen."

FOR THE NEXT TWO WEEKS, LIFE onboard the *Miss Cora* took on a slow, monotonous pace punctuated with a day or two of frenzied activity when we could actually set the net out and catch fish instead of just cruising around "looking."

We looked for fish more often than caught them.

I busied myself learning to cook on an oil stove or watching the scenery slide from somewhere on deck. Southeast Alaska was beautiful, but after a while one beautiful bay looked much like another, distinguishable only by an abandoned cabin on one point or a cluster of treacherous rocks on another.

Joe was a contained whirlwind whether we were working or only looking: talking on the CB, steering the boat, scribbling notes. Marilyn was a skinny shadow wedged in the wheelhouse, watching out the windows so she could yell "jumper!" whenever she could. The more fish jumping to shake their egg sacs loose before spawning, the more fish there were around to catch. I'm not sure she ever saw a jumper before Joe did, but she made more noise about it.

Dennis chain-smoked and gazed silently over the transom. JJ read from his throne in the seine skiff, or if was too rainy, in his bunk. My crewmates only came together when we were working on deck, or at mealtimes, when sullen silence grew preferable to the crew's petty squabbling and Joe's malicious teasing.

The pretty silver bracelet from Anders and the plea to come home from Brad stayed in their separate compartments of my pack. I kept meaning to think about them and about my future. Instead, at night I climbed into my sleeping bag in the narrow, dark bunk, and fell instantly asleep.

Everything that didn't pertain to seining started seeming less real than my dreams; everything not on the ship or within eyesight, a figment of my imagination.

One morning, we prepared for yet another opening, the darkness exacerbated by thick fog. Joe carefully maneuvered the *Miss Cora* in the pea soup while I was in the galley cleaning up after breakfast. Suddenly, the boat was thrust in reverse and Joe bellowed, "All hands on deck! All hands on deck!"

Running outside, I saw another seiner looming out of the fog, headed directly toward us.

Joe turned on every light on the *Miss Cora* and sounded the ship's horn nonstop.

Dennis and Marilyn grabbed bumpers and gaff hooks, ready to fend off the other boat. JJ unhooked the seine skiff, jumped in it and roared a safe distance away.

I stood on deck, frozen, not believing my eyes.

"It's the *Joya*," Dennis said. "Shit, they're trying to cork us."

"Joe won't let them," Marilyn said, her voice a mixture of awe and fear.

A shot rang out.

I looked up at the pilot house and saw Joe leaning out the open window waving a pistol.

Joe fired once more—into the air, I think—and the *Joya* gave way, turning to starboard once she was clear of the *Miss Cora*.

Joe sounded a last blast on the *Miss Cora's* horn as though blowing a raspberry at the departing boat.

JJ brought the skiff back to the boat and held his empty coffee mug out to me. "How 'bout a cup for the road?" he asked as though nothing had happened.

"Some help you were," Dennis said to JJ. "Running away like that."

"Standing by to pick up survivors!" JJ said, winking. "Women and children first, of course."

"Hey, Cookie, you look a little green," Joe said jovially when I brought him a cup of coffee. "Don't worry. Those SOBs won't try to cork me again any time soon," he said with great satisfaction.

After that opening, we resumed our tedious cruising around looking for fish. This evening as I did the dishes, Joe got out a cribbage board. Dennis hastily went out on deck and Marilyn buried her nose in a crossword puzzle book. That left JJ to accept Joe's challenge. I listened as they bantered back and forth.

"Fifteen two, four and a double run makes twelve," Joe bragged.

"Two, four and there ain't no more," JJ lamented.

When Joe was winning, he attributed it to skill. When he lost, it was bad luck—never his opponents' superior skill. My grandfather had been like that, too, a vicious but kindly card shark playing Crazy Eights with his young granddaughter like it was high stakes poker. When I was older, he taught me cribbage.

After JJ lost two games, he admitted defeat. Joe chuckled and rubbed his hands. "Okay, who's next?" he asked. "Cookie, your turn!"

I slid onto the galley bench, won the cut, and dealt the cards. My hands were waterlogged, the cards worn. It seemed to take forever to deal six cards each. Joe cut a jack.

"Thanks," I said.

He looked annoyed.

"Fifteen two, fifteen four and a pair is six," he said and started to scoop up his hand.

I stopped him and recounted. "Fifteen two, fifteen four, fifteen six, and a pair is EIGHT," I said, adding the two points he'd missed to my score.

Joe harumphed, there is no other word for it, and played a little more cautiously. Dennis drifted back inside to watch. Marilyn openly rooted for me.

When I lost the game, Joe gathered up the cards. "She cooks *and* plays crib. We could do worse."

Ketchikan

AFTER A BETTER-THAN-AVERAGE OPENING IN MID-AUGUST, Joe announced we were going to take the fish directly to the cannery in Ketchikan instead of off-loading them onto a tender.

"Home!" exclaimed JJ.

"Showers!" whooped Marilyn.

"Bars." Dennis clasped his hands and rolled his eyes heavenward.

"Better prices," Joe said. "We'll be there about noon. Don't head for town until we've taken on fuel. No dinner on board. We pull out tomorrow morning at 8:00. If you're not back on board, you get left behind. Capiche?"

We capiched.

I was on deck with my crewmates when we pulled into Ketchikan.

"Welcome to the armpit of Alaska," Dennis said.

"Don't walk around after dark," warned Marilyn. "Ketchikan is the first port of call in Alaska, and a lot of losers and drifters wash ashore here, too broke to go further."

"Besides, there are a lot of loggers here, and everyone knows loggers are a rough bunch," cautioned Dennis.

"Not like fishermen," I joked.

"No, not like fishermen," Marilyn responded seriously.

I gathered up my dirty laundry, which was everything I owned, and strode up the dock, swaggering a bit like I belonged there. I scanned the boats as I passed, hoping to see one I recognized from Petersburg. No such luck.

In the harbor office, the disheveled clerk retrieved my mail, not even asking for ID. He was balding with a paunch and the broken blood veins on his nose of a serious drinker. What did I expect? A tall, good-looking Norwegian giving me a silver bracelet and kissing me like someone who'd been searching for years and finally found me?

I looked eagerly through the envelopes: a letter from my parents, one from my sister, even one from Brad. I went back through the letters slowly, hoping I'd missed one from Anders. I hadn't. I tucked letters in my pocket and continued into town.

The store fronts were shabby, the window displays dusty. Disreputable-looking men loitered on the sidewalks, eyeing me with too much interest. Two armed customs officials walked by holding clipboards and walkie-talkies, their presence both ominous and comforting.

Petersburg always seemed peaceful and friendly, but this place creeped me out. I wanted to return to the security of *Miss Cora* but forced myself to walk on, more scurry now than swagger.

No one looked up to greet me as I entered the laundromat. No music played softly in the background. No mothers with sticky-faced children were gossiping and passing babies around. Just a bunch of transients guarding their laundry like it was everything they owned, and I guessed it was. I shoved everything I owned into an empty washer, found a nearby plastic chair, and opened my mother's letter.

Dear Elizabeth,

Dad is slowly getting his strength back and now walks to the end of the street and back. Soon, we'll be playing tennis at the Country Club although the doctor says only one martini afterwards, ha ha.

Your sister is doing well and looking pregnant. We went shopping last week and bought some darling maternity clothes. Hard to believe my baby is all grown up and having her own baby.

Isn't it time you grew up, too?

Love,

Mom

Emotions churned through me like the clothes swirling in the washer: relief that my dad was doing better, guilt that I wasn't there, and irritation that my mother could still get my goat.

Most of the time on the *Miss Cora,* I felt good about myself and the fact I had done what I set out to do, even if it was just working on a fishing boat. Mom's letter made me doubt myself anew, made me wonder why I was living on a cramped fishing boat with four other smelly people getting rained on by jellyfish. Was this what happened when you went with the flow, you started circling the drain and couldn't get out?

I opened the letter from Charlene next. A smiley face grinned inanely from the outside of a greeting card. She knows I hate smiley faces, so it must be her idea of a joke.

Dear Lizzard Breath,

Douglas and I are fine except the little sprout inside gives me heartburn. Dad is weak but doing better. Mom is worried and frustrated. I keep telling them, Not all who wander are lost. See, I read the Tolkien book you gave me last year.

I'm enclosing a prayer card to remind you that Saint Charlamagne watches over you while you are away wandering. But I do hope you will come back in time to see the little sprout emerge.

Love,
Charlamagne the Great

She had included a 2x3 inch laminated prayer card depicting a stern, ornately robed man with crown and sword. The caption read: "Prayer of Saint Charlemagne: a prayer of great protection from accidents, enemy aggression and evil spirits."

Maybe, just maybe, I had judged my sister a bit too harshly.

Brad had written to me on flimsy, crinkly airmail stationery, like when he had written to me in France, as though Alaska wasn't part of the United States, as though the distance between us was temporary, not permanent.

Dear ~~Lizzie~~. Maddie,

It sure was good to see you. I'm just sorry you had to leave so soon. I understand now you need your space. I get it. But your mother said you'd be back in the fall and I want you to know I'll be waiting.

The fire still burns.
Brad

I shivered despite the warm, humid, laundromat air which caused condensation to crawl up the windows like wet worms. The harsh overhead lights fizzed intermittently, electrocuting bugs. I watched my clothes churn in the front-loading washer like a kaleidoscope whose pattern I couldn't discern. As though, if I stared hard enough, I could figure out why Brad had written—and Anders hadn't.

WHILE MY CLOTHES DRIED, I TOOK my ditty bag into the washroom as excited as if I was going to a fancy spa. The sterile, utilitarian stalls were a far cry from the calm, soothing Zen ambiance of those places, but I didn't care.

I wanted to stay under the hot water forever, washing away all the dirt and smells and self-doubt that clung to me like dried fish slime. Instead, my four quarters' worth of hot water barely lasted until I rinsed off. By the time I emerged, still damp but at least not dirty or soapy, my clothes were dry. I lugged them back to the moored boat, eerily devoid of life. My crewmates and skipper were gone. I didn't want to stay either. I was utterly sick of the *Miss Cora*, but had nowhere to go.

I decided to be a townie for a few hours instead of a fisherman. I shrugged out of my raingear and rubber boots, choosing instead to disguise myself as a real person by wearing tennis shoes and the turquoise raincoat I had worn when I arrived in Alaska two months earlier. It seemed a lifetime ago.

Thus camouflaged, I set off to explore Ketchikan. Dodging mud puddles, I squished by one gift store, three hardware and marine supply stores, two banks, several nondescript office buildings, one large market, and at least four bars.

A large "Liquid Sunshine" gauge outside a storefront proclaimed Ketchikan the "Rain Capital of Alaska" with an annual average of 12 feet of rain. The record was sixteen feet. Petersburg, I noted, received "only" nine feet per year and Los Angeles a paltry fifteen *inches*. The liquid sunshine was getting my tennis shoes and light raincoat soaked.

I ducked into a bar with the promising name of the *Merry Mermaid*. Men perched at the bar looking like they had grown roots there. One or two looked up hopefully at my entrance and then returned their attention to the bottom of their glass. As my eyes adjusted to the gloom, I recognized Marilyn playing pool in the back. As far as I could tell, she was the closest thing to a mermaid in there and if she was merry, it was only because the nearby table was cluttered with empty shot glasses and beer cans. Before she could see me, I retreated back out the door. I craved companionship from someone, anyone, other than the four people I had been confined with on the *Miss Cora* these past weeks.

I passed several windowless bars, screwed up my resolve, and entered one without dried vomit on the pavement. A dozen pairs of eyes swiveled toward me. The new Maddie reminded herself she had as much right to be there as anyone. Ignoring my prickling skin, I found an empty bar stool. I thought about ordering cognac but there was no tall, handsome Norwegian to drink it with me.

"Wine, please," I asked.

"Wine? What's that?" the bartender asked, deadpan.

"Michelob Lite?" I tried again.

"Miller or Bud," he replied.

"Bud Lite, then."

"Bud Bud or Miller Miller," he said, "But you can have a glass."

The man beside me straightened up and indicated the stack of dollar bills piled carelessly on the counter. "I'm buying," he told the bartender. To me, he said, "I'm Fred."

"I'll get my own," I said, but the bartender had already taken a ten-dollar bill from Fred's pile.

"Keep the change," Fred told the bartender. The careless generosity of drunks never failed to amaze me.

A large pot-bellied man squeezed in beside me, so close I could smell stale tobacco and fresh beer. "I'll have a PBR and get whatever the little lady wants," he announced grandly. I didn't know when he'd last brushed his teeth but it wasn't recently.

"I've already bought her a drink." Fred glared at his competition and skootched his bar stool closer to mine.

Someone else wedged themselves between me and the newcomer, leering at me.

"These losers bothering you?" he asked. "Let's grab a table over there." He waved in the general direction of the gloomy interior.

The man looked for a moment like Ron. The beer I swallowed tasted like bile. I thumped my glass down on the counter and turned to go.

I couldn't.

I was hemmed in by men jockeying for position, the prize they vied for all but forgotten in their alcohol-infused aggression. I leaned back from the two men snarling at each other in front of me, right into the chest of the man behind me. "That's right, darling," he said, in boozy camaraderie. "Let's you and I get cozy."

Fred got to his feet and shoved the man. He shoved back and Fred's stool toppled to the floor. The man on my right threw a punch. Or maybe the other man did. Or Fred did. Or both, or all. Stools crashed to the floor. Glass broke.

I felt in my coat pocket for the little paring knife, but I'd left it in my wool jacket when I'd changed into civilian attire. I wouldn't have used it, I'm sure I wouldn't have, but I would have felt better.

I heard a sickly thump as someone's fist connected with someone's face. I screamed.

The bartender waded in among the brawling men, pulling them apart. "You!" he said glaring at me, "Out."

"Me?" I sputtered. "I haven't done anything!"

An arm in a red plaid shirt sleeve grabbed my elbow and used his body as a shield while pulling me out of the fray. I let myself be led out of the bar.

"As far as the bartender's concerned," the stranger said sympathetically, "*you're* the one causing trouble and *they're* the ones going to stay and buy more booze, not you."

I sagged against the wall, blinded by the daylight.

"You okay?" he asked.

I blinked a few times until my eyes stopped tearing up. I saw a man a little older than me with kind eyes looking at me with concern. His clean Carhart jeans were cut off at the ankles so as not to get caught on his boots which were leather, not red rubber. I knew by now the signs. He was a logger, not a fisherman.

"I'm Chris," he said, leaning against the building between me and the front door. He stared at a spot above my head, tensing whenever the door opened. Several departing men looked toward us but left us alone.

"I'm Maddie." I took several shaky breaths. "Thanks for rescuing me."

He shrugged. "Never a good idea to get in the middle of a bar fight."

"It happened so fast!" I exclaimed. "I've never been in a bar fight before."

"I could tell." he looked at me and grinned. "You looked like a deer in the headlights."

I could feel my adrenalin leach away. "I need to sit down."

"There's a bus stop across the road."

"Busses in Ketchikan?" I exclaimed.

"Well, bus stops, anyway."

Chris was nice-looking in a medium sort of way: medium-length brown hair, medium brown eyes, medium tall, medium good physique. When we sat on the bench, his presence was reassuring, not threatening. I slumped against his shoulder, wishing it was someone else's.

Before I could stop myself, I kissed him.

All the sexuality I'd so carefully suppressed while on the boat came flooding back. I wanted to keep going, to let down my guard and see if

I was someone a normal guy could want. Just enjoy the here and now, as Rachel always urged me to do.

Except I knew by now that all too soon, the here and now would be over and once it was over, everything would still be the same. I'd still be a lonely girl on a fishing boat, maybe even lonelier than before.

"You sure have a nice way of saying thank you" Chris said.

"More like good-bye," I said, and, recognizing a good exit line, I left.

I couldn't remember when I'd last eaten and I was famished. Wong's Chinese restaurant lured me inside with its flashing neon dragon and cheap bamboo lanterns and a menu that didn't include a single thing made with salmon or canned vegetables. A hugely pregnant young woman showed me to a table.

"Do you have wine?" I asked.

"Red or white?"

"Chablis? Cabernet?"

"House or house."

I sighed. "White, please."

While waiting eagerly for food I didn't have to cook, I re-read the letters I'd received that morning. I thought about calling my folks, but decided against it. Mom said everyone was okay there. Whatever I had to say back could fit on one of the postcards I'd bought on the way here. Let my folks try reading between the lines of a postcard instead of me trying to interpret the static and silences of a long-distance line.

I addressed a fresh postcard to Brad and then stared at it a long time. When I finally realized I had nothing to say to him, I ripped it up.

I really wanted to write to Anders. I had so much I wanted to say but knew it wouldn't all fit on a postcard. And, I didn't know exactly what to say. He said I'd hurt his feelings, and for that I was sorry. But I wasn't sorry I had gone fishing. I wished he had written first.

The waitress arrived with my food. In my previous life, I would have found it mediocre. To my deprived palate, it was ambrosia. I ordered another glass of wine.

The bill came with a fortune cookie. The fortune read, "There can be success in retreat but no honor in surrender."

"I don't understand my fortune," I complained to the waitress.

"Who does?" she replied.

Tipsy and tired, I walked back toward the boat. The phone booth at the harbor was empty and I was inspired to dial Bear's number in Petersburg. I chewed my nails as the phone rang and rang. Finally, the old man answered. "Ya?"

I cleared my throat. "Hi, Bear, this is Maddie."

"Who?

"Maddie. Hi! How are you?"

"Who is this?"

"It's Maddie." I said loudly. Not Darlene, I wanted to add. "I'm calling from Ketchikan. Is Anders there?"

"Who?"

"Anders. May I speak to Anders?"

"He's not here."

"Oh…Will he be back later?"

"Ya."

I took a deep breath. "Do you know when he'll be back?"

"No, not really."

I waited.

"He's gone up Petersburg Creek.' Bear finally admitted. "Staying at Haftor's cabin. Be back tomorrow. You can call then."

"I can't, we leave in the morning. Tell him I called. Please."

"Ok."

"Tell him Maddie called."

"Ya sure. Goodbye." He hung up.

Frustrated, I fished a blank postcard out of my purse, addressed it to Anders, and wrote, "My fortune cookie says there can be success in retreat but no honor in surrender. What the hell does that mean? Maddie."

The Broom Goes Up

Two more boring, beautiful days slid by as we cruised around "looking for fish." Then, as we entered Dahl Bay, Marilyn's calls of "jumper" came with such increasing frequency Joe finally told her to knock it off. Dennis stopped looking bored and JJ stopped studying.

"So, we'll set here on Sunday?" I asked JJ.

"These fish won't be here on Sunday."

Seeing my crestfallen look, he grinned, "But more are coming in behind them."

"As many as are here now?" I asked.

"Maybe more!"

When I brought Joe a sandwich at noon, I stayed to watch him watch the water. Every once in a while, he scribbled something in the log book beside him.

"What are you doing?" I asked, hoping he'd answer me for once.

"Casing the joint!" he said jovially, and thrust out his coffee cup for a refill.

When Joe steered the *Miss Cora* out of the bay the next morning, I was crestfallen.

"Just wait," JJ told me. "Joe's a sly one. You'll see."

Joe made a great show of taking the *Miss Cora* north to Dixie Bay, staying to the middle of the channel and chatting more than usual on the open radio frequency. We anchored there overnight amid the normal smattering of jumpers. Nothing like we'd seen in Dahl Bay.

The next morning, JJ raised a finger to his lips and pulled me over to the base of the pilot house where Joe and his controls reigned supreme. Joe called the *Annalee* on the open radio channel and then told him to change to "their normal channel," ostensibly so they could talk in private.

Instead, Joe clicked the mic knob twice and without preamble, hollered into the radio, "Hey, Mike, you wouldn't believe how strong the run is up here in Dixie Bay…Oh crap!" Joe clicked the mic off and set it down, chortling.

I looked at JJ, puzzled.

"Joe never forgets what radio channel he's on," JJ replied, grinning.

We snuck out of Dixie Bay at dusk. With the shadows lengthening and the *Miss Cora* hugging the shore, we observed strict radio silence as we returned to Dahl Bay. This was clearly a clandestine operation. No one made any noise on deck and I took care not to clang the pots together in the galley. The *Annalee* was already anchored in the bay, dark but for her anchor light. Their crew helped ours tie the boats together without the usual boisterous insults, just a quiet word here and there. The bumpers between our two boats rubbed together like an old married couple on a saggy mattress settling down for the night.

Joe and Mike exchanged a few quiet words on deck, then Joe herded us inside. "Big day tomorrow," he said. "Hit the sack as soon as you're done eating."

The next morning, I made oatmeal for the subdued crew, and grilled white bread smeared with margarine on the stove top to simulate toast. By the time I cleaned the galley, our two boats had been untied and were traveling farther into the bay.

Like a dog turning in ever tighter circles prior to settling down, Joe nosed our boat around a spot in the bay only he could discern. At 6 o'clock sharp, he gave the word for JJ to start towing the seine skiff around.

Marilyn didn't even get a chance to use the plunger before Joe yelled at JJ to bring his end of the seine net aboard so it could be cinched and the fish inside captured. As the net was slowly pursed, the cork line on top was pulled under the water by the weight of the fish inside.

Joe stopped the winch from lifting more net on board and the *Miss Cora* listed toward the overflowing net. I lost my balance, sinking to my knees on the slanting deck and clutching the swinging net for balance.

Joe, sweaty and red-faced, yelled at JJ to counterbalance the weight of the fish-laden net by using the skiff to pull on the opposite side of the *Miss Cora*. He yelled at Marilyn and Dennis to use the smaller auxiliary power brailler to bring some of the fish on board to lighten the load. He yelled at me to get out of the way and not stand under the power block like an idiot.

There were so many fish in the net, hundreds could swim frantically over the cork line to freedom.

"They're getting away!" I shouted as though no one but me could see what was happening.

"It's them or us," Dennis replied shortly.

I looked around for a life vest, which no one ever wore on deck. They were too awkward to work in and besides, fishermen know that if something goes wrong, they probably wouldn't survive long enough in the cold Alaska waters to be rescued.

Joe threw the plunger at me like a javelin. "Push more corks under. We need to release more fish!"

Between some of the fish being brought on board with the brailler and some being released over the cork line, the load of fish lightened enough so that the net could be brought on board and the fish spilled on deck in the usual manner. Only this time, I found myself up to my knees in wet, flapping fish which filled the deck from stern to bow. My crewmates and I whooped and hollered. Even Joe cracked a smile.

"Don't bother icing them," he said. "Shovel them down in the hold and let's get some more!"

Joe took the boat back to the mouth of the bay for another set. This time, we barely got the net out before he hollered to bring to bring it back on board, so we didn't capture more than the boat could handle. We set one more time before the tender Joe had summoned pulled into the bay and other seiners, smelling success, followed. We off-loaded our record catch, then went back to work. It was dark when Joe called it quits. I was shaking with exhaustion, but the adrenaline kept me going.

My exhausted crewmates napped where they could on deck while we waited our turn to off-load onto the tender. I shucked off my raingear and went inside to scrounge dinner. After heating up soup and making sandwiches, I climbed down to my bunk, pulled my sleeping bag over me, dirty jeans and all, and let sleep drag me swiftly under.

The rattle of the coffee pot roused me the next morning and I staggered up to the galley to find Joe making coffee.

"Sorry, Joe. I must have overslept." I expected his wrath to rain down on me like the stinging and hot jellyfish that burned me as I helped bring in the net.

"Figured you all needed a little extra shut-eye this morning," he said cheerfully. "Let's have pancakes, I'm starving."

After breakfast, a commotion on deck brought me to the galley door. Joe was directing JJ to climb the rigging.

"Hey, Cookie," he said. "Grab the broom and bring it here."

Mystified, I did as ordered. Marilyn took the broom from me, upended it, and passed it up to JJ. He tied it to the mast, bristles up.

"Broom in the mast means we're a highliner," Joe explained with immense satisfaction. "Yesterday's haul put us over 100,000 pounds for the season. Didn't think we were going to make it."

"Most of them won't," Dennis said.

For once, Marilyn didn't correct him.

The broom stayed there the rest of the season, a battered flag that, having survived a tough battle, now flew in tattered splendor though the rest of the war.

We spent the next several weeks cruising around deserted bays between weekly 24- or 36-hour openings when we could actually fish. Joe and Marilyn looked for jumpers and I tried to find something to do between meals, the real focus of our days.

I played word games with JJ.

"A tower of giraffes."

"A steal of seals."

"A wake of buzzards."

"A prickle of porcupines."

I made Dennis play cards with me, usually something mindless like rummy or Crazy Eights. Cribbage was reserved for the skipper, and tended to leave someone feeling seriously out of sorts.

I asked Marilyn if she had any books to read. She loaned me some outdated magazines. I read articles about movie stars I'd never heard of, completed all the half-finished crossword puzzles, and took all the personality tests. Turns out whether I am a romantic or pragmatist is unclear but Peachy Keen is definitely my lipstick color.

An old Rubik's Cube on the galley table would yield its secrets only to JJ, although I almost solved it once or twice. I thought about borrowing JJ's anatomy book, figuring the pictures might be interesting even if the text wasn't. Then I discovered a Zane Grey novel and was bitterly disappointed to discover the final pages missing.

One day, I heard Dennis shout from the deck, "Killer whales at ten o'clock."

I rushed outside.

"They're orcas," observed JJ. "Dolphins, not whales."

"Voracious killers," said Dennis.

"Of marine animals," JJ said.

"What's for lunch?" Marilyn asked, bored.

Casting around for something to say over our sandwiches, other than commenting on the weather (rainy) or the fishing (poor), I asked who the *Miss Cora* was named after.

Joe pushed his plate away and climbed up to his perch.

"What'd I say?" I looked at the stony faces of my crewmates.

Dennis shrugged.

Marilyn said, "Joe doesn't like to talk about it."

JJ took pity on me. "Cora was Joe's daughter. She fell overboard when she was ten years old. Drowned. Joe was supposed to be watching her. But he was drinking too much in those days."

"My God, that's awful," I said. "Why doesn't he change the name?"

"Bad luck to change a boat's name," said JJ. "And maybe he doesn't want to. Maybe he wants to punish himself, remind himself why he doesn't drink anymore."

JJ went out on deck. Dennis went below. Marilyn went back to her magazine. I made brownies.

I spent the rest of the summer as a bona fide salmon fisherperson. I loved living and working on a boat, being a self-sufficient but integral part of the world around me. I loved the excitement of setting the net and not knowing what would be in it when we brought it on board. I loved cruising around the wild, deserted bays of Southeast.

I did not love the jellyfish. I did not love the constant bickering, the undercurrent of tension Joe promoted instead of squelching. I did not love being dirty and bored and celibate.

I both loved and hated the isolation. It was a relief not to be inundated with paternal nagging or romantic demands, but I was lonely. This new life of mine offered freedom and independence but at what price? Out here, I was no one's friend, no one's daughter or sister. Certainly no one's lover. Who was I? I was starting to realize I was just me. I was starting to like it.

Everyone grumbled at what a lousy fishing season it was but, not knowing any different, I was content. At the cannery, I was always figuring out how much money I had made that day or that week. Out here, money became irrelevant. I spent none, and didn't know how much I made. Joe complained constantly about expenses but never mentioned profits. "I'll make a tally at the end of the season," was all he said.

Fishermen are gamblers, and I came to understand Joe was no different. Fishermen were always betting on the next set, the next bay, the next opening, never knowing for sure, after all that work, what would be in the purse. Skippers learned to read the signs and keep a careful log of past results which they guarded like gold. Good skippers knew all the tricks, but sometimes they guessed wrong, or something went wrong with the equipment, or everything went right but the fish didn't show or the weather turned bad. Every set was like the throw of a dice and if this roll was a bust, there was always the next. It was impossible not to get caught up in the anticipation that the next set or the next opening or even the next season would be better. If you didn't think that, you didn't last long in this fickle business. Dennis, I was sure, wouldn't last long. JJ could probably take over his uncle's boat, if he wanted, but he didn't want. About Marilyn, the jury was out.

Me? I was okay for now—and the here and now was all there was.

Fisherwomen Don't Hug

"MAKE A BIG BOWL OF POTATO salad," Joe said one day as he passed through the galley on his way to the pilot house. "Enough for two crews."

"What's up?" I asked his back. Shrugging, I got to work boiling potatoes and chopping celery and onions.

When we pulled into Kopakoff Bay for the night, the mystery was solved. The *Annalee,* a seine boat skippered by a friend of Joe's, was moored in the bay. When we pulled up beside her, Grateful Dead tunes blared from a tinny tape player and a barbeque grill smoldered on the stern.

"Party time!" Dennis announced gleefully, reading the smoke signals correctly. He rushed on deck to place protective bumpers between the two boats as the *Annalee's* crew took the ropes JJ threw and tied our boat off to theirs. The heavenly smell of sizzling burgers wafted over to the *Miss Cora. A moveable feast,* Southeast Alaska style.

"Grab the salad and let's eat," Joe said in an unusually cheerful voice as he passed through the galley.

I picked up the industrial sized bowl of potato salad and prayed I wouldn't drop my precious cargo overboard as I crossed. A familiar pair of arms reached out from the Annalee's side to take the salad bowl from me.

"Rachel!" I exclaimed.

"Maddie!" Rachel grinned.

We might have hugged except our two crews were watching and it was much too girly a thing to do.

We clasped the big salad bowl between us instead, grinning at each other.

"What are you doing here?" I asked.

"Long story," she said. "Food first."

She led the way to a cooler at the end of a makeshift table and pulled out two beers.

"I can't drink," I said reluctantly. "Joe will fire us."

"That's why the party's over here, so Joe can pretend not to know."

I took a long, satisfying swallow. The cheap beer tasted like champagne and the smell of burgers had me salivating. I looked at the two crews milling around the deck. After their initial curiosity, they paid us no mind. Laughter and good-natured ribbing filled the air. For once, Marilyn and Dennis weren't bickering.

The two skippers filled their plates and disappeared inside the *Annalee,* which seemed to be the signal for the others to grab plates and descend on the food.

"We'd better grab some grub before those maggots eat it all," Rachel said.

We loaded up our paper plates and, by mutual agreement, made our way to the bow for what passed as privacy onboard a ship. I found a coil of rope to use as a seat and held Rachel's plate as she overturned a bucket and dragged it close. I watched, fascinated, as she took a big bite of the juicy burger. I'd never seen her eat meat before.

"What?" she asked.

"You're dripping."

She wiped her mouth on her sleeve and took another bite.

"Okay, now tell me what the hell you're doing here?" I demanded.

"Same as you. Working. Making money." She took another swig. "Sven needed someone to fill in while one of his crew went to a funeral. I jumped at the chance. Kinda like my friend Maddie did. Jumping at chances."

"I did, didn't I?" I had felt foolish and frightened much of the summer but now I saw my actions differently. Foolish and frightening, true, but also adventurous and brave. "Joe said he'd try me out for one trip. He's never given me a compliment, but he hasn't fired me either."

"I hope Sven likes my work as much," Rachel said. "Being out here is much better than slaving away in the cannery, for sure. You were right, Tanaka's a male chauvinist pig."

"At least he didn't try to rape you, like that asshole skipper Ron."

"Tanaka's more bark than bite," Rachel agreed.

"Ron was all bite and no brains."

"Men are bastards," Rachel said automatically, without the bitterness which used to accompany this pronouncement.

"With a few exceptions," I added. "My dad. Allen. Jimmie."

"Reed," Rachel said softly.

"Maybe Anders."

Just naming them aloud seemed a brave thing to do out here where so much could go wrong. Where so much could go wrong, but where anything seemed possible.

She polished off her potato salad with gusto. "Mmmm, is this your mom's recipe? I love your mom's potato salad."

"I was hoping the paprika on top would disguise the fact that I had to make it with Miracle Whip."

"You hate Miracle Whip."

"Exactly."

"My mom always left something out of hers. Or burned the potatoes," Rachel said.

"How do you burn boiled potatoes?"

Rachel shrugged. "I think it's genetic. Sven had me cook a couple of meals and then told me to cease and desist. The crew cheered."

"You were never much of a cook," I said.

"Yeah, but now I have to work on deck, pitch fish into the hold, all that stuff."

"I have to get up before anyone else, cook three meals a day, keep the coffee pot full."

"Poor Madeline," Rachel said, pretending to play a violin.

"The good thing is, no one is picky. If I make brownies from a mix, they think I'm Julia Child." Rachel licked hamburger juice from her fingers.

"So, you're not a vegetarian anymore?" I asked. "That would be about impossible on the *Miss Cora*."

"It *is* impossible on the *Annalee*. If I didn't eat meat, I'd starve."

"Well, it suits you"

"What?"

"Eating. You look good. Not so skinny. No circles under your eyes." I leaned over and playfully pinched her cheek. "You have roses blooming in your cheeks."

She batted my hand away. "You make a terrible bubbe." But she looked pleased. "How's your dad?"

"Recuperating slowly but surely. I can't tell if he likes being fussed over by Mom and Char, or hates it."

"Probably a little of both. I always liked your dad."

"But not my mom?" I teased.

"Oh, you know. She blames me for corrupting her poor, sweet, innocent daughter."

"Well, don't tell her different."

We finished our meal as the long, slow Alaskan twilight smoothed the edges of the spruce trees and softened the jagged rocks on shore. The *Annalee's* bright stern light cast dramatic shadows onto the deck, but its light didn't penetrate our cozy perch.

I relaxed in the faint buzz of the beer, the almost indiscernible sway of the boat at anchor, the good food, and the comforting presence of my friend. Rachel got up and returned with more beer.

The pop and click of the can sounded loud in the quiet.

"Hey, Rach…"

"Hmm?" She took two Oreos out of her pocket and handed me one.

I took a deep breath. "When Ron came to the door of our house that night, was he really looking for you?"

It was silent so long, I thought she hadn't heard.

I took another deep breath. "If so, I'm sorry. I shouldn't have taken your job."

"Yeah, it really pissed me off at first," Rachel said slowly. "But, as it turned out, I dodged a bullet."

"You did, at that," I agreed.

"Serves you right," Rachel said without rancor.

I stuck my tongue out.

We twisted our cookies apart and I licked the icing off mine.

"Here," Rachel said, handing me half her cookie—the half with the icing. When I glanced at her in surprise, her obsidian eyes, usually mirrors reflecting emotion back rather than windows allowing feelings out, looked at me transparently. There was a warmth in them I wasn't used to seeing.

I started to wave the cookie away, knowing she liked the filling best, too. But then I took it, licked the icing off, and flung the remaining chocolate wafer far into the darkening sea like a miniature frisbee. Rachel followed suit and we watched seagulls appear from nowhere to squabble over the cookies.

Joe emerged from the *Annalee's* galley like a tornado bringing its own weather system with it. "Get a move on, girls," he shouted. "You, too, Maddie!"

This time we did hug good-bye.

A WEEK LATER, WE WERE BACK in Ketchikan. When I got to the harbor office, Joe had already collected the mail and left with it. That seemed thoughtless, if not downright mean. But it probably didn't matter anyway. I did my laundry, took a shower, ate cashew chicken and drank white wine at Wong's. Once we cleared harbor the next morning, Joe distributed the mail. I quickly flipped through my small stack, but there was nothing from Anders.

Mom wrote that Dad was feeling better and Charlene was over her morning sickness. She wondered what in the world I was doing there and when would I come to my senses? She enclosed a recipe for lasagna.

I crumpled her letter into a ball and threw it overboard. Sorry, mom, no ricotta cheese on board.

Charlene sent me an invite to her baby shower. I kept that.

The final envelope was from Brad and contained only a generic tape cassette on which he'd written "Maddie's Song." We had often sent tapes back and forth when he was in Boston and I in France. He would expound on recent political events: the Pentagon Papers, Watergate, Tricky Dick. In return, I sent him love poems I recorded in French. I expected he would know their meaning even if he couldn't understand the words. I think now I expected too much.

I borrowed Marilyn's tape player and went on deck. After a few scratchy seconds, Brad's voice came on. "Maddie, I wrote you a song. It's your song. I wrote you Maddie's Song." A few soft guitar chords and then he started to sing.

A few months ago, I would have been ecstatic to have him write me a song. I would have worn out the tape listening to it. I would have learned the words by heart.

Now, suddenly, I was outraged. How dare he write my song. It was my song to write, my song to sing. Not his.

I jammed my finger on the stop key as though doing so before any more words spilled out would save my life.

Instead of his seductive song, I heard the boat's engine throb beneath me, the swoosh of the hull slicing through the water, the wind whistling in the rigging.

I ejected the tape and flung it as far as I could into the sea. Seagulls cawed and fought to grab it, losing interest as soon as they discovered it was a piece of junk, not food. I thought I would feel regret or curiosity or even sadness as I watched Brad's song for me disappear beneath the boat's frothy wake.

Instead, I felt the motion of the boat cutting through the vast and beautiful world around me, the wind taking my breath away, the salt spray forming rainbows in our wake, the fresh smell of salt water. The sight, the smell, the wonderful, heady exhilarating feel of freedom.

Marilyn came up beside me. "This was mixed in with my mail." She handed me an envelope.

The letter was from Anders, postmarked Fairbanks. He must have gone back to school. I tore it open.

> The I Ching says "Retreat is not the same as surrender. Surrender means yielding to the power of another. Retreat is a regrouping of your forces before moving forward."
> I think this means you should dump that California guy and come visit me.
>
> Anders

My heart spiraled upwards as only a heart with one wing can do.

North or South?

A WEEK LATER, THE SEASON WAS OVER. The *Miss Cora* was tied up in Ketchian for the winter and everyone was planning to leave as soon as we got our paychecks. No one asked for my address nor I theirs, but I did make blueberry pancakes by way of saying goodbye. I scrubbed the galley until it shone, then went outside where the others were washing down the deck and rigging with detergent and fresh water.

Marilyn came by mopping the deck and—playfully, I think—sloshed water on my rubber boots. I stuck one boot out as though for her to scrub it, which much to my surprise, she did. I struck the other one out and asked, "Where's Joe?"

"In town getting our paychecks," she answered, making a few swipes over my boot with her mop.

"Hallelujah!"

"What are you going to do next?" she asked.

"Get to the airport, for starters. You?"

"Go back to Spokane, I guess." She shrugged. "Joe hasn't said yet whether he's hiring me back next year. You coming back?"

"Whatever I do next summer won't involve jellyfish," I told her.

"Smart." Marilyn moved away, scrubbing the deck savagely to erase every last piece of fish scale and jellyfish slime.

I returned to the foc's'le and shucked off my old jeans and work shirt. They smelled of diesel and fish—*eau de fish*, indeed. At the bottom of my pack, I dug out the black underwear, the green tee shirt, and the black jeans that hung loosely on me now. I slipped the silver hoops on my ears and the silver bracelet on my wrist. My shaggy hair needed a trim but no way was I wearing the red bandana.

I left my pack at the galley door and walked to the bow. The usually busy harbor was quiet. The local fishing boats were moored in their winter quarters. The tourists and waterfowl had flown south. The fishermen had departed.

Empty of boats and people, I noticed how many signs were everywhere. Directions. Arrows. Instructions. Warnings. Earlier in the summer, I'd been surprised to realize there were no location signs on the complex waterways of Southeast Alaska. You had to decipher different kinds of signs in order to navigate. Now the harbor signs seemed bossy and intrusive.

I went to the side of the boat and took the little paring knife from my pocket where it had resided since the *Misty*. JJ came up and looked at me curiously as I flung it into the water.

"A burial at sea for something I don't need anymore," I explained.

We watched the ripples from the sinking knife spread out and subside. He nodded toward shore. "Fireweed's done blooming."

"When fireweed turns to cotton, summer will soon be forgotten," I chanted.

JJ nodded. "We'll make an Alaskan out of you yet."

He held out his hand for me to shake. "Good-bye, Maddie. Remember to take the journey. Don't let it take you."

Then he was gone.

Joe climbed over the gunnels, paperwork in hand. He gave a mock salute with a sealed envelope, then handed it to me. "Not the best season, but not the worst, either."

I was dying to know what I'd earned, but didn't want to find out in front of Joe. Good or bad, it was what it was. I put the unopened envelope in my pocket.

"Mexico, right?" Joe said gruffly. "This should buy you some tacos and *cerveza*."

He looked proud at knowing this much Spanish.

"Adios," I said. "Thanks for giving me a try."

"You want a job next summer, let me know," he said.

I retrieved my pack and walked up the ramp, effortlessly avoiding the mud puddles at the top. A middle-aged woman was getting into an idling taxi and I hurried to the driver.

"Can you give me a ride to the airport?" I asked. Sharing taxi rides was how it was done in this small town

"Sure, hop in."

I crammed my pack into the trunk and climbed in. The other passenger nodded once, then we both looked out our windows. All I saw were the masts of anonymous boats. They all looked alike from a distance. My home away from home these past two months was now just another seiner. The taxi pulled away.

God, I was sick of the rain and sick of seining. Sick of everything that went with it: red rubber boots and rain gear and fish slime. Bland food and crowded, smelly quarters.

Sick of jellyfish.

At the airport, I'd catch the flight to Seattle. From there, the red-eye to L.A., and voila—I'd surprise my parents. They would be so thrilled to see me. Mom would take me shopping for new clothes, Dad and I could sneak out for ice cream—or maybe we would take a walk instead. I could tease Charlene about her pregnancy weight, and then tell her how beautiful she looked.

At the airport, I hurried to the ticket counter.

"One ticket south, please," I said, like a woman would say who knew where she was going.

"The afternoon flight has already left."

"What? It's already gone?"

"There's room on the plane tomorrow."

"Tomorrow?" This was not going according to plan.

Seeing my distress, the woman tapped her keyboard.

"If you hurry, you can catch the northbound flight to Anchorage and then double back to Seattle on the red eye."

The woman in back of me shifted an infant on her hip and the man behind her called to a friend to order him a beer, he'd meet them in the bar.

"Okay, one ticket to Anchorage." As I reached for my wallet, the eagle's beak on the bracelet nipped my wrist. "Just out of curiosity," I asked. "Can I get a flight to Fairbanks from there?"

The clerk checked the monitor. "Yes. From Anchorage you can catch the flight south to Seattle or north to Fairbanks. Whichever way you go, you need to get going."

Yes, I did need to get going. No more retreating, no more going with the flow. I would just walk off the plane, collect my backpack, push open the door, and see what was out there.

~

ACKNOWLEDGMENTS

I always felt I had at least one book in me, but I didn't realize it would take almost a decade to write with many friends and mentors providing support and assistance along the way.

Shortly after moving to Redmond, I wormed my way into the EZ Writers critique group which reviewed endless drafts and dished out indispensable advice. Special thanks to Mary Krakow and Amanda Curley who have journeyed with Maddie and me for the past five years.

The Central Oregon Writer's Guild offered an encouraging community of fellow writers and monthly meetings focused on improving our craft. COWG President and OSU-Cascades writing instructor Mike Cooper became my personal "tough love" writing guru, encouraging, demanding and always believing.

Jennifer Silva Redmond was of immense editorial help and an inspiration to follow on her own journey as a newly published author. My final editor, Eva Long, cheered me on as my energy was flagging to help Maddie and I navigate the murky waters of self-publishing and make it over the finish line.

I owe a special debt of gratitude to Cathy Edgerton, fellow Alaskan, friend, and proof-reader extraordinaire. Thanks also to friends who read all or parts of the early manuscript and provided invaluable feedback, including Candy BelAir, Sandy Ayres, Peggy Carlson, and Rebecca Lucas.

Gayle and Jim Eastwood were particularly helpful with enthusiasm and technical information. Sue Paulson graciously allowed me to browse through her newspaper collection of 1970s *Petersburg Pilots*. Others who shared their memories of fishing and living in Petersburg include Bill Conner, Erik Rosvold, Brian Kandoll, Clyde Curry, Glorianne (Glo) DeBoer Wollen, Jean Curry, and Grant Trask. Over the years, Petersburg residents Steve and Desi Burrell encouraged my writing, fed me fresh seafood, laughed and cried with me, and trounced me at cribbage.

Other friends read bits and pieces over the years; I hope they're happy with the final product.

I have tried to be as factually accurate as possible, given fishing technology and the town itself have changed dramatically over the past fifty years. Any errors are mine alone. If you spot mistakes, let me know and I'll buy you a beer in Kito's Kave or the Harbor Bar by way of apology.

To all who have accompanied me on my journey, both in life and in writing, please know my heart is full of gratitude. If I have forgotten you here in print, please know you are etched forever in my heart.

"We must be willing to let go of the life we've planned,
so as to have the life that is waiting for us."
Joseph Campbell

LYNDA SATHER arrived in Alaska on a whim, as many do, and stayed for forty years, as many do not. She worked a variety of jobs in Southeast Alaska before settling in Fairbanks, Alaska, where she managed communications for a public school district and for a pipeline service company.

She has a B.A. degree of marginal value in French literature from U.C. Santa Cruz and a much more useful master's degree in Professional Communication from the University of Alaska Fairbanks. Her work has appeared in *Alaska* magazine, and the Central Oregon Writer's Guild 2023 and 2024 Anthologies.

When not writing, Lynda enjoys traveling, hiking, writing and playing pickleball.

A Smack of Jellyfish is her first novel.

Please visit LyndaSather.com.

9 798990 778900